Lyns s was born
bookworm. A careers adv
writing wasn't a "good o
little bit of everything, including make-up artistry, teaching and doing admin for a chocolate fountain company.

Now, she has finally fulfilled her dream and is writing full-time. When not writing, she drinks tea, eats lots of cake and dreams of owning her own island in the Outer Hebrides with a sheep called Steven. It'll happen one day.

twitter.com/Lynsey1991
instagram.com/lynseygram

Also by Lynsey James

The Luna Bay Series

The Broken Hearts Book Club

The Sunflower Cottage Breakfast Club

The Silver Bells Christmas Pantomime

Standalones

Just the Way You Are

A Season of Hopes and Dreams

A Winter's Wish Come True

THE SINGLE DAD'S HANDBOOK

LYNSEY JAMES

This paperback edition 2021

1

First published in Great Britain in ebook format
by HarperCollins*Publishers* 2021

Lynsey James asserts the moral right to be identified
as the author of this work

A catalogue record of this book is available from the British Library

ISBN: 978-0-00-840262-4

This novel is entirely a work of fiction. The names, characters and incidents portrayed in it are the work of the author's imagination. Any resemblance to actual persons, living or dead, events or localities is entirely coincidental.

Printed and bound in Great Britain by
CPI Group (UK) Ltd, Croydon CR0 4YY

To Gran

You would've loved this one

Prologue

This is for them.

Every stroke of the pen, every word I write; it's all for them. My two favourite people, the little team that I desperately wish I didn't have to leave behind.

Cancer is a bastard.

I look down at the letter I've just written and tears spring to my eyes. I've been doing this for a while – distilling everything I want my husband and daughter to know into short, easily read letters – but today I'm struck by just how sad this is. I'm thirty years old and should be in the prime of my life. Evan and I should be that annoyingly perfect couple, still blissfully happy after ten years of marriage, and I should be the best mummy in the world to Violet. Instead, I'm preparing my family for a life without me because cancer has wiped away our future.

It's not bloody fair.

My hands ball into fists and I screw my eyes shut, resisting the urge to scream. Evan and Violet are downstairs, playing a game of some sort, and I don't want to ruin it. That's all they need; me screaming like a banshee and frightening the life out of them. I imagine them together, just for a second, Evan lifting Violet into his arms and spinning her around while she giggles. For that brief moment, the sadness and tragedy melt away, and I almost forget how ill I am.

Maybe I could join them, just for a little while. It wouldn't do any harm, would it? Might even make me feel a bit better. Evan will fuss and try to send me back to bed, but I want some carefree, silly time with Violet. We could play a game or read a book or...

Pain ripples through my body as I try to get out of bed. Every muscle feels as though it's on fire and my breath is immediately ripped from my lungs. I sink back onto the pillow and try my best to stifle a sob. Even the simplest of things, like going downstairs to see my family, are becoming harder.

There isn't much time left. I can feel it in my bones. My body is slowly giving up the fight and soon, I'll be nothing more than a collection of memories. A name that Evan can't bear to say, and Violet doesn't quite remember. I'll whisper at the edges of their thoughts, looking for a way in, determined to stay with them as long as possible. I don't want them to forget me. Even thinking about it breaks my heart.

That's why this book of letters is so important. I glance at it as it lies upturned on the bed, its glossy purple cover catching the weak sunlight. Hidden within its pages is my legacy, everything I want Evan and Violet to know but won't be around to tell them. I'll be here whenever they need me, giving them a gentle nudge or some words of advice. As long as they have this book, I'll never be gone. Not really.

I pick it up and put my pen to my lips. It's time to write another letter.

Chapter One

A pair of red shoes.

Size-seven stilettos, to be precise.

That's all it takes to derail my morning routine, which was starting to fall apart at the seams anyway. In the seconds before it happens, I'm in the kitchen, throwing a haphazard packed lunch together and keeping one eye on the clock.

Twenty minutes before we absolutely have to leave the house.

There's still a lot to do. I have to brush Violet's hair into as neat a ponytail as I can manage. We have to locate her pencil case, jumper and shoes, which have all gone missing in the three days since we bought them. I have to make sure I don't leave the house wearing my pyjamas and hair like a scarecrow.

A word to the wise: try to get more than two hours of sleep the night before your child's first day at school.

I take a deep breath and force myself to calm down. *Everything will be fine*. I repeat it in my head like a mantra and let the beat of the words wash over me. Violet will have a lovely day, and nothing will go wrong.

Then, as if fate is determined to prove me wrong, she stomps into the kitchen wearing the red stilettos.

'Look what I found, Daddy! Can I wear them today?'

When I look up and see her standing in the doorway, her tiny feet barely filling a quarter of the shoes, my heart stops. My hand hovers in mid-air as jam drips off the knife I'm holding, landing in sticky splodges on the kitchen counter.

How the hell did she find those?

'Can I, Daddy? I like the colour and look how tall I am!'

A lump rises in my throat and for a second, I think I might cry. I step out from behind the island counter and crouch down in front of her, hoping my sadness doesn't show on my face.

My voice cracks. 'No, baby, you can't wear these today.'

Her brow creases and she folds her arms. 'Why not?'

What is it with kids and the word *why*? It seems like one day, they latch on to it for dear life and won't let go, much to their parents' dismay. When they realise that one simple word can unlock the answers to a whole world of questions, that's it.

'Look at them – they're far too big.' I gesture to her tiny fairy feet. 'Did you find the shoes we bought a few days ago, the ones with the butterflies on the front?'

She shakes her head and I let out a frustrated groan. We're definitely going to be late now, which will earn me a telling-off from Violet's teacher. At the school's New Parents' Day, Miss Thompson made it clear that she wouldn't tolerate lateness or what she called 'sloppy standards'. Anything less than military precision wouldn't wash with her.

'Go and have another look. I'll be up to help you in a minute.'

'But I want to wear these ones!'

I press my hands to my eyes as a headache brews. I sense an almighty tantrum coming, but I hope to God I'm wrong.

'You'll fall over in them. So please just go and try to find your proper shoes. Have a look for your jumper and pencil case while you're at it as well. And try to be quick – we're running really late.'

'No! The butterfly ones are too small and make my feet sore.'

Great, now she tells me. This had better just be an excuse not to go and find them; if they're really too small and she didn't say anything in the shop, we're screwed.

'Are they really too small or are you just kidding? Because remember, the lady in the shop asked you if they fit OK and you said they were fine. She asked you quite a few times before she put them in the box.'

Please God, tell me the shoes are fine and I didn't spend two hours and thirty-five quid in a stuffy shoe shop on the hottest day of the year for nothing.

Mercifully, she decides to admit defeat. 'They're fine, but I like these better because they're a nice colour. Whose shoes are these? Are they yours?'

I look down at them and a lump forms in my throat. They've been languishing at the back of my wardrobe for a long time, yet I can remember the last time their owner wore them as if it were yesterday. I can picture the bright, sunny smile on her face as she danced in loops around the kitchen, tugging at my hands and inviting me to join in. With all my might, I push the memory away. If I let it consume me, we'll never get out the door.

'No, they're not mine.' I sneak a quick glance at the clock. Time is running out, like it always seems to be, and I still have a jam sandwich to make.

'Then whose shoes are they, Daddy? "Whose shoes!" That sounds funny.'

She starts giggling and stomping around the kitchen, seemingly forgetting about her lost school shoes. My already fraying nerves become even more strained as potential hazards jump out at me. She could hit her head on the hardwood floor, bang into one of the granite counters, or pick up the jam-covered knife I've stupidly left within reach…

'Dance, Daddy!'

Violet staggers over to me and makes a clumsy, ill-timed grab for my hands, almost slipping over when she lurches forward too quickly, but I manage to save her in time.

'Watch yourself – you could've banged your head!'

'I know all the planets in the solar system,' she says, smiling up at me with pride as if nothing happened. 'Can I tell you them? There's Earth, Venus, Mars—'

My patience snaps like an overstretched thin piece of elastic.

'Violet, please! We don't have time to talk about planets right now. Take those shoes off and go and find the ones with the butterflies on them.'

She looks startled. I didn't mean to speak so loudly or to sound so on edge. She absolutely loves space and enjoys telling me facts she's learned from all the documentaries she watches. Normally I let her carry on until she runs out of steam, but today I'm too tired and stressed for a fact marathon.

'Violet, I—'

I heave a sigh of frustration as she runs off towards the stairs without letting me finish my apology. It's not even nine yet and everything's going to shit. This has to be some sort of Evan Harper personal best.

I turn to look at the discarded stilettos and my breath hitches in my chest. Invisible fingers curl round my heart and begin to squeeze. While it's silent, I close my eyes and picture her. She's walking towards me, slightly unsteady after too many glasses of wine, with her arms outstretched. Even now, after all this time, she still makes my heart leap. Her honey-blonde waves are falling over her shoulders and her large green eyes are crinkled at the corners from smiling so much.

'Come on, you,' she says, lacing her fingers with mine. 'Stick some music on and dance with me.'

It takes everything I have to open my eyes again. My heart aches and my bones are heavy with grief. That was the last good day before everything changed. Remembering it is always hard.

She should be here on her daughter's first day of school, but she isn't.

She should be here telling me not to panic and helping Violet look for her shoes, but she isn't.

She should be here, wishing her good luck, showering her with kisses and making today seem like a big adventure.

But she isn't, and I miss her like hell.

Ten minutes later, we still aren't out the door and my stress levels have reached their peak. The kitchen looks like a bomb has struck it, I'm still not dressed and Violet's jumper is still missing. We've located her shoes and pencil case though, so that's progress. My sanity has got lost somewhere along the way, but we're not likely to find that anytime soon. She's decided now is the perfect time to start a game with her toys and has told me I can't play because I'm 'shouty and angry'. Nothing makes you feel like a shitbag quite like being excluded from a child's game.

To make matters worse, my phone is ringing, and I don't know where it is.

'Violet, come on! We have to leave in a few minutes,' I yell as I head down the hall, trying to follow the noise. No wonder she called me 'shouty and angry' – I've done nothing but shout since I found out I'd slept through my alarm. Actually, it was two alarms, set fifteen minutes apart.

I hear movements upstairs and hope she's putting her toys away rather than starting a new game. If I can get us out the door without spontaneously combusting, it'll be nothing short of a miracle.

My phone rings again and this time, I figure out where it's coming from: it's wedged between the sofa cushions in the living room.

'Hello?'

'Mr Harper? This is Jean from the Fraser Robertson Funeral Parlour. Sorry to call so early, but as you're a previous customer of ours, I'm phoning to ask if we could conduct a short feedback survey. We're updating our website and if you could give us a couple of sentences to add to our testimonials section, that would be great.'

I take the phone away from my ear and frown at it. Have I just heard this woman correctly? She wants to do the whole 'how was it for you' thing about my wife's bloody funeral, two years after it happened?

'I'm sorry, but now really isn't a good time. I have to get my daughter ready for school.'

Jean isn't about to give up that easily though. 'Just a couple of quick questions, Mr Harper, please. It would help us to improve our service. First of all, were you satisfied with the service we provided?'

I sigh and roll my eyes. Bugger it, I'll play along for a couple of minutes. We're going to be late anyway.

'To be honest, I was too busy grieving for my wife to notice what the service was like. The flowers were nice, but there was a bit of a mix-up with the song choices. We ended up listening to "Good Riddance" by Green Day instead of "You Send Me" by Sam Cooke, and a lot of people thought it was in poor taste.'

Jean is silent for a moment as she digests what I've just said. There are various attempts at an apology, but they all seem to die on her tongue. Appropriate really, since this is the most bizarre conversation about death I've ever had.

'Don't worry, it was totally my fault,' I assure her. 'The sound system at the church blew a fuse, so I tried to play the song off my phone and messed the whole thing up. It was the only laugh we got all day, actually. Claire would've loved it.'

Another couple of questions follow – How supported did I feel during the planning process? Were Claire's wishes carried out as I wanted? – and I answer them as best I can without actually thinking about the day of the funeral.

Once Jean has everything she needs, she thanks me for my time and hangs up. Just as I'm about to call Violet downstairs, my phone rings again. Without thinking, I accept the call, assuming Jean forgot to ask an important question about the sausage rolls we had at the buffet or the stern expression on the chief mourner's face.

'Look, Jean, I know you're trying to improve your website, but I really don't know what more I can tell you.'

'Guess who?'

My back straightens and I only just manage to resist the urge to hang up immediately. It's been a while since I heard that voice.

It belongs to my best friend in the whole world. At least she used to be.

'Hannah.'

'Got it in one.' She either hasn't picked up on the fact that I'm not pleased she called, or she doesn't care. Both are equally likely. 'Guess where I am right now?'

'Well the last time you remembered to get in touch, it was Sri Lanka. But since that was, what, four months ago you could be anywhere. I'm going to go with somewhere in the Arctic Circle.'

'Indonesia, actually. And it was amazing, but I decided to come home for a while. Got into Edinburgh Airport about an hour and a half ago. Are you free later? We need to talk.'

Typical Hannah: she breezes in from wherever she's been on her travels and expects everyone's plans to fit in with her. I'd give her a piece of my mind if I weren't so bloody exhausted.

'Let me guess, some guy's followed you home and you need me to get rid of him again. Who is it this time? Has Beau, the over-privileged yoga instructor, made a comeback? Or is it Julio, the language student?'

The last thing I need is another showdown with one of Hannah's boyfriends. She falls hook, line and sinker for them before realising too late that they're absolute arseholes who aren't worth her time.

'No, not this time, smartarse.'

'Well, I'm sorry but I can't see you today. I've got to take Violet to school, then I'm going to work. It'll have to be another day.'

A silence stretches between us and discomfort sets in. Hannah's never quiet; she's always a bundle of fun, excitement and noise. That's why Violet loves her so much. People are drawn into her one-woman carnival and want to be part of her world.

'Look Evan, I'm trying to be nice here so let's park the bullshit for a minute. I won't take up a lot of your time and I'm not looking for an argument. Let's just have a coffee and catch-up. It's been too long and there are things I need to say.'

I close my eyes in resignation. She won't take no for an answer.

'Fine. I've got a tour right after I drop Violet off, but I can be free after that.'

'Great. Text me when you're finished, and I'll meet you at Costa on George Street,' Hannah says before hurrying through a goodbye.

I stare at the phone for a few seconds, frowning. As far as I knew, Hannah was having the time of her life travelling. So why is she coming back to the city she was so desperate to get away from?

Chapter Two

The good news is we're only five minutes late to school in the end.

The bad news is Violet has taken a seat on the low stone wall separating the playground from the pavement and won't go inside. No amount of begging or pleading from me will change her mind.

I'm sitting here with her now, staring out at the deathly silent playground and wondering what the hell to do next. Short of picking her up and carrying her into the building while she screams blue murder and gets me arrested for child endangerment, I've got nothing.

'Are you ready now?' I ask.

I look down at her. Her elbows are on her knees, propping up her chin as she stares at the ground. When she finally meets my eyes, her lower lip wobbles and she looks like she might be about to cry.

'I don't want to go,' she mumbles. 'Want to stay with you.'

I'm tempted to scoop her into my arms, give her a big squishy cuddle and take her back to the car.

'Baby, I know you're nervous, and it's OK to feel like that.' I stroke her hair and rest my hand on her shoulder. 'But today's going to be really exciting. You'll meet lots of new people and learn cool things you can tell me about when we go home. And it's just for a little while. I'll be back to pick you up in a few hours.'

She slides off the wall and for a glorious second, I think I've won. Alas, victory is snatched away from me at the last minute as she climbs onto my lap. I hold her close and smooth some hair away from her face. We didn't have time for a ponytail today, but it doesn't matter. She looks ridiculously cute anyway.

'We can't stay out here all day, kiddo,' I tell her. 'You've got some learning to do. Everything will be OK – you'll have lots of fun.'

I'm not sure if I'm saying that for her benefit or mine. I think it's a little of both; I want to get her excited for the day ahead while also calming my own nerves about leaving her.

It doesn't work.

Violet bursts into tears and buries her head in my

neck. For a moment, I'm frozen, thrown off by how upset she's become. Is this just first-day nerves or something bigger? My frazzled, sleep-deprived brain has an argument with itself about what I should do next. Should I try to find out what's wrong, give her a hug, *what*? I don't want to do or say anything that makes her feel worse, but sitting here like an idiot isn't helping.

Get it together, Evan. Your little girl's crying; you have to do something.

'What's wrong?' I ask. 'Is it because I shouted at you earlier about your shoes? I'm sorry, I didn't mean to—'

She shakes her head and clings tighter to me, like she's afraid I'll disappear if she doesn't hold on. I gather her shaking body close to mine, shushing her and gently rocking her to try to calm her down.

'Shh, come on, it's OK,' I whisper. 'Don't cry, Daddy's got you.'

And then it comes: three words that have the power to split my soul in two.

'I want Mummy.'

My heart shatters into a million grief-stricken pieces. I don't know what to say to make her feel better. No combination of well-placed words will take that particular pain away; I know that from experience. Claire was such a huge part of both our lives; the three of us orbited around each other and the love we shared was fierce and beautiful. Losing her broke something in me; it cast dark shadows over everything and gave all the love, warmth and happiness inside me plenty of places to hide. Having my own pain to bear is bad enough, but seeing Violet suffer makes every fibre of me ache.

I look down and notice she has her jumper on back to front. *Bollocks.*

'I miss Mummy,' Violet sobs. 'I wish she was here.'

'So do I,' my voice trembles as I desperately try to hold myself together. 'I miss her so much. But she'll always be with us, in here.' I point to where her heart is. 'We'll never forget her, I promise.'

Gently, I reach up and wipe some tears from her cheeks. This is supposed to be a happy day, full of excitement and possibilities.

'Were the nice shoes Mummy's?' she asks. This is the fifth time she's brought them up since we left the house and I can't swerve the subject any more.

'Yes, they were her favourites. She liked to wear them when she was going out dancing.'

A smile tugs at the corners of Violet's mouth and she rubs at her eyes.

'Are you ready to go in?'

There's a brief pause and she nods. I place her down on the ground, take her hand and walk her into the building. This marks the first step in a new chapter of Violet's life. She's off to become the person she's destined to be.

And it all starts with her first day at school.

Can a place miss a person? Our house misses Claire, I'm sure of it. Her memory is carried in every room and sometimes, I swear I can hear the whole building creak and sigh under the weight of its grief. It's not hard to see why; she picked it out in an estate agent's window not long after we got married and fell in love as soon as we walked through the door. It needed a lot of work, but Claire was determined to bring it back to life and she did. She's everywhere in here, from the cherry-red kitchen units to the sunny yellow sitting room and polished wooden floorboards. There used to be flowers everywhere when she was alive, but not anymore. If she were here now and saw the large jardinière in the hall was empty, she'd go mad. Every time I walk past it, my chest tightens. It's a swift kick in the guts, reminding me that the love of my life is gone.

The shoes are still in the kitchen, their vibrant red popping against the hardwood floor. For a short, painful second, it's as though she's still here.

Her absence sneaks up on me again, pressing down on my already weary shoulders and making my bones ache. The grief books piled up at the side of my bed said this would stop after a while, that I would somehow learn to consign her to a memory. 'A while' hasn't happened yet.

I catch my reflection in the hall mirror as I walk past. I look as exhausted as I feel. There are dark circles under my eyes, my face is pale, drawn and covered in stubble, and my hair is like a haystack. I was too busy rushing around this morning to notice, but now I can see how much of a state I'm in. I'll have to fix myself before I go to work; I might be in the business of scaring people for a living, but I usually leave that up to my business partner James.

There's a small avalanche of stuff littering my bedroom floor. Violet's had a good rummage, by the looks of things. This must've been where she found the shoes; half the wardrobe is still packed with Claire's things. I should probably take them to the charity shop and keep some bits for Violet, but I can't. How could I banish her from the house she loved so much? Remove all traces of her as if she never existed?

I take a moment to look through some of it. Her favourite summer dress, the delicate cream fabric sprayed with pretty, colourful flowers. The red coat she'd wrap round herself on cold mornings, along with its matching scarf. Her purple wellies, still sprayed with flecks of mud from our final family day out. Crammed on the top shelf near her handbags is her collection of beautiful headscarves that she loved to wear during her treatment. I haven't dared to touch them since the day she died, as though she might come back and tell me off for moving them.

So many memories packed into a tiny space. Our painfully short story told in a series of bright primary colours and patterns.

Fuck, I miss her.

'And here, on Victoria Street, we have Thomas Weir's house, reported to be the most haunted house in Scotland. He was known as the Wizard of the West Bow and was executed for witchcraft in 1670. Legend has it that a phantom coach roams the street late at night, pulled by headless horses and ridden by the devil himself. Some say the devil's looking for Thomas Weir. They say he wants to take him back to the underworld, where he truly belongs.'

The crowd doesn't look very interested and to be honest, I don't blame them. My delivery is a flat, soulless monotone, devoid of any kind of passion for my subject. I'm privileged enough to be able to walk around the most beautiful city in the world, telling ghost stories, yet here I am sounding like I'm talking about the history of the root canal.

This isn't how I want to do things, and it certainly

isn't how I was when I started my ghost-tour business ten years ago. When Monsters, Murders and Magic Tours burst onto the scene, I came alive when I talked about the city's murkier history and my presentations zinged with passion and enthusiasm. Now, I run my tours on autopilot and it shows. I've become like the tour guide who inspired me to do this, whose disinterest in the subject and dull delivery made me turn to James and say 'I could do better.' I give my groups facts and stories, but nothing of myself because I don't have anything left to give. The shred of the old me that's still hanging around in the hope I get my shit together screams at me to get my act together.

Today, the added distractions of wondering how Violet's getting on at school and the reason behind Hannah's sudden return are taking my mind even further off the task at hand. As much as I try not to let them overrun my thoughts, they do and I can barely concentrate on what I'm saying. Not that it matters, judging by the group's collective lack of interest.

I soldier on with my story, even though I lost them about three stories ago. I'd give anything for even one murmur of curiosity or a question, but none come. The group is talking amongst themselves and completely ignoring me. Only a few of them arrived together so if nothing else, everyone has made a new friend. They don't have a clue about Thomas Weir and his phantom coach – which was once my favourite story to tell.

My mind throws up an image of Violet, curled up in the corner of her classroom waiting for me to come and get her. I shake my head as I try to dislodge it.

'If you're ready…' I point in the general direction of where we're headed next. 'We'll continue.'

I suspect the only reason they're following me is because they don't know the city very well. If we pass a Five Guys or a cosy-looking pub, I'm fucked.

Chapter Three

After a painful hour of trying to engage with my tour group, it's time for me to hang up my frock coat and top hat for the day. We had about half the people we started with by the end, which is pretty standard. Now, we'll get to discover how many new ways there are to say 'it was shit' in the online reviews.

'Evan, don't take this the wrong way,' James says as he wipes his makeup off, 'but you were an even bigger miserable bastard than usual today.'

'Was I? I didn't notice.'

James looks at me, his head cocked to one side. It's his signature who-are-you-trying-to-kid? look. He knows I'm lying; even a total stranger could work that one out.

'I'm fine, mate, really. There's no need to worry.'

'Come on, man, I'm not stupid. I know your heart

hasn't really been in the tours since Claire died, but today was bad even by recent standards. Tell me what's wrong. We've been scaring the shit out of people for, what, ten years now? I see more of you than I do my husband.'

My mouth opens and I briefly consider telling him how awful I feel inside, my mess of a morning with Violet, and Hannah's sudden return to Edinburgh. Annoyingly, the words won't arrange themselves in the right order, so none come out. I have to steer the conversation towards safer territory, away from the sensitive but well-worn topic of 'What's Wrong With Me'.

'I'm serious, everything's fine.'

He looks at me for a moment, searching my face for any clue about what I might be hiding, then gives up.

'You know if you want me to do the tours, you only have to say,' he says, putting his hand on my shoulder. 'Or we could hire someone else. You didn't take much time off when you lost Claire – maybe a holiday would be good for you.'

'We've been down this road before: you don't like the storytelling, I can't jump out at people like you do and we can't afford to hire someone else. It's always been the two of us and that's the way it's going to stay.'

James looks worried, like he thinks the next words out of his mouth will sour the atmosphere.

'We can't keep going like this,' he says. 'When we first discussed changing things up so you didn't have to lead all the tours, you said you'd bounce back and that you were just in a rut because Claire died. It's been nearly two years, Evan, and your heart just isn't in it anymore. It kind of hurts to see, actually, because you used to love the tours so much. You drew people in, made them believe in all the myths and legends and stuff. Now, you just talk at them. And, like it or not, sales are down, mate. Something needs to change. *You* need to change. What would Claire want your life to look like right now, mate? You know it wouldn't be this.'

My teeth clench and I take deep breaths as I try not to show how utterly pissed off I am. This is a carbon copy of a conversation James and I have had hundreds of times, and it always ends the same way: I get defensive and storm out, or he gives up when we can't find a solution. I know ticket sales are down, just like I know about the snarky reviews people leave about me and my 'face like a constipated squirrel'.

'I *will* bounce back,' I insist, 'it just takes time. Anyway, who would we get to run the tours instead? Some hard-up drama student who thinks he's playing Hamlet at the Globe? I don't bloody think so. We built this business together, James. Everything's going to be fine. Sales will bounce back – they always do towards the end of the year. And I'll … well, I'll be fine too.'

There's a fierce desire to protect my role within the business, even though my passion for storytelling has long since died out. Sitting in the office poring over our dire finances doesn't sound fun, and James's flair for the dramatic means he's the one best suited to making people jump. If I didn't tell the stories, no matter how shit I may have become, there would be no place for me.

Luckily for me, James has reached the point where he decides to throw in the towel.

'How about a pint tonight? There's a new barmaid in the Halfway House you'd like the look of.'

He raises his eyebrows in a you-know-you-want-to fashion. Irritation prickles across my skin. *Not this again.* The only thing I hate talking about more than my feelings is the possibility of finding love again.

'You know I'm not ready to start dating.'

My voice comes out strangled and small thanks to the lump in my throat. It stays put when I try to swallow it down.

James drops his gaze to the floor and clears his throat. This isn't the first time he's tried and failed to get me back into the dating game. He's getting fed up with me, judging by the look on his face.

'Claire would want you to be happy, you know. She'd hate seeing you like this.'

I look up at him and feel my blood boil. Since I lost Claire, people have tried to use what they think she would want or feel to get me to do what they think is best. I don't appreciate it from anybody, least of all my business partner. That isn't what riles me most though; I'm annoyed because he's absolutely right.

'No offence, James, but you don't know what it's like to lose the person you thought you were going to spend the rest of your life with. You're lucky – you've got your person and you don't have thousands of days without him stretching out in front of you. I had to watch her die, knowing there was nothing I could do about it.' I gather up my things to leave. 'Don't forget to lock up when you're finished.'

'Evan, I'm—'

I'm gone before he can say another word.

She's ill.

Someone's hurt her.

She's in trouble and needs my help.

These are just some of the possibilities I've come up with for why Hannah's asked me to meet her as I wait at an outside table at the Costa on George Street. I curl my hands around my large cappuccino to fight against the slight chill in the air. Summer is losing its grip on the city; you can tell by the bare trees, the shorter nights and the breeze that makes the golden leaves dance on the pavements.

'Hey, you.'

I look up and see the whirling dervish that is my best friend standing in front of me. Her brown hair is streaked with sunshine, a smattering of freckles dances across her nose and cheeks, and her hazel eyes are sparkling with her trademark curiosity. She's wearing a pair of pale denim shorts, a white lacy top with spaghetti straps and a brightly coloured kimono. Her wrists are covered with bracelets and she's wearing several chunky, exotic-looking rings. She's a rare, colourful creature who's just blown in from a faraway land, full of wonder and secrets.

'Hey, long time no see.'

It comes out like a dig and it kind of is. I haven't seen her in eight months; our contact has consisted of a handful of fraught, awkward phone calls, and I've had to drop everything to come and see what she wants.

'You look like shit,' she says as she pulls her chair out. 'Like a Muppet with insomnia.'

'Thanks. You look like someone who said she'd stick around to help me after Claire died then buggered off to south-east Asia and asked me to vet tenants for her house. Oh wait, you are.'

Hannah sighs and chuckles. 'Are you ever going to forgive me for that?' Our friendship has taken a beating, but we're laughing with each other and that's a good sign.

'I don't know. If I ever forget about Angela and her collection of spiders and snakes, I'll think about it. Her albino python really took a shine to me.'

Silence falls as we sit at opposite sides of the table, studying each other like we've found an ancient artefact buried in the sand. How do I feel about being in her company? How does she feel about being in mine?

'So what are you doing back?' I ask, passing her the coffee I ordered her as a peace offering.

'Travelling isn't all it's cracked up to be, you know.' She takes a sip and a contented smile spreads over her face. 'All those travel bloggers make it look a hell of a lot more glamorous than it actually is.'

I roll my eyes. 'Are you going to tell me the truth? Because believe it or not, I've got things to do.'

Well, sort of. I'd planned to head home and listen to Claire's favourite songs on Spotify while looking through our photos.

'All right, all right…' Hannah pauses for a moment and stares down into her coffee. 'I did a lot of thinking while I was away … about how things have been since Claire died. We haven't exactly been the best of friends, have we?'

'Bit of an understatement.' I risk an uncertain smile. 'We've barely spoken to each other.'

We look at each other for a moment and she winces in agreement. 'Kind of hard to when I was gallivanting round the world, eh? That's why I decided to come back. I wanted to see if we could get back to how we used to be. I missed you and Violet when I was gone and I want to make things right again. I've been a crap godmother and an even worse best friend, but if you let me, I can change that.'

I recognise something in her eyes: it's the same pain and loss I've been struggling with since Claire died. It's so easy to forget Hannah's been hurting all this time too.

'Um … OK. Yeah, we'll see.'

I want to say more, but I can't. Her reason for coming back has caught me off-guard; I'd assumed she wanted to see friends or go to a festival.

Hannah allows a small smile to pass her lips before she pushes her chair away from the table. 'Well, this was fun,' she says, 'but I'd better get going.'

We lock eyes for a moment and she folds her arms in a silent challenge: *tell me to stay and I will.* I'm not sure what to say or even if I should say anything. I have a habit of making things worse when I open my mouth.

'I'm sorry, you know,' she says, shifting her gaze to the pavement, 'for everything. For what it's worth, I'm sticking around the city for a while and I'd love to spend time with you and Violet. If you both want to, that is.'

I make an attempt at a smile that probably ends up

giving weight to all those constipated-squirrel comments. There's so much I want to say to her. I want to tell her how much it hurt when she left and how devastated Violet was when I told her Hannah had gone away for a while. That Claire and I made her Violet's godmother because we trusted her to be around when Violet needed her, but she wasn't.

But the words don't come. They're lost somewhere in my exhausted brain and I can't root them out.

'Right, well…' Hannah says, shifting awkwardly from foot to foot. 'I'll see you around.'

She walks off down the street, looking smaller and more human than the statuesque creature that greeted me a little while ago. Something inside me calms as I watch her go, and I realise I haven't felt truly settled since she left. In the back of my mind, I've worried about her getting hurt or needing my help when I can't get to her. I'm still mad as hell at her for going back on her promise to help me when Claire died, but one thing is for certain.

I've bloody missed her.

What would Claire want your life to look like right now, mate? You know it wouldn't be this.

It's those annoyingly accurate words of James's that

have me clambering up the loft stairs that afternoon. They shook something loose in my head that I haven't thought about in a long time, and I'm going to dig it out from its hiding place before I change my mind.

The book of letters Claire made before she died is exactly where I left it, the tell-tale patch of purple peeking out at me as though it's whispering, 'I'm over here, come and pick me up.' My breath hitches in my chest when my fingers close around the book and bring it out of its hiding place. I wasn't sure if I was ready for this, but now I'm holding it in my hands, I realise this is the perfect time to look at it. My disastrous morning, plus the conversation with James, brought it back to my thoughts, so it seems like fate is guiding me.

If I read a couple of letters, maybe I can pretend for a few glorious minutes that she isn't gone.

Chapter Four

I fling the book open in front of me as soon as I get downstairs. The house is still a mess and there isn't much time before I need to pick up Violet, but I have to read at least one letter. This is something she took the time to make for me, and I'm lucky enough to have it in my lap. I open it at the page marked by the Post-it note that says *Read me First.* That's as good a place to start as any.

'Here we go. What did you want to tell me, Claire?'

Dear Evan,

Welcome to The Single Dad's Handbook, your comprehensive guide to life without me when I pop my clogs! I hope my demise is suitably dramatic – who wants to leave this world quietly? Not me, that's for sure. So many things are up in the air right now – how many more rounds of chemo I'll have to face before the doctors admit defeat, the colour I'll dye my new teeny tiny tufts of hair, how sick I'll be from one day to the next. Despite all these things, one thing is certain in my mind: I'm going to die. Dr Fielding is trying to be positive, saying we still have hope, but the results speak for themselves. The first round of treatment didn't work and this one isn't doing the job either. The Big C is winning and I'm not.

That's why I've decided to create this book, to help you navigate a world without me. Not because I'm big-headed enough to think you'll fall apart without me; I just want you to have something to refer to when everything seems difficult and scary. You and Violet make such a great team, but even the best ones need a little help sometimes.

I don't want to die, Evan. I'm terrified. All the blogs I've read have talked about making peace with it, preparing your loved ones as best you can and creating memories. I wish I could be as strong and brave as them, but I'm not. As I'm writing this letter, I'm thinking about how bloody unfair my imminent death is. I'm thirty years old and I have so much to live for. You and Violet, my job, my friends, all the things I still want to achieve in life. If I had my way, I wouldn't leave any of you behind. You're my team and I love you all so much.

But hey, let's be positive for a second. They might find a miracle cure, or Phil and Grant (yes, I've named my tumours) might decide to piss off and leave me and my tits in peace. You may never have to know this book exists. We'll count every page you never have to read as a blessing.

This book is not a cure-all (if only it were!). It won't magically drag you through grief and drop you on the other side. It won't cook dinners or look after Violet or arrange my funeral. It'll just be there, giving you a gentle nudge in the right direction until things feel a bit less shit. I'd like to think of it as a map of your new life, the one that doesn't include me. Maybe you'd like to write to me too? When things get a bit too much, you can just scribble a note to me in a notebook. It'll be like I'm not really gone and you never know, it might help you work some things out. Your choice, but I think it's a good idea.

It's time to start living again, Evan. Your new forever starts right here.

Love always,

Claire

Tears are streaming down my face by the time I get to

the end. I wipe them away and turn to the letter titled *My Funeral*, eager to devour more of her words.

Dear Evan,

You won't like this letter, but please don't skip past it. It's important, I promise. We need to talk about my funeral.

Depressing subject matter, I know, but bear with me. I've had a lot of time to think about this – more than anyone my age should – and I have a few little requests. Nothing too out there, just some acrobats, doves and an ice sculpture of me in all my post-chemo glory…

Kidding! Although if you want to take those ideas and run with them, I wouldn't object. The main things I want for my funeral are joy and colour. Nobody is allowed to wear black and tears are a definite no-no. Scrap the eulogies and tell funny stories instead. Oh, and I don't like funeral marches. Why not play some ABBA instead, or Sam Cooke? We have a ton of songs that mean something to us, so choose the happiest one and get everyone to sing along.

I know you hate talking about my death – don't think I haven't noticed you subtly changing the subject every time I bring it up! I don't like it either, to be perfectly honest. But it's going to happen, sweetheart, and a lot sooner than we think. I'm not going to tell you what snacks to have at the wake (although if you want to have sausage rolls, that would be great) or how to mourn me when I'm gone. These are just some guidelines for you to follow during arguably the worst time after you lose someone. I love you so much and the idea of leaving you breaks my heart. Take all the help you can get from those around you. We're lucky enough to have an amazing team of people in our lives and I know they'll all want to pitch in.

And please don't worry about money. The funeral plan documents are in the bedside table next to the life insurance stuff. You never know, there might be enough for a horse-drawn funeral cortege and a customised headstone! All jokes aside, I'm counting on you to make sure people have a good time and remember me the way I want to be remembered: someone who was so in love with life and memories and the world. Someone who was so much more than the illness that claimed her life. You'll do a great job, I know it.

Love always,

Claire

For the longest time, all I'm capable of doing is looking at the page while my hands shake. I'm surprised to find just how many of her wishes I managed to fulfil without reading the letter. The only area I slipped up on was the tears. I sat in the front pew, wearing a red T-shirt she'd bought me, bawling my eyes out.

A mirthless chuckle bursts out of me as I remember all the times I told her she'd beat the disease. Yet she knew. I thought I could see quiet resignation in her smile, but convinced myself I was wrong. It was there though, all through the worst year of our lives. What must it have been like, knowing she wasn't going to make it? Now all that's left of her is a gravestone at the local cemetery and occasionally some mysterious bouquets of her favourite flowers that I definitely haven't left there. There's no note to say who they're from, just a bunch of purple violets propped up against her headstone.

I think about what happened the last time I saw her, and the words I didn't say. If I'd just stayed a few more seconds, I could've told her what she wanted to hear. I'd have been with her when… A stab of guilt makes my insides twist themselves into knots. My eyes are drawn back to the book, still open on my lap. I look at the Post-its that tell me what each letter is about, and tears prick the back of my eyes. Claire's written a letter for every scenario she would miss. She's covered everything from puberty and dating advice to Violet's wedding and beyond. I have to resist the urge to read all of them in one sitting. My fingers trace over some of the lower Post-its, but I snatch my hand away before I can turn to any of them. Claire has specified when each of them should be read and I want to respect her wishes. Plus, if I disobey her, she'll likely find a way to come and haunt me as payback. I like the idea of writing to her though. Maybe I'll scribble down a few lines a day and see how I go.

Claire thought I was capable of being Super Dad; it's obvious from the letters I've just read. If she could see me now, she'd be so disappointed.

Maybe this book can finally help me become the dad I want to be. The question is: where the hell do I start?

Fancy dinner one night this week? Lorna's got someone she'd like you to meet. Four of us could go to Cosmo? D x

Oh Jesus.

This is all I need – my best friend Dave and his wife Lorna doing their matchmaking routine again. I've told them I'm not ready to date, but they won't listen. They seem to think that if they invite me out enough times to discuss my woeful lack of a love life, I'll give in and go out with one of Lorna's friends or colleagues. This is the first time Dave's mentioned a double date though. Usually, they take me out on my own and try to get me drunk enough to agree to a blind date.

Since being direct hasn't worked so far, I have to

come up with increasingly creative ways of saying 'no bloody way'.

I've told you, mate: leave matchmaking to people like Paddy McGuinness. Lorna's friends deserve better than an awkward double date with a widower whose Mastermind specialist subject would be the life and times of Peppa Pig. Let's not bother, eh? E x

Dave texts back to tell me I haven't heard the last of this and that Lorna will probably be in touch to try to persuade me.

She can do her worst, as far as I'm concerned. I'm about as likely to go on a date as I am to embark on a trip to the North Pole wearing a pair of denim hot pants.

Anyway, I have much more important things to focus on, such as becoming the dad Claire thought I could be.

I'm waiting for Violet at the school gates and I've brought the book with me, so I decide to read a letter.

Given where I am, it could only really be the one labelled *First Day of School.*

Dear Evan,

So today is the big day – our little button is starting school!

How did this happen? Wasn't it just yesterday she was trying to climb the stairs?

In reality, she's still the cutest two-year-old in the world and is sitting next to me on the bed, flicking through The Tiger Who Came to Tea. Her first day at school is a long way off, but as I won't be there, I wanted to write down some tips and advice in case you need it. You're a great dad and this will all come naturally to you, but hey, I'm dying. Indulge me, eh?

Tip number one: DON'T PANIC! Easier said than done, I know, but do try. Violet will be excited about the adventure ahead, but she'll be nervous too. School is a big deal for any kid, let alone our little adventurer. So try to pretend you're not playing every worst-case scenario in your head and emphasise just how much fun she'll have. Tell your awful-but-brilliant jokes, give her plenty of squishy cuddles and let her know everything will be OK.

Tip numero dos (check out that Spanish!) is make fellow parent friends. You don't have to join the local 'yummy mummies' group, although they'd be lucky to have you, but having some friends who know how bloody hard parenting is will be good for you. You can share anxieties and experiences, ask questions and have a laugh. When I'm gone, you'll need all the support you can get. And it's always nice to have someone to stand with at pick-up and drop-off.

My third piece of advice is a little request. When you pick her up after her first day, take her for ice cream at our favourite place. You know the one: Mary's Milk Bar on Grassmarket. We had some great times there, didn't we? Remember when we… No. I'm not taking a trip down memory lane or I'll end up even angrier at Phil and Grant than I already am. Anyway, it'll give you both a chance to have some fun and breathe after a busy, exhausting day. Get her two scoops of her favourite flavour. It's strawberry now, but it might have changed by then. Oh, and some cookie dough for yourself. If you'd like to get me one, mine's a vanilla with rainbow sprinkles. Ask about Violet's day, splodge ice cream on her nose and make her laugh. Just don't cry over me or I'll never forgive you!

Love always,

Claire

I run a hand over my face and sigh. Today definitely hasn't been the first day that Claire imagined for Violet. And now, as I look around the silent playground, I'm not even sure I've got the right pick-up time.

This doesn't feel right. God, I wish someone would turn up so I don't feel so uneasy.

My wish is granted when a group of women walks through the school gates, deep in hushed conversation, and stands just outside the old caretaker's cottage opposite me. They all look impeccably groomed with long, glossy hair in various shades of gold and caramel, and they're all wielding rose-gold iPhones like they're using them to plot world domination. The ringleader is standing in the middle, wearing a brown leather jacket and dark tailored jeans. She seems to be holding court with her friends, judging by her brisk hand gestures and her sweeping gaze to ensure she has their rapt attention.

They're about as far away from who I'd usually talk to as possible. But Claire wanted me to make friends with the other parents and I want to at least give it a go. A mantra from one of my grief books pops into my head: *do one thing a day that scares you.*

Today, talking to these fellow parents will be my thing.

'Um … hi.'

I raise my hand in an awkward greeting and the group's eyes swivel onto me. Suddenly, I'm an unsuspecting gazelle who's wandered up to a pack of lionesses instead of a thirty-two-year-old man looking to make some new friends.

The ringleader is the first to step forward, and I mutter, 'Bollocks,' under my breath. I'd hoped one of the other group members might've beaten her to it, but no such luck. I wouldn't want to get on the wrong side of her either; she's smiling at me, but it's not what I would call friendly. Predatory, maybe, but not friendly.

'Hi there.' She takes a step towards me, her smile broadening. 'I don't think I've seen you in the playground before. Are you new?'

'I am. My daughter just started school today, actually. I-I'm Evan. Evan Harper.'

The ringleader regards me for a moment, her head tilted to one side and her arms crossed over her chest. I'm the polar opposite of her crowd with my faded T-shirt, mop of wild brown curls and my battered Converse. Her talon-like fingernails drum out a beat on her expensive jacket as she makes up her mind about me.

'Renee Wilkes.' She extends a manicured hand and I shake it. 'This is Lisa, Miranda and Steph.'

She nods to each of her friends in turn and they wave or smile at me. They all look friendly enough, even if they're a lot more polished than I am.

'So…' Renee takes a few steps back towards her group and regards me with something between suspicion and intrigue. 'Your daughter's just started school here. What's her name?'

'Violet. She's in Miss Thompson's class.'

'That's the same class as Arabella!' Renee squeals in delight and claps her hands. 'She's my youngest. Violet should join us next time we all have a playdate.'

All I can manage is 'Um,' which Renee seems to take

as an acceptance. She grabs my phone and adds all their numbers into the contacts. And just like that, I'm initiated into what looks like a very elite group. In the space of five minutes, I've gone from having no fellow parent friends to being invited out by the local yummy mummies group. Claire would be proud. She did say they'd be lucky to have me, after all.

Chapter Five

As Claire's letter instructed, I take Violet to Mary's Milk Bar for some celebratory ice cream. Claire and I spent a lot of time here at university, back when it seemed like we had our whole lives to love each other.

Fuck, I miss her.

I look up ahead and see a woman with her child, deliberating over flavours like it's a matter of life and death. Jesus, how long does it take to choose some ice cream? Kids like anything with sprinkles and adults always know what they're going to get before they reach the counter. What's taking them so long?

Calm down, Evan. Everything's fine.

When I breathe in, the unmistakable scent of vanilla hits me. Claire's favourite flavour.

Coming here was a mistake. I have to go.

The final straw comes when 'What a Wonderful World' by Sam Cooke starts playing.

Our song.

I can't do this. I thought I could, but I was wrong.

'Come on, let's go. We need to leave.'

I take Violet's hand and hurry towards the exit, dodging and weaving through the mounting crowd. A vile, burning taste travels up my throat and, for a moment, I'm certain I'm going to be sick. That'd be the icing on the cake of a very tough day: vomiting in front of a bunch of strangers in an ice-cream parlour.

'But Daddy, I wanted to get Mummy's favourite ice cream!' Violet protests as I wrench the door open. 'And you said I could have a treat!'

'We'll think of something else, and we'll come back here another day, I promise.'

When we finally make it to the street, the fresh air helps me to steady myself. It's warm and muggy and there's still the slightest trace of vanilla on the breeze, courtesy of the ice-cream shop, but I can breathe much easier.

'Come on then.' I take Violet's hand. 'Let's go home.'

She sighs and nods, resignation set into her little face. Her shoulders slump as we walk back down Grassmarket, and my heart hurts.

'How about we pick up some food on the way home?' I suggest. 'You can pick a film for us to watch too.'

Violet nods, but doesn't even look at me. I'm definitely not winning any Dad of the Year awards today.

'Can you make Mummy's pasta?' She looks up at me with hopeful eyes. 'The yummy one with all the colours.'

Oh, bugger. Claire's roasted-vegetable pasta was Violet's favourite, but I've never been able to make it the same way. It's been so long since we've had it, I can't even remember all the ingredients.

'Um … the thing is, baby—'

The look on her face stops me in my tracks. How can I disappoint her again? Not only have I screwed up the plan Claire set out in her letter, I can't even make a simple bowl of pasta. Top-class parenting from me today.

Renee and her group throw me a lifeline when they invite Violet and me to the local Playzone with them later that afternoon. I'm a bit surprised; I hadn't expected an outing with them so soon, and I thought it might come in the form of an embossed gold invitation with a dress code.

'I don't like Arabella – she's a poopyhead,' Violet grumbles as I drive our clapped-out Honda into the car park. 'Can we go home?'

'You only met her today, why don't you give her

another chance? You never know, she could end up being your best friend.'

I catch Violet's glare in the rearview mirror and gulp. She looks like she's about to turn into the kid from *The Exorcist,* but I hope to God I'm wrong. The car is in a bad enough state without her splattering green vomit all over the upholstery.

'Look,' I say, hoping some tactical bargaining will work, 'how about we stay for an hour? If you're not having fun, we can go home. Deal?'

Violet sighs, which is good enough for me. We get out of the car and walk towards the doors, where everyone is waiting. Renee approaches me, arms wide for a hug and a huge grin on her face.

'You made it!' Before I can reply, she throws her arms around my neck, lingering just a little too long and placing her hands on my chest when she pulls back. It takes her a couple of seconds to notice Violet. 'Oh, hello, sweetie! Are you ready to have some fun?'

Violet stares hard at Renee and doesn't reply, just folds her arms over her chest and purses her lips.

'Of course she is! Let's head inside, it's getting cold out here.' My voice is a little too cheerful and I pray to whoever might be listening that we're not about to enter epic-shit-fit territory.

Once we're inside, it takes a couple of minutes to convince Violet to go and play with Arabella, Maisie,

Freddie and Ruby, but she eventually – mercifully – stalks off towards the play area with a backward glance to let me know I'll be paying for this later.

When they disappear into the primary-coloured paradise, Renee raises her eyebrows. 'Is she always so ... reluctant to mix with other kids?'

I bristle a little, but try not to show it. 'She's not reluctant, just shy. Some kids thrive in big groups, but Violet's always been happy in her own company.'

Silence falls and I get the awful feeling that the four of them are judging Violet. She's always been a unique kid with her own interests and way of doing things. I've never questioned it because she's always seemed happy socialising on her own terms. And, though I hate to admit it, I've had more than enough on my plate the last two years and some things have slipped through the cracks.

Renee forces a smile and mutters without really saying anything. A swift subject change is called for and, to give her credit, she does it in style. She leans in close to me, after checking her friends are engrossed in a conversation about someone who's apparently run off to Marbella with the guy who tiled her bathroom.

'Listen,' she purrs. 'I don't want us to get off on the wrong foot. You know sometimes you can just get a *feeling* about someone? Well, I have the feeling we could be really good friends. My husband works away a lot, so why don't you bring Violet over to the house one day? While the kids play, we could ... get to know each other better.'

A jolt of shock rings through my body when Renee places her hand on my arm. *Oh, bloody hell.* What do I do now? My eyes dart around the room, looking for solutions and coming up empty. I haven't been in the dating world for almost fourteen years and I don't think becoming Renee's bit on the side is the best way to re-enter it.

'Bloody hell, Renee, leave the poor man alone!' Miranda says with a cackle. 'Look, he's wearing a wedding ring. He's married, like you seem to keep forgetting you are.'

I turn my attention to the platinum wedding band I haven't taken off since Claire put it on my finger one sunny July day twelve years ago. It's never entered my head to stop wearing it. I still feel married to Claire in every sense of the word.

'So, Evan,' Miranda says, twisting round to face me, 'what does your wife do? It's so refreshing to see a man taking on the childcare duties while the woman pursues a career.'

She flashes me a smile that says 'Got you out of that one, didn't I?' I open my mouth, expecting the truth to come out. That Claire died of breast cancer and it's the worst thing to ever happen to me.

Instead I say, 'She's a doctor, works as a registrar in paediatric oncology at Sick Kids. Bloody amazing at it, she is too.'

The women smile in reverence, while I'd give anything for the ground to swallow me up. I'm not sure why I lied; maybe because it let Renee know in no uncertain terms that I'm not interested, but also because things were just so much better when Claire was alive.

'She sounds like quite a woman.' Renee's voice is edged with bitterness.

I nod and swallow the lump in my throat. 'She was. I mean, *is*.'

Renee is about to reply when she's interrupted by a piercing scream followed by *"Mummyyyyyyy!"* It's coming from the ball pit and we all instinctively head over there to see what's going on. When we get there, I see Violet standing on the side of the ball pit, looking like butter wouldn't melt, while Arabella is flailing around in the middle, sobbing her heart out.

As my daughter gives me her most innocent smile, I get the distinct impression we won't be invited back to Playzone ever again.

Before I know it, I'm storming across the car park with Violet's hand tightly clasping mine.

'OK,' I say. 'Walk me through what happened one more time.'

'Arabella was too scared to go in the ball pit, so I helped her. But then she started crying and I don't know why.'

I turn round to look at her. 'Violet, she was crying because you pushed her in! You know not to do that kind of thing, so what were you thinking?'

She doesn't answer immediately, just looks at the ground like she's trying not to smile.

'It's not funny – Arabella could've been seriously hurt!' I know the chance of injury in a pit of plastic spheres is minimal, but that's not the point. 'If she didn't want to go in, you shouldn't have made her.'

Violet sticks her chin in the air. 'I was helping, Daddy, and you said that was a nice thing to do.'

I grit my teeth and decide to take the matter up again when we get home. Being outsmarted by a five-year-old doesn't rank amongst my finest moments and I don't want to make things worse by arguing with her in a car park.

'Arabella's mummy was looking at you funny,' she says as I strap her into her car seat. 'Like Rapunzel when she sees Flynn Rider, but you don't look like him, Daddy. His face is nicer than yours.'

'That's right, Violet, turn the knife,' I mutter.

When she's safely inside, I close the door and lean

against the car for a moment. What a bloody day it's been. A brief stir of chatter catches my attention and I see a cluster of people making their way towards the soft-play centre. I bet *they* won't have to leave early because their kid shoved someone into a ball pit.

Violet and I sit side by side on the couch when we get home, plates of spaghetti hoops on toast in our laps and *Alvin and the Chipmunks* on TV.

I decide to attempt a conversation. 'So, did you have fun at Playzone? Were the other kids nice?'

My master plan is to segue nicely into asking what really happened with Arabella because there's definitely something she isn't telling me.

'I like *Alvin and the Chipmunks*.' She doesn't take her eyes off the TV.

The conversation is killed stone dead in less than ten words.

I'm not ready to give up yet. 'Tell me what happened at the ball pit again, I forgot.'

Silence.

Just then, the doorbell rings. A sigh of relief escapes me as I get up to answer it. Whoever's waiting outside has no idea how grateful I am for the interruption. I'm banging my head against a brick wall with Violet, but perhaps she'll feel like talking later.

The smell of cheese reaches me before my mum's greeting does. She's holding a tray of lasagne that's almost bigger than her face and is looking up at me expectantly.

'Wow, you brought lasagne. Again.' The smile on my face is a little strained at the edges. She's brought the same thing round for dinner at least twice a week since Claire died, as though the layers of pasta, meat and cheese are the only thing keeping our fragile family unit together.

Mum's smile widens and she's practically hopping from foot to foot with excitement. 'And a little surprise. Look who it is!'

She steps aside and my stomach drops instantly when I see Hannah on my front path. She's standing with her feet together and her hands clasped in front of her, a sheepish glint in her eyes tempering her megawatt smile.

'Hannah. Nice to see you,' I say through gritted teeth.

After the way we left things earlier, I can't believe she's turned up at my door. I didn't exactly give her the warmest welcome. Mum looks between us and frowns as she makes her way into the hall, thrown off by the sudden change in atmosphere. She heads through to the kitchen as she usually does to put the lasagne in the oven. Hannah tries to follow her over the threshold, but I step in front of her.

'What are you doing here?' I ask.

'I wanted to see Violet – I *am* her godmother after all.'

I scoff and my jaw tightens. 'When it suits you.'

She exhales sharply and runs a hand over her face. 'Evan, I said I'm sorry, but I can't make amends if you don't give me a bloody chance.'

'How do I know how long you'll be sticking around for, Hannah? How do *you* know? You've spent the last two years gallivanting round God knows where—'

Mum calling my name from the kitchen brings our confrontation to an abrupt halt. I reluctantly step away from the door and Hannah skips into the hallway as if nothing's wrong.

Mum shoots me a look. 'Don't think I didn't hear the pair of you snapping at each other like stray cats. And when was the last time you tidied up in here? The kitchen's filthy.'

I roll my eyes and lean against the counter.

'Not now, eh, Mum? I'm not in the mood.'

The oven door bangs shut and she twists round to face me, hands on her hips and a stern expression on her face.

I'm in the shit.

Her expression softens unexpectedly at the last second. 'I know you've already said no to this, but if you wanted Violet to come and stay with me for a while, just until you get yourself back on your feet—'

'No. For the last time, she's staying here.'

Even the notion of her going to stay with my mum makes my stomach lurch. Mum first offered a couple of days after Claire died, when it was clear I wasn't coping. Now, I'd like to think I have my shit a little more together than back then, even if it's less than I would like.

'Evan—'

'No, I'm not discussing it anymore!'

Violet comes running into the kitchen with her favourite space book.

'Daddy, can we read about the planets, please? I know all their names but some are tricky to say.'

She waves the book at me while fixing me with one of her Bambi stares. Damn genetics for making her inherit her mother's eyes.

'Not now, Violet, I'm talking to Grandma. Go and see if Hannah wants to read it with you.'

Her smile disappears and her whole body seems to deflate with disappointment.

'But I want to read it with *you*.'

'Violet, I don't have time right now, OK? Now do as you're told!'

I screw my eyes shut as soon as the words leave my mouth. They came out much louder and harsher than I'd intended. Before I can apologise, Violet storms off towards the living room.

'Well, you're everybody's favourite today, aren't you? First you get into an argument with Hannah and now you've bitten Violet's head off. Congratulations, son, ten out of ten.'

'Get off my back, Mum. Please. It's been a long day and I'm tired.'

My eyes are stinging from lack of sleep and no amount of massaging is making them feel better. I could do without another argument today since I've had three already.

'Evan, I've had enough of this. I know you miss Claire, but you've got to pull yourself together. Do you think she'd want you arguing with Hannah and stopping her from seeing Violet? Of course she wouldn't. Things might be tense between the two of you, but she can't make things right if you don't let her. And, like it or not, you're all Violet's got left. She deserves the best, not whatever the hell you're doing right now.'

My blood begins to boil, cutting through the swathes of fog that cloud my thoughts. Mum's not telling me anything I don't already know, but that last remark cut below the belt.

'I know, all right? I know I'm screwing things up because Hannah and I are barely speaking and Violet's shoving kids into ball pits. Believe me, I know everyone deserves better, so spare me the lecture. I'm trying my bloody best here, so do me a favour and get off my case.'

I stalk off to the living room and find Violet and Hannah on the rug, huddled round Violet's space book. They're deep in discussion over whatever planet they're reading about and may as well be a galaxy away. So much for protecting Violet from getting hurt again. She's welcomed Hannah back with open arms and allowed her to slot back into her life as if she'd never been away. It'll be a different story when Hannah decides she wants to go travelling again. I'll have to pick up the pieces like I did last time. They don't notice me standing in the doorway. I've never felt more disconnected from the people around me; all my efforts to keep them close and hold on to them have failed. Evidently, I'm doing nothing except pushing them away. I've disappointed my mum, snapped at Hannah, and Violet and I may as well be strangers.

Things need to change.

I need to change.

Chapter Six

Dear Claire,

You know I've always been a believer in fate and that things or people find you at exactly the right moments. Well, if ever I needed one of those gentle nudges from the universe, it's now. Violet and I need something – anything – to bring us back together. We've drifted apart since we lost you and I hate it, especially when I remember how close we used to be. I want to be the dad you thought I could be. I want to be Super Dad.

Renee and her friends are gathered round the old caretaker's cottage when Violet and I arrive at school. A note of terror runs down my spine when I spot them looking at me with barely concealed contempt.

Violet's transgression at the soft-play hasn't been forgotten by the looks of things. My days of having fellow parent friends are over before they've even begun.

'Why don't you go over and say sorry to Arabella again?' I suggest. 'Maybe you two could still be friends.'

Violet looks up at me with narrowed eyes, as if I've just suggested she runs away with the circus.

'But she's a *poopyhead*!'

'Don't call her that; it's not nice. Where did you learn that word anyway?'

'Netflix.'

Before Violet can elaborate, the bell rings and she runs off to line up with the rest of her class. She takes her place right at the back and, one by one, the lines of children make their way inside.

When I arrive at the office, I change into my costume and look at myself squarely in the mirror. The passion I used to have for my job must be locked inside somewhere; that kind of love doesn't just disappear. So, how do I tap into it? How do I make work fun again? My business depends on me finding that fire, so I'd better look bloody hard for it.

James hovers in the doorway for a moment when he arrives, not sure whether to join me. We look at each other, locked in a stalemate, neither of us having the guts to break the unnatural silence first.

'I'm sorry. For yesterday. I was a complete moron,' I say.

Little by little, the pressure eases out of the atmosphere. I begin to relax, but not completely. James is standing in the doorway, his face blank. He's usually an open book, but I can't read him this time.

'I just thought taking a break from the tours would give you a chance to relax a bit, that's all.'

He comes in and shuts the door behind him. I hand him a mug of coffee that I made a few minutes ago, hoping it'll go some way to making up for being such an arsehole. We sit on the battered old desk we got when we first rented this office.

One apology just isn't going to cut it. 'I'm really sorry. I know things have been shit for a long time because I haven't been handling things as well as I should. But I want to be different. I want us to get the business back on track and if that means you taking over the tours until I find my mojo, that's what we'll do.'

It kills me to say it, absolutely rips me in two, but I know it's necessary. The tours brought me so much joy and fulfilment when we first started, and, one day, hopefully they will again. But right now, for the sake of the business, I have to step back.

'It won't be forever, just until you feel ready to come

back,' James says, patting my shoulder. 'Why don't you do today's one as a kind of "see you later", then I'll take over tomorrow? How does that sound?'

'Deal.'

I slide off the desk and put my hand out for him to shake. He clasps mine tightly and brings me in for a hug. A huge weight has been lifted off my shoulders, but there's sadness lurking behind my carefully crafted smile. Part of me is still clinging on to my place in the business, frightened to let go in case I can't come back.

One final adjustment of my top hat, and I'm ready to go. My farewell tour starts right here.

I wander down Princes Street two hours later, lost and lonely and in desperate need of distractions. There's a voice in the back of my head saying it's only a matter of time before I'm booted out of the business altogether, and I wish it would shut the hell up.

I'm just outside the giant Waterstones so I head inside in the hope that its miles of shelves will clear my head. Maybe I can pick up a new bedtime story for Violet? We've read *Ratburger* and *Gangsta Granny* more times than I can count, along with her Tom Fletcher and Judith Kerr books.

The children's book section is on the ground floor and

quite honestly, it's paradise. The walls are bright, there are comfy beanbags so kids can lose themselves in fictional worlds, and the choice is magnificent. I'm not altogether sure what I'm looking for as I slowly browse the shelves. Something to bridge the gap that's formed between us since we lost her mother would be good, but I can't think what section that would be in.

'Everything OK?'

A woman of about fifty with a sunny, welcoming smile approaches me, looking very keen to help. Her name badge says *Margaret*. She looks so kind that I feel bad for taking up her time when I don't even know what I want.

'I'm looking for something for my daughter. She's five and she loves space and aliens. We lost her mum a couple of years ago and since then, things have been a bit ... difficult for us. I want to get her something we can enjoy together, but I'm not sure what to choose.'

Margaret's smile widens and she swings into action, whizzing from shelf to shelf picking up armfuls of stuff. If she has her way, I'll be spending a fortune on picture books, puppets and puzzles. She motions me over to a couple of free beanbags and dumps the pile of things between us. It looks like an archaeological dig in bright primary colours. The next ten minutes are spent looking through all manner of items that a child like Violet would adore. There are games and puzzles connected to classic children's stories, taking the characters from between the pages and placing them right in front of the kids who love them. If money were no object, I'd buy them all. There are puppets from *The Very Hungry Caterpillar* and *The Gruffalo*, but we already have those.

And then I spot it.

It's near the bottom of the pile, but beams out at me as if trying to attract my attention. *This is what you need: me! I'm right here, pick me up.*

An audio copy of *Ask an Astronaut* by none other than Tim Peake. This is perfect. Violet will love learning all about life in outer space and listening to it together will give us a chance to bond.

'You said your daughter loves space and aliens, so I thought that would be a good one,' Margaret says when she catches me looking at it. 'We have the paperback in stock too, but since she's only little, it might be more fun to use the audiobook. She'll feel like he's in the room with her, telling her all about space.'

My heart swoops as I pick it up. This is a step in the right direction and it'll hopefully lead Violet and I to where we need to be.

'Thank you so much. You've been wonderful.'

She takes me over to the counter and I pay for the CD.

When I'm done, a little cloud of happiness carries me back onto the pavement. There's a long way to go before I'm Super Dad, but I've made a start.

Chapter Seven

About dinner. How about we make it lunch today, just the three of us? Lorna and I are both on annual leave. Promise we won't discuss your love life. What do you say? D x

I shake my head, a smile playing on my lips as I sit in the office the following morning. This is Dave's fallback plan that he deploys whenever I say no to being set up. He gives it a day or two then, at Lorna's behest, gets in touch again with that well-worn 'friendly dinner' ploy. They pretend they *don't* want to discuss my love life, and then it magically comes up in conversation anyway.

My attention strays back to the paperwork in front of me for a moment until my phone buzzes again. It's another text from Hannah, asking again if Violet and I want to hang out tonight. She's sent a couple already today, but I haven't replied. Swallowing hard, I turn back to Dave's text and type out a response.

I say we've been here before. Can't we just go out for a pizza and enjoy ourselves? Being single and grief-stricken isn't as bad as it sounds, you know. E x

My eyes are drawn to the storyteller costume laid over the back of a chair, just waiting for James to slip into it. The ache in my heart grows, but I know this is the right thing. I walk over and pick up the top hat, smiling fondly as I look at it. You wouldn't think a slightly moth-eaten hat could hold ten years' worth of memories, but it can.

Putting it on won't do any harm, will it?

I slip it on and adjust it in the mirror, trying to get it to sit at the right angle. It was a charity shop find, back when James and I decided to go into business together, and it had seen better days then. What happened to the guy who put on this hat ten years ago? Surely, he must still be around somewhere; he can't have completely disappeared. There must be a way to bring him back again.

My phone ringing draws me back to the present. When I look at the screen, I see that it's Dave calling.

'Can I just say that if they were giving out an award

for the World's Saddest Bastard, you'd win hands down?'

Dave has such a rich, warm voice that he can make the worst insult sound like a motivational speech. A smile kicks up the corners of my mouth.

'And I'd accept the award with dignity and grace,' I reply. 'Seriously though, mate, you don't expect me to believe it'll just be a normal lunch with no dating talk, do you? I know what you two are like, remember. I'm not ready to get back out there again. No blind dates, double dates, nothing. I like things the way they are.'

There's a short pause before Dave speaks again. If I know him and Lorna as well as I think I do, she's given him some rebuttals to use in case I'm not into the idea. Their ultimate goal is to get me to go on a double date with them; any suggestions of it just being the three of us are complete rubbish.

'OK, you got me. There's a friend of Lorna's we really want to introduce you to, and we were going to use this afternoon to talk you into it. She's funny, really smart and she likes ghosts too! You two would have tons to talk about. But now you know about it, how about we invite her along? You two could chat and see if you like each other.'

I think about what the last couple of years have been like. I've barely scraped through with my sanity intact. Not the ideal time to get myself a love life.

'I appreciate the thought, but no, thanks.'

'Come on, mate,' he begs, throwing himself on my mercy. 'Lorna's really keen on the idea. There's no pressure, but it could be fun to meet someone new?'

He doesn't understand what he's asking me to do. Going out with someone who isn't Claire means admitting I'm not married any more, and I just can't do that.

Luckily, Dave manages to stop me in my tracks.

'Hannah thinks it's a good idea.'

'You talked to Hannah?'

Something about that doesn't sit well with me. Hannah and I have always been aware of each other's love lives – a little too much at times – but the idea of Dave discussing mine with her makes me squirm. I wonder what she thinks of my reluctance to date again and my determination to hold on to Claire's memory.

'I rang her to ask if she thought setting you up was a good idea and she said yes. Just come to dinner and give this mate of Lorna's a chance. If you don't like her, fair enough, but you can't stay out of the game forever. It doesn't have to be a date if you don't want it to be.'

The hope in Dave's voice kicks me in the guts. I'm backed into a corner now. Maybe I should say yes, just this once, and when it doesn't go well, they'll hopefully see how *not* ready to date I am.

'All right,' I sigh in resignation. 'Count me in.'

Dave gleefully informs me that he's off to tell Lorna the good news and that I've just won him ten pounds. Apparently, they had a bet on about whether or not I would agree to go on the double date: Dave said yes, Lorna said no. Before I can protest, he tells me that he had faith in me from the beginning and rushes through a goodbye.

The office is silent once more, save for some traffic noise coming from outside, and I only have my thoughts and the depressing business accounts for company. Ticket sales are down, we're in a bad way and need to do something drastic to avoid going bust.

I cast them to one side and focus on the other thought occupying my mind instead. The one that's terrifying the life out of me.

I'm going for lunch in a nice restaurant with a woman who isn't my wife.

Dear Claire,

Today, something big is happening: I'm going on my first official date since you died. Even the notion makes my heart rate spike and my head spin. You were – and still are – the love of my life; how am I ever meant to meet anyone else? I've had second, third and fourth thoughts about it, but I'm not backing out. Maybe I need to do this so I can be a better dad to Violet. Perhaps getting out there and meeting new people will bring me back to life? If all else fails, I can flee the country and change my name – always good to have a backup plan.

I close the little notebook I've started scribbling notes to Claire in and stuff it back inside my bedside drawer. I popped home to get changed and had the urge to tell her what's happening today. Writing to her brings a peculiar sort of comfort; it's as though she isn't really gone. At the moment, my plan to skip the country to start a new life somewhere else doesn't sound too bad. Spending time with Dave and Lorna has helped so much since Claire died – even if they've now made it their mission to find me a girlfriend – but this will be different. There will be four of us gathered at the table instead of three and no matter how many times Dave and Lorna say it's not a date, that's exactly what it bloody is.

I'm the first one to arrive at the Omni Centre, a huge glass building on Greenside Place guarded by two large metal giraffes. Cosmo is inside, along with a host of other restaurants and a giant Vue cinema. I stand outside to wait and although I know Dave and Lorna won't be far behind, there's just enough time for panic to take hold.

Dave might've said it didn't have to be a date unless I wanted it to be, but that's not what this friend of Lorna's will be expecting. It's probably been pitched as a date to her, so our expectations will be totally different. As my fear escalates, my thoughts flit from *What the fuck was I thinking?* to *Oh shit, have I dressed appropriately for this?* in a matter of seconds. My tan-coloured trousers, charcoal blazer and grey T-shirt looked OK when I left the house, but now I worry it looks like I just don't give a toss.

Any hopes of heading home and thinking up an excuse to text Dave are shot down when I hear a familiar voice calling my name. My heart plummets to my boots when I see Hannah walking down the street, waving enthusiastically.

'Hey! You haven't been waiting too long, have you? My taxi was late. Bloody roadworks.'

I frown. 'Um … no, I'm just waiting for Lorna and Dave to show up. Are you meeting someone here too?'

Unease grows in my stomach. Something stinks here; I'm definitely on the back foot.

Hannah laughs and pulls a face. 'I'm meeting *you*, you daft sod. Didn't Dave tell you?'

My phone buzzes. It's a text from Dave.

Don't be mad, dude, but I lied to you earlier. You're not meeting us for a double date, you're having lunch with Hannah. She told us she wants to sort things out with you, but you've been avoiding her, so we came up with a ruse to get you to meet her. Bit sneaky, I know, but you two have

been friends forever. Just talk to her, eh? Oh, and have fun.
D x

My lips twist into a scowl. Bloody Dave; he always has to try to do the right thing.

'You didn't know, did you?' Hannah says. 'He said he might not tell you in case you didn't show up.'

'No, I didn't know. Listen, I appreciate what you're trying to do, but it's really not necessary. There's nothing to sort out; we cleared the air over coffee, remember?'

She tilts her head to one side and puts her hands on her hips. Her eyebrow raises a fraction – her signature don't-fuck-with-me look.

'Really? Then how come I literally had to surprise you at home to get any time with you and Violet? I've asked you to hang out at least half a dozen times and you haven't replied once. I'm trying here, Evan, but you're not making it easy for me.'

Despite the sadness in her eyes, I bristle. 'What? Hannah, you've had it easy for the last two years. You got to travel and see all these beautiful places, while I was back here trying to hold myself and Violet together. You said you'd stick around and help until things got a bit easier, but you didn't. And don't get me wrong, I know you must've had your reasons for leaving, but it was so sudden. One minute you were here, the next you were gone and I … I missed you. Anyway, like I said, it's water under the bridge. There's nothing left to resolve.'

I take a couple of steps up the street, back towards Princes Street and wherever the hell I've left my car. My thoughts are trying to knit themselves back together after Hannah's unexpected arrival.

'Turning down a buffet, Harper? That's not like you.'

I turn to look at her and catch that smile of hers. The one that can hide a million secrets and still feel like home.

She folds her arms across her chest. 'If we're as fine as you say we are, and the past is in the past, we should be able to have lunch together, right? Seems a shame to waste a perfectly good meal.'

She stands there looking at me, challenging me. My face twists into awkward shapes as I consider her offer.

'Fine,' I say eventually, 'but only if I can eat my weight in prawn toast.'

'So...'

'So...'

Jesus, this is awkward. I scrabble around, looking for something to talk about. I'll take anything at this point, even something controversial.

'How are your noodles?' I ask, gesturing to her plate.

Hannah chuckles and twirls some around her fork. 'They're good actually, not too noodly.' She pauses and purses her lips. 'Is this what we're reduced to now? Talking about bloody noodles?'

My cheeks flush and I rub at the back of my neck. 'Sorry, I just… Well, I thought I was going on a double date today and this has thrown me off a bit.'

She flashes me a sympathetic smile and goes to reach across the table for my hand, thinking better of it at the last second.

'Yeah, I understand that. But hey, you're thinking of dating again? That's great. It's a shame to deprive the world of that Evan Harper charm. You knew how to use it when we were younger, if I remember.'

My shoulders slacken and I manage a smile. 'You know, you're the first person who hasn't said it's what Claire would want. Or called me a miserable bastard, for that matter.'

She shrugs. 'Well, why tell you something you already know?'

Our gazes lock for a moment, as though we're trying to work each other out. Testing our boundaries, seeing how far we can push our well-worn banter.

I watch her fingers delicately trace the handle of an upturned mug in front of her – a leftover from the breakfast service – and a memory whispers to me.

'Do you remember that morning with the terrible coffee?' I say.

Hannah's gaze snaps upwards and meets mine. An uncertain smile plays on her lips and she considers me for a moment before answering.

'Of course I do – it was the day after my dad's accident.'

A lump forms in my throat. When I look at her, I can tell we're both reliving the moment we found out Ken Russell had been in a car crash.

'You were so scared.' My fingers twitch as I think about taking her hand, but don't. 'I'd never seen you like that before.'

She adjusts herself in her seat, as though the memory is making her physically uncomfortable. I wish I'd kept my mouth shut instead of veering off down memory lane.

'I remember being at the hospital while he was in surgery and…' She trails off and runs a hand over her face. 'And trying to remember what the last thing I said to him was. All I could think was, "God I hope he knows how much I love him".'

I nod. 'He did,' I insist. 'And he still does, if his Facebook posts are anything to go by. He can't get enough of those travel photos of yours.'

Hannah's face breaks into a smile and my tense muscles begin to relax. Our eyes meet again and I study them. Have those subtle gold and amber hues always been there or am I imagining things?

'I hope so.' Her voice is small until she shakes herself like she's dislodging some painful memories. 'You were great that night. I remember you sitting with me and Mum in the hospital corridor, telling us everything would be OK even though you weren't sure.'

She opens her mouth to say more, but shrugs and picks up her wine glass instead. A series of tiny vignettes flash through my mind. The still silence of my flat, pierced only by Hannah's shaking sobs. Wrapping her in my arms and gently stroking her hair so she'd sleep. Standing in my kitchen the next morning, utterly exhausted, and rustling up the worst coffee in the world. And, of course, the totally unexpected thing that happened a few minutes later.

She's staring at me expectantly now, waiting for me to speak. I've been lost in my own thoughts for too long.

'I just did what anyone else would've done,' I say, smiling. 'Nothing special.'

Hannah snorts. 'You need to learn how to take a bloody compliment. You took care of me, made sure my mum had everything she needed, visited my dad every chance you got…' She trails off for a second. 'You were there for me and my family when we needed you and I didn't return the favour. Christ, no wonder you're angry with me. I never thought of it like that before.'

Her hands run through her hair, pulling it into a loose ponytail at the nape of her neck before letting it fall again. Her mouth is set into a thin, worried line and her eyes are shining.

'You must miss Claire so much,' she said when she looks at me again. 'I came really close to losing my dad, but I didn't. He's still here, but you … you lost the love of your life.'

The pain hits all over again, going for a gut punch this time. I style it out behind a quick smile, but she's not fooled.

'Every single day,' I admit without thinking. 'Some mornings, I roll over expecting to find her on the other side of the bed. When she's not there, it's … well, it's shit, to be quite frank. Reminds me all over again that she's never coming back. I just … I never thought I'd have to live without her, you know? I thought the cancer would just be a really shit thing that happened to us and that we could keep going. Now it's just me here, trying to be and do everything, and feeling like I'm fucking it all up.'

Hannah doesn't reply right away, just looks at me with barely concealed pity. Sweat prickles on my skin and I rub the back of my neck, feeling exposed and vulnerable. Like I've shared too much, at the wrong time, with the wrong person.

'Give yourself a break, eh?' she says. 'I couldn't do what you've done – I'd have gone to pieces if I were in your shoes. In fact, I *did* – I missed Claire so much that I went off travelling! But you … you stayed and made a life for you and Violet. That's something to be pretty proud of, if you ask me.'

She reaches over the table, certain this time. When her fingers touch mine, I pull back and clear my throat. I should've known she'd want to build on our shared moment of vulnerability. Part of me wants to reciprocate, but I can't quite bring myself to. Why does letting people in, even someone I've known a whole lifetime, have to be so hard?

'Oh, erm…' She retreats back to her own side of the table and wraps her arms around herself, looking confused and a little hurt. 'Sorry, I…'

I shake my head and take a sweeping glance around the room. Nope, no convenient holes in the floor to swallow me up. God, I'd give anything for a distraction.

I'm more than a little spooked when my phone rings.

'Mr Harper?' The voice at the end is sharp and officious. 'It's Tracey from St Joseph's. We need you to come and collect Violet. She's fallen ill.'

Chapter Eight

Keeping a clear head as I dash to Violet's school isn't easy. Although it's probably a sore stomach or sickness bug, a series of much worse scenarios plays in my head and scares the shit out of me.

I clamber out of the car and sprint across the playground as fast as I can. There's a class gathered outside holding a huge colourful parachute while children take it in turns to run under it to the other side, but I'm so focused on getting to Violet that I spot them too late. The teacher lifts the parachute high as I barrel towards it and with just seconds to spare, I manage to duck underneath and emerge at the opposite end.

'Thanks,' I yell over my shoulder as I head towards the office.

A short woman with dark hair, who introduces

herself as the Tracey who called me, buzzes me into the building and smiles kindly at me. My hair is clinging to my face in sweaty clumps and my heart is pounding furiously in my chest.

'Don't worry, she's fine,' she says as she leads me to where Violet's waiting. 'A bit of an upset tummy by the sounds of things.'

I frown. 'She seemed fine this morning. Maybe she's eaten something dodgy that hasn't agreed with her.'

Tracey glares at me over her shoulder and her nostrils flare with indignation. Great, I've been in the building five minutes and managed to land myself in the doghouse.

'Our canteen has a gold hygiene certificate, Mr Harper,' she says. 'If you want more information, it's on our website.'

Before I can tell Tracey that I'm not about to have Environmental Health down here taking swabs from the kitchens, Violet pops into view. She's sitting on an uncomfortable-looking chair, her head bowed low and her gaze on the threadbare carpet.

'Hey.' I crouch in front of her and put my hand on her shoulder so she looks up at me. 'You ready to go home?'

She nods and holds her arms up, motioning for me to lift her. It catches me off-guard a little – I can't remember the last time she wanted a hug from me – but I lift her into my arms and balance her on my hip. She buries her face into my shoulder and I stroke her hair. This may be the nicest moment we've shared in a long time.

I thank Tracey, who scuttles back to her office, probably to put the whole school on high alert about the troublesome parent casting aspersions about their hygiene. I carry Violet into the playground, away from the main building and past the swanky IT room that cost an absolute fortune. We head towards the gates and to our right, there's the class from earlier with their parachute. The teacher spots me and gets her class to lift it as high as they can, but I smile, shake my head and keep walking. No more daring acts for me today.

When she's securely in her car seat, I touch the back of my hand to her forehead.

'You feel a bit warm.' I smooth some hair away from her face. 'The lady on the phone said you have a sore tummy too. Did you feel unwell this morning before school?'

'No, just after we did numbers. I felt sick and my tummy started hurting. It hurts here too,' she says, pointing to her chest.

I kiss the top of her forehead and climb into the driver's seat. Suddenly and without warning, Violet lets out a loud yelp of pain and starts clutching her chest. A note of panic pinballs through my body, setting off every alarm bell in its path. This is looking way too much like a heart attack for my liking. Are they common in five-year-old girls? Why don't I know this?

'Violet, are you OK? What's wrong?'

Her hands are pressed to the centre of her school jumper as she wails in agony. I pull away from the school as quickly as I can without breaking the speed limit.

'It's OK, everything's going to be fine. We're going to the hospital and the doctors will help you get better.'

All I get is a sob in response, but at least she hasn't passed out on the back seat. Terror threatens to take hold, but I use all my strength to fight it off. Now isn't the time to panic, not when I have to get my little girl to the hospital.

Please let her be OK. Please don't take her away from me.

In a scene reminiscent of *Casualty,* I burst through the doors of Edinburgh Royal Infirmary's A&E department with Violet in my arms. She's still crying and murmuring, 'Ow, my heart,' every few minutes, but at least the screaming has stopped. No matter what happens while we're here, I won't forget that first piercing scream anytime soon.

'Hi, my daughter has just started having chest pains. I had to pick her up from school because she had a sore stomach, but when I put her in the car, she started screaming and holding her chest.'

How the receptionist behind the desk understands me is anyone's guess, since I sound like I've run an ultra-marathon, but she directs us over to some seats and tells me a doctor will be with us shortly. Sitting down does nothing to ease my panic; in fact, it makes it worse. I know how quickly situations can change in a hospital. One minute, everything's fine and the next a doctor is telling you the person you love is gone.

That was what happened with Claire. I left her for no more than twenty minutes to grab a quick cup of coffee. By the time I got back, she was gone. She died alone and it was all my fault. One of the nurses, a kind woman named Carol, told me not to blame myself. In her experience, she said, a lot of people wait to be alone before they let go so their loved ones don't have to see them die. That didn't make me feel any better.

With shaking hands, I get my phone out of my pocket and scroll through my contacts. I wish Hannah were here; she's so good at putting things in perspective so panic doesn't take over. I can't call her now though; I ran off in such a panic to get to Violet that I didn't even tell her where I was going.

I try Mum first, but she doesn't pick up. A moment later, I get a text saying,

Sorry, love, at Pilates. Speak soon x.

In a way, I'm glad. This is just the sort of thing that would lend weight to her idea that Violet is better off with her.

Dave and Lorna are both off the table. Their jobs as a police officer and firefighter don't leave them with a hell of a lot of time to rush to my side when I need them. James is out doing tours all day, so he can't come down either.

OK, then; time to swallow my pride. I fire off a quick text to Hannah, telling her what's happened and apologising for dashing off earlier. Whether she'll turn up or not, I have no idea, but I certainly wouldn't blame her if she didn't.

'Daddy, this hurts,' Violet says, pulling her face away from my shoulder to wipe her eyes. 'Will the doctor make me better?'

'Of course they will, sweetheart. We just have to wait a few more minutes, OK? Is it as sore as it was in the car?'

'No, it feels burny and hot now.'

My panic levels rise. I weigh up the merits of collapsing to my knees and screaming, 'Someone help my baby!' but that will probably delay things further as security wrangle me out of the building. Times like these are where being a single parent goes from bloody hard to really bloody hard.

Over Violet's shoulder, I see Hannah run into the building and wave her over to where we're sitting. Her wild curls are flying round her shoulders and I notice the fear in her eyes. A pang of guilt hits me as I think of how rude and standoffish I've been to her since she came back. I thought her promises of being there for Violet and me were hot air, but she's proven me wrong.

'Hey,' she says, taking a seat next to us. 'What's happening? Have you been seen yet?'

'Not yet.' I adjust Violet on my lap so she's not pressing down on my thigh muscle. 'The school called to tell me she had a sore stomach then she started having chest pains in the car, so I brought her here.'

'You did the right thing. It's probably something minor, but it's always worth getting her checked over.'

You did the right thing. A lead weight lifts off my shoulders when I hear that. Hannah strokes Violet's hair and she lifts her head off my shoulder, giving a bright smile.

'Hey you,' Hannah whispers, grinning at her. 'Are you feeling better now?'

'My heart feels burny. It's not very nice.'

'That doesn't sound so good. We need to get you better, don't we? You've got lots of space adventures to go on.' She looks at me and puts a comforting hand on my arm. 'I'll go and have a word with the receptionist, see if I can speed things up a bit.'

There's a shakiness to Hannah that I haven't seen for a while. It's there in the way she moves and speaks, a fault line running through her. Maybe I recognise it because I have one myself. She's worried about Violet like I am, but there's something more to it. She hasn't been back here since she quit her midwifery job nearly two years ago, so that probably has a lot to do with it. She clutches the desk as she waits for the receptionist to speak to her, throwing a seemingly carefree smile my way. It's taken a lot for her to even walk through the hospital doors today, even more to do what she's doing now.

Bravery isn't always running under massive parachutes, James Bond style. Sometimes it's walking into a place that terrifies the life out of you because your goddaughter and best friend need you.

'Someone's going to come out in a couple of minutes,' she says when she sits back down. 'She's down as a priority because she's so young.'

My head gently taps the wall behind me and I let out a sigh of relief. Finally, the end to this nightmare is in sight. Soon, we'll hopefully be back at home eating fish-finger sandwiches in front of a film.

'Thanks for being here,' I whisper. 'I was going crazy waiting by myself. And I'm sorry for just running off and leaving you earlier – when the woman from the school said Violet was ill, I panicked and didn't think.'

'Don't worry about it,' she says. Hannah reaches over and takes my hand, giving it an affectionate squeeze. It's a simple gesture, but it brings huge comfort. Nothing says 'I'm here for you' like a gentle hand squeeze.

Trapped wind.

Violet wasn't in grave danger, like I thought when I burst into the hospital. She had *trapped fucking wind*. The doctor did his best not to laugh when he told me and sent us off with a box of antacids.

Jesus Christ, it's been another rough day.

Glass of wine in hand, I lift Claire's book from the coffee table onto my lap. Bedtime with Violet was surprisingly easy, but not in a good way. She got her pyjamas on and climbed into bed, refused a story and said goodnight. In fact, she barely spoke to me at all. It was as though the nice moment when I picked her up from school had never happened. I'd have preferred a screaming match; at least there would've been a dialogue.

I flick to the one marked *When You Feel Like the Worst Dad Ever* and my chest tightens. Claire really did think of every high and low moment I was likely to experience without her.

I start to read.

Dear Evan,

Parenting is hard. With or without a life-threatening illness, it feels like a minefield sometimes and it's impossible to get everything right. Mistakes happen no matter how hard you try. This letter is a pick-me-up for when you feel like the worst dad in the world. Is Violet angry with you? Did you forget something important to her or get things wrong? Whatever's happened, you're bound to be feeling pretty low. So, let me cheer you up.

Remember the day we found out I was pregnant? To say we were shocked is the understatement of the century! A baby wasn't in our plans; we were going to go travelling round South America. Instead, we swapped carnivals in Rio de Janeiro and Machu Picchu for antenatal classes and jaunts round Mothercare. Yet, through the shock and the 'How the hell did this happen?' I knew we were in for the best adventure of our lives. For the last two and a half years, Violet has proven me right. And you've been amazing every single second. The 2am trips to get ice cream, the dirty nappies, Phil and Grant's unwelcome appearance: all of it. Your bond with Violet is incredible. Every time I watch you play with her, talk to her or bounce her on your lap while she giggles, my heart melts. You've got this, even if it doesn't always feel that way.

Whatever mistake you've made, Evan, it can be fixed. Always remember that. Hell, you used to say that to me when I was stressing over my clinical placements and never-ending exams. Every parent out there is just doing the best they can, exactly like you. Sometimes, things go wrong – it happens. But you're a fantastic dad, so stop being hard on yourself and go and talk to her.

Right now.

Go.

When you've sorted things out, make your famous chocolate pancakes and stick on a Disney film. Sing along embarrassingly loud to Tarzan or Tangled or Mary Poppins and let the argument melt away. You know more than anyone that life is too short to dwell on the bad things. Mistakes aren't important in the long run. What matters is how you make things right again.

Love always,

Claire

Chapter Nine

Mornings with Claire were always my favourite. There was something about a sunrise that made her even more beautiful. She'd open her eyes, give a lazy smile and stretch her arms up to the ceiling then say, 'Good morning,' her voice heavy with sleep. Then we'd drink coffee together out in the garden and watch the sun peek over the Salisbury Crags. It was a little slice of heaven before work and real life got in the way. Mornings lost their charm when she died.

Today, however, some of that magic is back, thanks to some delicious chocolate pancakes. Violet has a huge smile on her face as she tucks into them. I've also set up my laptop to play *The Little Mermaid* while we eat, so I'm winning all the dad points today.

And I'm not about to stop there.

'How would you like to go for ice cream after school?' I suggest as I clear the plates away. 'I was going to take you yesterday, but we had that little emergency with your tummy, didn't we?'

Violet slides off the kitchen chair and runs over to me as fast as her little legs will carry her. I bend down, scoop her up into my arms and pepper her face with kisses as she balances on my hip. The giggles that burst out of her make my soul happy. These are the kind of moments I want with her: happy, carefree ones where the chasm of grief between us doesn't seem quite so large.

'Come on, let's get you ready for school.'

I set her down and she dashes off towards the stairs. If we can make it through the day without any hospital trips or me having to run under a parachute, I'll count it as a success.

Mary's Milk Bar: take two.

Things go a lot smoother this time because I'm prepared. Even hearing 'What a Wonderful World' doesn't throw me off like it did last time. Violet's chatter about her school day helps me hold things together and, before we know it, we're sitting on a bench facing Edinburgh Castle. Grassmarket is almost empty as people head back home from work or school, but here we are. The sun is shining, we have delicious ice cream and for once, nothing has gone wrong. We even have a scoop for Claire – vanilla with rainbow sprinkles.

'Who lives in Edinburgh Castle?' Violet asks.

'No one's lived there for years – it's a tourist attraction now. Did you know the rock it's sitting on was made when a volcano erupted three hundred and forty million years ago?'

Her eyes widen with wonder as she looks at the castle then at me. '*Really?* Did it hurt the dinosaurs?'

I shake my head. 'This was way before the dinosaurs, about a hundred million years or so. Can you imagine a stegosaurus or a triceratops stomping all over Princes Street Gardens? They'd ruin the floral clock.'

Violet laughs and the sound catches me off-guard. I can probably count on one hand the number of times I've made her laugh since we lost Claire. Without warning, she takes a dollop of ice cream on her finger and plops it on my nose.

'Hey!' I chuckle.

I do the same to her and she bursts into more of those glorious giggles. Before we get into a full-on ice-cream fight, I get to my feet and reach for her hand.

'Come on you,' I say, 'we'll share this on the way home.'

I show her the portion of ice cream I got for Claire and her face lights up. We begin making our way home and for the first time in a long time, I think maybe we'll be OK.

Mum not only brings a tray of lasagne round later that night; she also insists on staying to cook it for us. I feel a rush of affection as I watch her take it out of the oven.

'Thanks,' I say, 'this looks great.'

'Oh, don't worry about it.' She smiles at me and joins me at the table. 'Did you have a nice lunch with Dave and Lorna yesterday? They were bringing a friend of theirs, weren't they?'

'It was … an experience.' I don't want to elaborate too much. 'I had lunch with Hannah instead. It's a long story. We had a good laugh and the food was decent. Can't ask for more than that. Then, of course, we had Violet's medical drama to contend with.'

She smiles kindly. 'Poor lamb, I'm glad she's OK now. Thank goodness it was only trapped wind. I was frantic when you called to say what had happened.'

I watch her for a moment, looking for signs of judgement, but don't find any. Little by little, I relax as I realise she's not about to suggest Violet coming to stay with her. We fall into silence and I drink in the sensation of a quiet night at home. There's something comforting about sharing dinner with Mum after such a hard day yesterday.

Mum shakes her head and laughs. 'So you didn't meet the love of your life then?'

'Been there, done that, remember?' I smile sadly and drop my eyes to my plate.

Mum doesn't say anything, but I can tell her mind is buzzing with thoughts.

It isn't long before we're finished. 'Fancy staying for a cup of tea?' I ask as I carry the dishes to the sink.

'Why not?' I can see she's tired, but jumping in the car and driving home can wait until after she's had a cuppa.

Mum asks how Violet is after her trip to the hospital and I tell her as I prepare the cups. As I move around the kitchen, I think about Dave and Lorna, their good hearts and their well-placed intentions. Although their double-date invitation had ulterior motives this time, they've made it clear they think it's a good idea. It's a subtle reminder I still have a life to live. One that doesn't include Claire.

'Mum ... do you think it's time for me to start moving on from Claire?'

She doesn't answer for a moment, just sits and appraises me. I can't tell what she's thinking; her expression's unreadable. Her thumb and forefinger frame her chin and her eyes are slightly narrowed.

'I'm not talking about *dating* necessarily.' I don't want

Mum on my back as well as Dave and Lorna. 'I'm talking about … I don't know, moving forward somehow.'

'Are you ready?'

'I don't know,' I admit as I pour our teas. 'Everyone seems to think it's time for me to be happy again. But I don't know – it feels like such a big step.'

Mum chuckles and rolls her eyes. 'You're thirty-two, not ninety-two! Hey, you could always try one of those, what do you call them, dating apps. If Rosemary down the road can get a Tinder account, so can you. She says it's a good laugh – you might enjoy it.'

I pass her a cup and join her at the table. 'It doesn't feel right to even consider meeting anyone else though. It feels like I'd be betraying Claire.'

My eyes drift up to the ceiling as my brain continues to pore over what's happened the past couple days. I had fun at lunch yesterday, even though I ended up saying too much to Hannah. Why did I let myself open up to her? We've always shared an implicit trust, but she left me right when I needed her.

'You wouldn't be,' she says, smiling warmly. 'I know you miss Claire, but you can't close yourself off forever. Violet's got all those grand plans to go to space, so you'll be rattling round here on your own unless you get out there and meet someone.'

I frown, losing myself in thoughts for a moment. Mum is right, but bloody hell, *Tinder*? Even the thought makes me feel sick with nerves. It couldn't work, could it?

Mum patting my hand snaps me out of my thoughts. 'Turn that brain of yours off for a while,' she says, smiling at me. 'Whatever you're stewing over can wait until tomorrow.'

My brow creases and I look at her with slight suspicion. 'How do you do that? Are you a witch and you just forgot to tell me?'

She chuckles and shakes her head. 'I'm your mum, Evan – I *always* know. Mums and dads have superpowers. Do you ever just know when something's bothering Violet?'

Not nearly enough. I do my best, but there's been such a disconnection between us since Claire died that I feel as though I barely know her any more. Not for the first time, I find myself longing for the days where I'd drive her round Edinburgh at 2am, watching as the city I loved slept but the little girl I loved didn't.

'Most of the time,' I reply, giving myself more credit than I deserve. 'We all miss some things though, right?'

I give her a wary glance, hoping she doesn't use this as another excuse to bring up Violet going to stay with her. Things haven't been easy since our three became a two, but I love her with everything I have. The thought of her being anywhere except this house makes my heart hurt.

'Evan, you know when I said Violet could come and stay with me…' Mum pauses to choose her next words carefully. 'It wasn't because I don't think you're up to being a dad. It was just to help you get back on your feet, that's all. Take the pressure off a bit.'

That doesn't make me feel any better. 'I know, Mum, but she's my daughter. It's my responsibility to take care of her. I might not be doing a great job right now, but things are going to change. I promise.'

She smiles a little uncertainly and puts her hand on mine. Our shared history unfolds in front of me: first we were part of a three, then a two when my dad decided he'd had enough of us and moved back to New York City. When I close my eyes, I can still picture the look on his face before he left for the last time. A flicker of remorse that disappeared seconds later.

'How come you never dated again after you and Dad split up?' I ask, looking at her.

She doesn't answer immediately and stares out of the window for what seems like hours. It's as though she thinks she'll find her response in the shadows of the Salisbury Crags.

'To be honest, I don't know. I loved your dad and it broke my heart when he went back to New York. I was never really sure if he left because he didn't like Edinburgh or because he didn't like me anymore.'

I put my cup down on the table and pull her in for a

hug. The idea of her blaming herself for my dad leaving kills me inside. 'It wasn't anything you did. He doesn't know what he's missed for the last twenty-three years.'

'Do me a favour,' she says with a small chuckle. 'Don't end up like me, rattling round on your own because you never got round to giving yourself another chance.'

If only you knew what happened when Claire died, you'd say that's exactly what I deserve.

Note to self: never enter the tricky world of dating apps alone when you haven't dated in fourteen years.

I've had Tinder for precisely two hours and I'm already in over my head. I'm not sure what possessed me to download it over breakfast this morning, but it definitely ranks among my worst ideas, alongside telling James I'd work from home today. He met Marcus, his husband, on Grindr and would've been a great resource for this kind of thing. The only problem is, I don't want anyone to know I'm doing this yet.

Bloody Mum and her harebrained ideas.

My phone buzzes with a notification, informing me that I've matched with Millie from Falkirk, who was the first person I swiped right on.

Great, now what do I do? Do I send a message or

does that look too keen and a bit stalkery? If I don't though, how am I supposed to meet anyone?

This is a *lot* harder than I thought it would be.

A loud knock on my door brings my brief venture into online dating to an end. I'm not sure who it could be; maybe it's Mum with more lasagne and life advice. If it is, I hope she's brought Rosemary with her so she can show me how to use this bloody thing.

Nope. It's Hannah.

'Hey.' I try not to look too surprised. 'What are you doing here?'

'Oh, I was just in the neighbourhood and thought I'd stop by.' She stops and winces. 'God, that sounds cheesy, doesn't it? I was … I was just wondering how Violet was after the other day?'

The real reason for her visit is hidden in her tight smile and the slight panic in her eyes, but I've got enough on my plate without trying to figure her out.

'She's fine. Nothing a couple of antacids couldn't sort out. You're a bit early to see her though, she's at school.'

Hannah chuckles a little too loudly. 'Don't be silly – I knew that! I just … I thought I'd pop round and ask, that's all. That's what good godmothers do, isn't it?' Her gaze falls on my phone, nestled in my hand with Tinder's home screen showing.

'Did I interrupt something?'

'What? No, why?'

My response comes too quickly and Hannah stifles a laugh. This is the downside to decades-old friendships; they know all your tells.

'Then why is a dating app open on your phone? Evan, you dark horse! I'm guessing this is something you don't want to discuss on your doorstep, so you may as well invite me in for a coffee and tell me what you're up to. I'll make the drinks, you do the talking.'

I roll my eyes and stand aside so she can come in. She's right; I don't fancy my private business being broadcast to the whole street.

'Make yourself at home, why don't you?' I watch her flit round the kitchen with an unexpected elegance, given her ridiculously high heels.

'Shut up.' She smiles over her shoulder at me. 'This is your fault really – you never move anything around so I always know where to find stuff.'

Once she's made two cups of coffee, we head through to the living room and I tell her about Mum's suggestion that I give Tinder a try.

'I've mastered the basics, like swiping, but I'm not sure what to do next,' I admit. 'To be honest, I'm not even sure what I'm looking for. It's not like I want a new mum for Violet or anything, just to meet some new people. But how are you supposed to say that on a dating app?'

Hannah leaves the armchair she's been sitting on and

joins me on the sofa. 'You have no idea how long I've waited for this. Pass me your phone.'

What follows is an intensive crash course in online dating. She teaches me some red flags to look for, helps me write a good bio for my profile and, most importantly, shows me how to enjoy using the app and actually have fun with it. We also flick through some profiles and choose two to swipe right on: a teacher named Rachel and a nurse named Jodie.

'Now we wait and see if you match with either of them. If you do, we'll send a message.' Hannah talks about it with the ease of someone who knows exactly what she's doing. 'And if you get stuck, just ask me. I've had a fair bit of experience with online dating – I met Julio on Badoo.'

Not exactly a ringing endorsement, considering Julio cheated on her with five different women and told her over Christmas dinner at my house last year. Throwing him out gave me an immense satisfaction that I didn't bother hiding.

'I'm still not sure about it,' I confess. 'Do people *really* meet like this or is it all a lie like smashed avocado on toast being the best breakfast ever?'

Hannah looks at me like I've just announced I'm joining a satanic cult. 'OK, first of all, smashed avocado on toast is *to die for*. Secondly, yes, people really do meet this way, Grandad. Just give it a go. What's the worst that could happen … you enjoy yourself?'

Great, that adds yet another member to the Evan Harper is a Miserable Bastard fan club.

'No, the worst that could happen is I go out on a date, end up being the victim of some sort of Black Widow serial killer, and Violet becomes an orphan.'

'Hmm, you've got a point. Who do you want to play you in the TV movie?' Hannah chuckles when she sees the terror on my face. 'Oh, don't look at me like that – I'm kidding!'

Chapter Ten

Once my initiation into the modern dating world is complete and Hannah has gone home, I settle down to read another of Claire's letters. I select the one titled *When Violet Asks About Me*.

Dear Evan,

Well, we got the worst news in the world today. Dr Fielding confirmed what I think we both knew deep down: I'm dying. I always imagined that I'd break down in hysterical sobs if someone told me I'd probably cark it before Christmas, but I didn't. You asked a lot of questions, trying to shape the news into something you could understand, while I sat there as if I'd just been offered a ham sandwich. Numb to it all, I think, and trying to push away all the fear, sadness and other things I didn't want to deal with.

I knew, of course. For a while now, I've felt time slip away from me, along with my strength and energy. Phil and Grant really are a pair of bastards.

This book has become more important than ever, so I'm going to use my remaining time to write as many letters as possible. This one is all about what I want Violet to know about me. Brace yourself, babe, it's a lot.

I want her to know the good, the bad and the downright ugly. You might avoid the conversation at first, to protect you both, but please don't put it off too long. I really would like her to know me as much as she can. Tell her I was hardworking and wanted to help people, but that I was also stubborn and hot-headed. Oh, and impulsive. Remember when I jumped off that cliff in Cornwall and terrified you and Hannah?

If talking to Violet about me is hard or hurts too much, let her get to know me through my favourite things: Jaffa Cakes, T-Rex songs, purple violets, Mary Poppins, Jilly Cooper novels (although wait till she's older before showing her those!). If she's looking for me, she'll find me in those things. There are tiny traces of me in all of them. I'm picturing her dancing around to 'Ride a White Swan' or 'Hot Love' and I have a huge grin on my face. I love the idea of her finding joy in things that mean a lot to me.

Tell her about my job and how it was always my dream to be a doctor. Tell her all my embarrassing stories and secrets, like the fact I didn't know gherkins were pickled cucumbers until you told me, and when I got so drunk I tried to leapfrog a traffic cone. I want her to know about my appalling sense of direction, what made me laugh and cry, and my amazing childhood back in Anstruther. Maybe we can take her there and show her the boats while we eat fish and chips?

It breaks my heart that I won't see Violet grow up. Hopefully this letter will give you some guidance on how she can get to know me. In fact, why don't you make a memory book together? You can pick out photos, tell stories and decorate it. That might ease some of the pain. What do you think? I want it colourful and sparkly with bright pink feathers!

Love always,

Claire

OK then – this weekend, it's time for Operation Memory Book.

Half an hour in a busy craft store on the outskirts of Edinburgh and I've locked eyes with half a dozen parents who silently agree it's far too early on a Saturday to be traipsing round the shops. Violet and I are gathering memory-book supplies – although I haven't told her exactly what the project is yet – and while she's loving life among the peacock feathers and pots of glitter, I'm dying for a coffee. No sleep plus an all-night greatest hits compilation of my biggest fears equals a grumpy Evan. Selected highlights include: 'Violet Would Be Better Off Without Me' and 'I've No Idea How to Be a Good Dad'. Tinder didn't help either; I matched with Rachel the teacher and thought about sending a message, but decided to wait until Hannah was there to supervise. I've enlisted her help to create the memory book, so hopefully she'll help me come up with a great first message while we're at it.

Man, I really need to sleep.

'Are we almost done, do you think?' I hope to God the answer is yes. How many decorations do we really need?

Violet looks up at me like I've just asked a really stupid question. '*No*, we still need buttons. Purple ones!'

Oh hell, we're never getting out of here. I'll be like Tom Hanks in *The Terminal*, wandering among the rolls of ribbon and stacks of oil paints.

We make our way to the buttons and Violet throws

herself into choosing just the right ones. I don't know what her criteria are and by the look on her face, I shouldn't ask. So I do the typical dad thing of standing to one side, holding the basket and wondering how much all this stuff is going to cost. I sneak a sideways glance at her and can't help but smile. She's in her element right now, among the colours, shapes and textures. Her eyes light up in wonder as she takes it all in. A tiny, happy moment that she hugely deserves after everything she's been through.

'Right then, are you ready? Auntie Hannah's coming over to help us with our project and we don't want to be late for her, do we?'

Almost instantly, Violet comes running over with the four packs of polka-dot buttons she thinks we'll need for today. It's funny how an incentive like your favourite auntie having lunch with you can speed up an important process like button selection.

Hannah arrives shortly after we get home, and it's time for the big reveal. Violet is desperate to know what our super-secret project is and I can't hold off any longer. While she sits on the living room floor, emptying our spoils onto the antique rug, I prepare to make my big announcement.

We've got sequins.

We've got glitter.

Now all we need is a…

'Drum roll please…' I pause while Violet slaps her knees in excitement, looking up at me. 'We are going to make … a memory book for Mummy!'

Violet's face lights up and my heart leaps. She looks over the moon – space pun totally intended – that we're finally going to stop avoiding the subject of her mother. And that she gets to play with glitter too, of course.

Hannah is on the rug with her, listening as Violet takes her through what we've bought. I spot a mischievous grin on Hannah's face as she reaches over to tickle her goddaughter, making her squeal with delight. Violet pats her arm and shouts, 'Tig!' as she runs away. My insides twist as I watch them have fun together. Hannah's a wonderful godmother; she treats Violet like an equal and knows how to cheer her up when she's sad. Seeing her have such a great relationship with my daughter is a little bittersweet because it's the kind of dynamic I'd imagined Claire having with her.

Hannah catches Violet around the waist and pulls her down onto the couch in a heap of giggles.

'Why don't you guys get started?' My voice cracks a little at the edges. 'I'll go and make some drinks.'

I walk to the kitchen as quickly as I can, clutching the counter to collect myself. I can't stay here for long;

Hannah and Violet will wonder where I am, and I don't want either of them to see me upset. My brain immediately begins breaking down what I have to do into smaller, easier chunks.

Step one: get the mugs.

Step two: fill them.

A voice behind me startles me and my hand slips, almost sending three mugs crashing to the countertop.

'Sorry,' Hannah says. 'I didn't mean to scare you. Are you OK?'

I nod and my brain switches on to autopilot as I prepare the cups and put the kettle on.

'Yeah, I'm fine. It's just hard, you know? Talking about Claire and thinking about her and missing her. It just hurts all the bloody time, Hannah. Anyone who tells you it gets easier is a liar. I let her down so much that last day in the hospital – I should've done more.'

Being vulnerable comes a little easier this time. This is the closest I've ever come to admitting what happened that day. Everyone thinks they know the truth, but they don't. I'm not the hero they believe I am.

'Hey, don't say that. You did more than enough; you were right there with her when she needed you most. That's what matters, nothing else.'

Oh, Hannah, if only you knew.

'You need to sleep.' She puts a hand on my back. 'You look done in.'

I sigh, grateful for the change of subject. 'I'm sleeping fine, honestly. Don't let the dark circles fool you – they add to my ghost-tour character. Well, they did anyway.'

'Did?'

'Yeah, um … James is doing the tours right now. I'm in the office looking at the financial statements and trying not to have a breakdown.' When I see the look of shock on Hannah's face, my thoughts immediately turn to damage control. 'It's the right thing for now, really. We had to do something to save the business and things are improving already.'

Hannah pulls me close for a hug. 'Oh, Evan, I'm sorry. I didn't know things were this bad. Is there anything I can do to help?'

Tears well up in my eyes as I hold her close. There's genuine concern in her eyes; I'd convinced myself it wasn't there when she left to go travelling. Now though, all the time I spent resenting her for having an escape route seems pointless.

'It'll be fine eventually – don't worry about it. James hasn't threatened to buy me out yet, so that's something!'

My laugh sounds more like a cat having its tail stood on, and Hannah notices. She pats my shoulder and I manage a smile.

'Listen,' I say, rubbing the back of my neck. 'I know I've been a bit of a dick, but it's good to have you back.'

Hannah smiles. 'Cheers. It's nice to be back home.

Now, how are you getting on with Tinder? Have you shown anyone the Evan Harper charm yet?'

I shake my head and tell her I've matched with Rachel, but have no clue what to say in a message. Then, with my best puppy-dog expression, I ask for her help.

Hannah shakes her head and smiles. 'What am I going to do with you? OK, I'll help you write a message. Consider me your online dating guru.'

'Come on, Daddy!' Violet shouts. 'I want to make the Mummy book!'

Chapter Eleven

A couple of hours later, we're almost done. The memory book encompasses everything Claire was: George and Sarah McDonald's daughter, love of my life, talented doctor and Violet's mother. I try my hardest not to notice the abundance of empty pages, the ones that will never be filled with photos and memories.

Surprisingly, remembering her doesn't feel as bad as I thought it would. Although I've come close to getting upset a few times, I've mostly felt *happy*. It's been nice going back over our years together, picking out the highlights and sharing them. Violet's favourite picture is one of me and Claire at our university's 90s night. I'm dressed as Peter Andre and she's Britney Spears.

'Daddy said you went away for a while,' Violet says

to Hannah, a little out of the blue. 'Did you go somewhere nice?'

Hannah doesn't miss a beat. 'I did. I went to lots of nice places. Would you like to see them?'

Violet nods and her attention is rapt as she looks at photos from Hannah's travels. I crane my neck to look as well, curious about what she got up to while she was gone.

'And this'—she points at her phone screen—'is when I was at a Holi festival in India. It's a special day to celebrate the beginning of spring. You can laugh, play and even make up with people you've fallen out with.' Our eyes meet for a fraction of a second. 'And look at all the beautiful colours.'

I look at the photo and notice the wide smile Hannah is giving the camera. Her skin is a painted rainbow, as if the colours of her soul are on show for the world to see. For the first time, I realise she didn't go away because she wanted to, but because she *needed* to. She needed to find herself – and that smile – again after Claire died. The two of them were good friends and her death hit Hannah harder than I realised.

'That's pretty,' Violet says with a wide grin. 'Can I be a rainbow too, Daddy?'

'You already are,' I tell her.

'I've actually got some news,' Hannah says. 'Since I've been back, I've been doing a bit of thinking about what I want to do next and … I've decided to go back to university. There's a great course in art therapy at Queen Margaret University and I've decided to apply for next year's intake.'

I smile as warmth rushes through me. I'd been hesitant about welcoming her back at first – more for Violet's sake than for mine – but she's staying, just as she promised she would.

'That sounds great. You'll be a really good art therapist,' I say. 'What made you decide to do that?'

'I took a lot of art classes when I was travelling and I love the idea of using art to help people who are struggling, maybe with grief or illness.' Her eyes are sparkling with excitement and she looks radiant. Hannah's always been a passionate person, and I can tell she loves this idea.

'Well, here's to you getting into Queen Margaret and becoming the world's most sought-after art therapist.' I lift my mug and clink it against hers.

While Violet's distracted by some bright, colourful feathers we bought, Hannah leans over to me.

'Why don't we come up with a message for you to send to Rachel before you bottle out of it? Get to it, Harper – I'm not taking no for an answer.'

Hi, nice to match with you! My name's Evan and I run ghost tours in Edinburgh. I love ghost stories, good food and Marvel movies. Tell me three things about you?

I look down at my phone screen, trying to figure out how one message took an hour and a half to write.

'There we are,' Hannah declares, wiping imaginary dust from her hands. 'It's simple, concise and doesn't give off any serial-killer vibes, unlike your first draft.'

I huff and fold my arms. 'Hey, there was nothing wrong with that.'

'Nobody starts a conversation with a stranger by saying, "Hey, wanna go on an adventure?" You may as well have asked if she was interested in becoming a crime statistic.'

'It did sound a bit like something Fred West would say, didn't it?'

'You're just a bit rusty, that's all. OK, you're *a lot* rusty, but you'll pick it up. Maybe don't send any messages without running them past me first though.'

When I look back at my screen, my stomach does a backflip. I've just sent my very first online-dating message and the magnitude of that is dawning on me, inch by inch.

'Just out of interest, is there any way of, say, deleting a message you've sent to someone else? Can you remove it from their inbox by any chance?'

Hannah fixes me with her sideways death stare and I shrink by several inches.

'I'll take that as a no.'

The cemetery is quiet when I get there, with a chilly early-morning breeze blowing through the overgrown grass. I try to come here to see Claire as often as I can, but sometimes life gets in the way and I don't make it for a few weeks.

Right now, however, I need some time here. Things have been mad lately and I need some peace and quiet to make sense of it all. I trudge across the grass, hardened by the cold weather we've had recently, and spot a bunch of flowers I definitely haven't left sitting at Claire's headstone.

A bouquet of wild purple violets – Claire's favourite – just like always.

Not this again.

I march over to the flowers and pick them up, looking for a note or something to indicate who might've left them. As usual, there's absolutely nothing. This has happened a lot since Claire died. They appear regularly in autumn and early winter, taper off in late spring and stop completely in the summer. Then in late August or early September, the cycle starts again.

I pick up the bouquet and place it at a headstone that's so covered with moss I can't make out the name any more. Nobody appears to have visited it for a while, so I decide they should have some nice flowers. I move back and sit in front of Claire's headstone with my knees pulled up to my chest, preparing to pour my heart out to an empty cemetery.

'Sorry I haven't been to visit you for a while.' I heave a sigh. 'I promise I haven't forgotten about you, it's just … things have been so crazy lately with Violet and everything else. She started school last week. You should've seen her, Claire – she looked so grown up. You'd have been so proud.'

A gentle breeze blows through the grass and ruffles my hair. The cemetery is quiet and still, separating me from the loud, busy world by a strong stone wall.

'People seem to think it's time for me to move on and find somebody new, which seems a bit scary. I'm not quite ready to let you go yet. Don't get me wrong, I know you're never coming back…'

My voice cracks a little and I take a second to compose myself, running my hand over my face. This is a lot harder than I imagined it would be. Visiting her grave is usually cathartic. I feel like I can spend time with her in a way, and voice my thoughts to her. Today, however, is different. Talking about moving on is never easy, not least when I'm sitting at my wife's graveside.

'I just can't seem to forget the life we had planned together, you know? We were going to have it all and then suddenly, everything was gone. I had a three-year-old daughter wondering where her mum was and no idea what to tell her, loads of neighbours who wanted to feed me lasagne, and this overwhelming sadness that felt like it would never go away. I finally feel like things might be getting a bit easier and that it might be time for some changes. I downloaded Tinder and even sent someone a message. Crazy, huh?'

When I stop talking, the silence of the cemetery weighs heavy on me. There's not another soul around and I become very aware I'm talking to thin air.

'I'm trying my best to be excited but… Oh, I don't know, there's just something weird about the idea of *dating*. I mean I did a bit of it when I was younger but then I met you while we were at uni and, well, that was it.'

I take a deep breath and rake my hands through my hair. My pounding headache is back, probably thanks to a stressful week of no sleep, school runs and the possibility of "getting out there again".

'Maybe I should just stop worrying and get on with it. How hard can it be, right? You just go out with someone and see what happens. If it doesn't go well, it's not a big deal. Obviously, I won't let Violet meet anyone until I'm absolutely sure they're a good fit. And it *would* be good to meet new people.'

The fog in my mind begins to clear, and I start to see how exploring new possibilities in my dating life could be fun instead of utterly terrifying. I get to my feet and look at the headstone. It's been a bit beaten up by the weather, but the inscription is still clear.

Claire Elizabeth Harper
Beloved Wife, Daughter and Mother

'I'll never forget you. But I think it's time I try to move forward. I hope you'll forgive me.'

Chapter Twelve

Making roasted-vegetable pasta should be a straightforward task.

You boil some pasta in a pot of water, put the vegetables in a roasting tin and stick them in the oven. Not exactly Michelin-starred stuff and there are no foams or reductions involved.

Why then did I have to put out two separate fires and make a desperate run to the nearest takeaway with Violet? The kitchen still smells of smoke and bitter disappointment, and there are dishes everywhere because I haven't been able to face cleaning up. When I told Violet I was making her mum's pasta, she was so excited because we haven't eaten it since she passed away. Chicken fried rice and prawn crackers didn't really hit the spot after that. I feel wretched for failing at such a simple task, but I also miss Claire even more than usual. Whenever she cooked, she'd always play music and rope me into dancing with her until the food was ready. We'd drink red wine and laugh and kiss. She had a way of making everyday life extraordinary; the simplest of things could turn into adventures with just a sprinkle of her magic.

She was so good at being alive. Even now, I still can't believe she isn't here anymore.

I've always been a big believer in signs. Not the ones from the Mel Gibson movie, but little nudges from the universe that help us choose the right path. When I was at my lowest after Claire died, I kept finding white feathers around the house, like she was trying to tell me she wasn't really gone.

After I tuck Violet into bed and come back downstairs, I get another sign that sticking with my dating adventure is the right thing to do. My phone vibrates and I find that Rachel from Tinder has replied to my message.

> *Hi Evan! Wow, three things about me… This is the part where I'm supposed to make myself sound cool and mysterious, right? Unfortunately, I'm neither of those*

things, so I'm going with honesty is the best policy. My name's Rachel, I teach seven-year-olds, and in my spare time I like to act and sing opera badly. Hopefully none of those things has put you off yet, haha! You sound cool though – anyone who loves ghosts and Marvel movies has to be. Look forward to chatting more. Rachel.

A reluctant smile spreads across my face. Rachel seems nice and relatively normal.

I go to type a message back then stop. If I send another message, there's a good chance she'll reply. Then I'll send another and she'll reply again. I'll officially be down the rabbit hole of online dating, with no escape routes and no Eat-Me or Drink-Me options to help point the way.

If Dave and Lorna were here, they'd be saying, 'It's only messaging, Evan – stop overthinking it. At the very least, you're talking to someone who isn't us, your mum, Hannah or your five-year-old daughter.' Hannah would tell me to stop being such a wimp and get on with it. In fact, she'd probably commandeer my phone and insist on writing the message for me.

So what do *I* say?

I take a deep breath and give myself a mental kick up the backside. I'm not being asked to make Da Vinci's *Vitruvian Man* out of cocktail sticks; all I have to do is reply to a message.

I start typing my response. I'm following the white rabbit, with no idea where the rabbit hole will take me.

It doesn't take long for that kind of thinking to land me in very dangerous territory.

I, Evan Michael Harper, am about to go on my first date in fourteen years.

I'm not sure exactly how it happened. One minute, we were talking about Captain America and the next I'd agreed to meet her for coffee.

While I'm in the St Joseph's playground, waiting for Violet to come out, I look at the message again.

That sounds great. How about we meet at Starbucks on the Royal Mile on Wednesday?

Did I really write that?

It's under my name, but it feels like the words came from a totally different person. Someone who knows what he's doing with this online-dating thing and feels confident in asking women to meet up for coffee. My leap of faith has earned me top marks from Dave, Lorna and Hannah: all talk of blind dates and double dates has now ceased.

Thank God for that.

Before I know it, my date with Rachel arrives. I change outfits six times before I find one that doesn't make me look like Beaker from the Muppets: a casual white shirt, a pair of jeans I probably paid way too much money for and a pair of dark shoes.

I stand in front of the mirror, trying to tame my hair and knowing I'm wasting my time. No matter what I do, it'll stick up at odd angles anyway. My stomach lurches as I realise I have to leave in ten minutes.

'I'm fucked,' I say to my reflection. 'Absolutely, one hundred per cent fucked.'

'No, you're not,' Hannah says from my bed while she helps herself to a family-sized bag of Doritos. 'You'll be fine, as long as you lighten up and relax a bit. You and Rachel have been getting on really well this week, so what's the problem?'

I turn to face her, still fiddling with my shirt cuffs. 'The problem is I'm nervous as hell and have no clue what I'm doing. Maybe this is a mistake. It's not too late to text and cancel, is it? I think I need more dating practice before I throw myself in at the deep end like this.'

Just as I go to grab my phone from the bedside table, Hannah lunges over and snatches it out of my reach.

'You are *not* cancelling this date, Evan Michael

Harper. It'll be good for you to get out there and start living again. Trust me, you'll thank me for this later.'

I make another grab for my phone, but she's too quick for me and does some sort of gymnastics move to get off the bed and over to the other side of the room.

'You can do this,' she says, smiling at me. 'I know it's scary, but sometimes you just have to take the leap and do it anyway. Remember when Claire jumped off that cliff in Cornwall?'

Only too well. My heart was in my mouth the entire time until she emerged from the water, whooping with joy and wanting another go.

Am I really ready to do this? Can I get out there and try again?

There's only one way to find out: I have to do what Claire did that day and jump.

My phone pings with two good luck texts: one each from Dave and Lorna. They both say how happy they are that I'm doing this and that everything will be fine. Lorna also says I should listen to my mum more because she's a genius, and that she wishes she'd thought of the Tinder idea herself.

I go back to getting ready for my date. I debate glasses versus no glasses, but eventually decide to go without. Violet once said they made me look like Peppa Pig's dad, and that's not really the look I'm going for today.

There's time for Hannah and me to read a quick letter from Claire. What other one could I choose but the one titled *When You're Out of Your Comfort Zone*? Maybe it will help me navigate this scary new territory I'm about to step into.

Dear Evan,

It's no secret that you love your comfort zone, is it? And who could blame you? You've made it into a beautiful, safe place, filled with things you love. If you had it your way, you'd stay nestled in there forever and shut out anything new or risky. But, my darling, you know that's no way to live. I've told you that often enough. When we met, your comfort zone was the past. You'd buried yourself in history books for years because you knew how things would play out. The past was safe for you, but the future wasn't.

When I die, your comfort zone will become a distant memory for a while. You'll have to do all sorts of things you never imagined: planning a funeral, clearing out my stuff, figuring out how to work the washing machine. And it'll likely scare the life out of you, but that's OK. A little fear never hurt anyone, did it? In a funny way, it's what keeps us moving forward. We want to move past the fear and get to a place of safety again. Only, when we get there, we find we're capable of more than we thought. And that's exactly what you'll discover too. You'll find you're the kind of person who can wash a load of clothes without dyeing anything a funny colour or find humour even in the darkest situations. You can't hide in your grief forever, and I wouldn't want you to.

So when you find you're out of your comfort zone, embrace your fear and dive into whatever new experience awaits you. Trust me, you'll be glad you did.

Love always,

Claire

She's right, as always. Burying myself in grief forever isn't the answer. Somehow, I have to build a new life, which means stepping outside my comfort zone and doing things that terrify me. As much as I'd perhaps like to hide from the world and keep my heart under lock and key, I can't.

I have to move on, and my journey starts today.

Rachel is already waiting for me when I get to Starbucks. She's average height with curly shoulder-length brown hair and large green eyes and is wearing a blue stripy jumper and dark jeans. She waves me over to the brown sofas by the window when she spots me and smiles enthusiastically.

I hold out my hand. 'I'm Evan, nice to meet you.'

'Rachel,' she replies, 'and likewise. You look a lot like your photo. That's a good start.'

We sit down and start the awkward portion of our date. Luckily, I've picked a good place for us to meet. The scents of cakes and freshly brewed coffee mingle in the air and there's a relaxed vibe about the place.

'So, you said you're from the Highlands originally?'

'Yeah, near Inverness; how about you?'

I tell her I lived in New York until I was seven then came to Edinburgh because my mum's from here. I edit out the part where my dad left a couple of years later; I don't want to bring the mood down or turn my date into a therapy session.

'I've always wanted to go to New York.' Rachel's eyes are wide with wonder. 'Did you live right in the middle of it, in Manhattan?'

'We lived in Greenwich Village, near Washington Square Park. I don't remember much about living there because I was so young, but it's an amazing city. You should visit sometime.'

'Maybe we could go together!' Rachel looks horrified and claps her hands to her mouth. 'Oh God, I'm sorry. I didn't mean for that to come out. Well I did, but it was meant to be a joke and… Oh hell, I'm really bad at this!'

In any other situation, having someone suggest a trip to New York on the first date would send up red flags all over the place, but it makes me feel better. There's something comforting about knowing Rachel's nervous too. Maybe we can navigate the scary world of a first date together.

Over coffee and cake, we set about getting to know each other better. Our respective nerves disappear after a few minutes and the conversation flows easily. Of course, it feels weird to be out with a woman who isn't Claire, but I do my best to adapt. It's going much better than I thought it would; I even think I might ask her out again, for dinner or to see a film.

Then the doll makes an appearance.

I get back from using the toilet and it's sitting on the table by Rachel's coffee cup. It looks like it might be Victorian, but isn't one of the pretty china dolls from that time. This one's eyes are crossed and it's looking at me with a vaguely demented expression. The skin is the colour of sour milk with two pops of pink in the cheeks.

Jesus Christ.

'Do you like her?' Rachel notices me staring at the doll and lovingly strokes its brown curls. 'Her name's Sally – I've had her since I was a kid. Isn't she beautiful?'

Beautiful isn't the first word that comes to mind when I look at Sally. Fucking terrifying maybe, but definitely not beautiful.

'Um ... yeah.' I hope to God I sound convincing. 'She's ... lovely.'

Goosebumps creep all over my skin when I look at her again. Although my job revolves around the macabre, I can't stand dolls. I want to get as far away from it as possible, but I force myself to stay where I am. It obviously means a lot to Rachel – although why she brought it with her on a first date, I don't know – and we all have that one possession with a long, rich history.

Rachel looks at Sally like she's the best thing in the world and even kisses the top of her head.

'I found her in an antiques shop when I was seven. She's got a really good story attached to her as well. Do you want to hear it?'

'Sure!'

Please don't be haunted, please don't be haunted...

'Well, when I bought her, the shop owner told me she's possessed by the spirit of a little girl. She died in a fire in 1875 and apparently, she was holding Sally when they found her.'

'Wow.' I fail miserably to keep the fear off my face. 'That's ... interesting. She doesn't get up and walk to your bed during the night, does she?'

'Now you come to mention it, I've found her on the

other side of the room from where I left her a few times before!'

I give Sally the side-eye, hoping she doesn't decide to visit my side of the table.

'Fascinating, isn't she?' Rachel scoops Sally into her arms. 'If you like her, you'll *love* the others.'

'Others? You collect dolls then?'

'Not just dolls, *haunted* dolls. I've got about twenty in total and they all have names. There's Beatrice, Margaret, Nelly, oh and I can't forget Harriet. You have to watch her – she's a bit demonic.'

As she goes back to counting off the names of her haunted dolls on her fingers, I can feel the chances of us having a second date disappearing by the second. When Rachel gets out her phone to show me photos of them, the final nail is hammered in the coffin. Overall, my first foray into the dating world has been a mixed bag. I make a mental note to add something to my dating profile when I get home: *Owners of demonic dolls, please look elsewhere.*

Chapter Thirteen

Dear Claire,

I've started dating again. It's all your fault, really; well, yours, Dave's, Lorna's and my mum's. Your letter about stepping outside my comfort zone was so inspiring that I said fuck it to my better judgement and arranged a date. I'll tell you all about it below, but suffice it to say it didn't go well.

Maybe this is the universe's way of telling me I should be on my own? That I should grieve you forever like some brooding hero from a classic novel. I may not have chosen solitude, but I'd like to think I wear it well. The haunted look is useful for ghost tours, so perhaps dating could jeopardise my career? Honestly, though, is it still too soon? Did you send the woman with the haunted doll to me for a reason?

My dating horror story gives my friends plenty to laugh about when I tell them that evening. They don't quite believe me at first and I can't say I blame them. Who would have thought that my first foray into the dating game would lead me to a woman with an obsession for haunted dolls?

Hannah gets the full run-down of what happened when I phone her just after I put Violet to bed. Normally I avoid phone calls like the plague, but the date isn't really something you can explain over text. So I've made myself comfortable on the window seat in the living room and cradle a glass of wine as I talk to her.

'*A haunted doll?* No way, you're winding me up.' Her laugh is just as goofy over the phone as it is in person. 'What kind of person would bring that sort of thing on a date with them?'

'Do you think this is a sign I should delete Tinder and forget about online dating? I feel like it was some kind of omen.'

She pauses for a moment. 'That depends. Do you *want* to forget the whole thing?'

I shrug, then remember she can't see me. 'I don't know. It seemed like a good idea before, but that date was pretty ... unique.'

There's shuffling on Hannah's end, like she's trying to make herself comfortable. 'Well, the way I see it is, if everyone let one bad experience put them off, nobody would get anywhere. I think it's worth giving it another shot, even if all you end up with is another funny story to tell.'

She's saying exactly what Claire would say: *don't let a rocky start put you off*. So as much as I might want to slink back to my comfort zone with my tail between my legs, I don't. When the phone call ends, I get swiping again and persevering produces a peculiar feeling: a fizzing in my stomach telling me I can do this. I can become the dad and man I want to be.

Before long, I have another date lined up; this one is with Meghan, a merchandise designer from Glasgow. We're going to the Edinburgh Dungeon and to my surprise, I realise I'm excited.

I've always been the kind of person who likes to be busy. Whether that's meeting people, telling them stories or playing stupid games with Violet; I like being in the middle of things and having plenty to occupy my brain.

Although I'm still relegated to the office while James treats the Old Town like the Globe Theatre, my brain is a hive of activity. I can't get my mind off the weird and not-so-wonderful date with Rachel. Perhaps it was my naivety, but I had no idea there were people out there who'd bring a haunted doll on a first date. Or any date at all, come to think of it.

There has to be a way to channel the chaos going on in my life into something positive. My eyes travel around the run-down office we haven't managed to decorate since we leased it. This room has been the site of our biggest triumphs and failures, so there must be some inspiration lying around.

I need a way to contribute to the business that doesn't involve sitting in this office day after day. Something that will help me make my mark and show James I'm still capable of being a part of things. My mind circles back over the last ten years, trying to pick up on the elements that made us a success. We each played to our strengths: me with my storytelling and James with his dramatic flair. We made the most of our surroundings, using the Old Town's history to its full advantage and adding spookier elements to ghost stories passed down through generations. We put on special events…

Wait a minute, that's it.

I should plan a special event to mark Monsters, Murders and Magic Tours' grand return to the ghost-tour scene. Halloween is soon, and what better time to do something spectacular?

My brain splutters into action, like a car engine that hasn't been started in way too long. Ideas start to form, slowly at first, then they come thick and fast. My hands scrabble around and grab a notepad and pen to write them down. I can feel a spark in my soul as fire spreads through my veins. I feel closer to the old me than I have in ages.

There's hope for me yet. I can become Super Dad, get back to the job I love, and find someone I can open my heart to.

I can do it all. I know I can.

By the time James comes back, my planning is in full swing. My brain has fired ideas left, right and centre, and I can see the event beginning to take shape in my head. Before I tell him though, he wants a quick update on my online-dating progress. I show him Meghan and tell him about our upcoming date to the Edinburgh Dungeons.

'I've got to hand it to you – I thought you'd have thrown in the towel after the woman with the creepy dolls. Good on you for sticking with it.'

'Mum would never forgive me if I gave up on it, and neither would Dave, Lorna or Hannah. My life wouldn't be worth living if I deleted the app now,' I say with a grin.

'Well, I'm glad you're not letting one slightly sinister date put you off. I was on Grindr for six months before the digital gods smiled on me and sent me Marcus.

Believe me, I had to wade through a whole lot of crap to get to him. You'll get there.'

James pats me on the shoulder and perches on the edge of the desk. His eyes travel to my notebook, much to my alarm.

'What have you been working on while I've been running the tours? Anything interesting?'

Before I can close the cover over, he picks it up and looks at all my notes for the spookathon. His eyes widen and a smile slowly spreads across his face.

'Mate, this looks brilliant. A scary-movie marathon, a special walking tour, stuff for kids… When did you come up with all of this?'

I rub the back of my neck and shrug, self-consciousness creeping up on me because he's seen my plans before they're ready.

'Well, I was at a bit of a loose end in here after I finished looking over the books. We're in a bit of a mess, but I think we could afford to do this at Halloween. Things have been a bit better since you took over the tours – we've sold more tickets and the negative reviews have stopped too. I haven't thought everything through and there's still a lot more to plan, obviously. Maybe I could even lead the walking tour while you jump out and scare people, just like old times.'

James passes the notebook back. 'Wait, *this* Halloween? Evan, we're nearly in September already.

This type of thing needs months of planning and we don't have the time. And do you really think you're ready to lead a tour again? You've had some time off and it's obviously doing you the world of good, but you've said it yourself that things are starting to pick up. Maybe we should get back on an even footing before you...'

He trails off, leaving the rest of the words hanging in the air unsaid. It doesn't take a genius to work out what they might be.

'Before I fuck things up again, you mean?'

James covers his face with his hands and makes an odd sort of grumbling sound before he looks at me again.

'Mate, I didn't mean it like that. It's just a bit ambitious for this year, that's all.'

I pick up the notebook and close the cover, keeping my grand plans out of sight. 'Do you remember the Halloween party we threw the first year we opened? Nobody came to it because we forgot to send out the invites – OK, *I* forgot to mail out the invites. Consider this event payback for that and all the other mistakes I've made. I'll do everything and if it fails, it's on me.'

He gets up and starts walking around the room, deep in thought. Part of me is offended at his lack of trust in me as a business partner, but it's understandable after the way things have been the last two years.

'All right, we'll do it. It'll be tight time-wise, but if we start now, we should manage it.'

He offers his hand and I shake it. It's official: our spookathon is happening.

Usually, Violet's favourite thing to do of an evening is spend time in her room, immersed in a world she's created with her imagination.

Tonight, however, I have something a little different planned for us.

We're in the living room, cuddled together on the sofa and listening to *Ask an Astronaut* for the first time. Little moments like this are why I started my Super Dad quest. I wanted to bond with Violet and find a way to bridge the chasm between us that Claire's death caused.

Finally, it looks like I'm starting to get somewhere.

We're learning all about spacewalking when I spot something odd on Violet's left arm. Maybe it's some paint from school that she forgot to wash off.

'Baby, what's that on your arm?'

She doesn't look at me and at first, I'm not sure if she heard me. She's really engrossed in our audiobook, after all. When I touch the mark as gently as I can, she winces and my worst fears are confirmed. It's a bruise.

'How did you hurt yourself?' My voice is soft and I look down at her until she meets my gaze. 'That looks sore. Did someone bump into you?'

She shakes her head, but doesn't elaborate and uses her hands to cover the bruise as best she can. It's hurting her to hold on to it, judging by the pain etched into her face.

'I bumped it in the book corner.'

She's not telling me the full story, but I don't want to push too hard in case she clams up completely.

'You know you can tell me if something happened at school, right? I won't get angry.'

Violet nods, but her mind has gone back to outer space. Have I missed something? Maybe I'm overthinking this and she really did bump it in the book corner, but I have a feeling she's hiding something.

Once I've put her to bed, I drag my body down the stairs and slump into a chair, the book of letters perched on my lap.

This is the only way to get out of my own head: diving into Claire's. A lot of the letters have to be read at specific times like Violet's university graduation or her first date. However, I rifle through the pages and come to one that says *When it's Time for an Adventure*.

That can happen whenever we want, so I decide to read it.

Dear Evan,

It's time for an adventure! Don't do that face you do, that what-the-hell-are-you-on-about one with the eye roll. For your information, I'm on the good stuff: tamoxifen. Yay, nausea and fatigue! Anyway, I'm writing this letter as a kind of wake-up call. My worst nightmare is thinking of you and Violet mourning me forever. My time might be short, but yours isn't. Somehow, things will move on and so will the both of you.

So, with that in mind, I want you and Violet to dedicate an entire day to magic and adventure. We live in a beautiful, historic city with plenty to do, so shake off the grief for a day and have some fun! Take her to the zoo or Camera Obscura or the museum – anything that takes some weight off and makes you smile. Maybe you could volunteer somewhere or find one of Edinburgh's secret beauty spots? Use that imagination of yours and come up with the most magical day possible.

You'll hate this at first. In fact, one of our friends – Lorna or Hannah – is probably looking over your shoulder to make sure you actually read this letter. Why? Because you'll think 'Why should I get to be happy when Claire isn't here anymore?' Well, my love, that is a complete load of bollocks. Even if you're determined to stay sad forever, what about Violet? She doesn't deserve to live a life of grief and neither do you. If you can't drag yourself out of despair for anyone else, do it for Violet.

Life is all about finding little pockets of magic wherever you can. Taking a day might help you find some of that again if you feel like you've lost it. You'll also teach Violet that life isn't based solely around schedules or work. It's also about moments, love, silliness and laughter. It'll be one of the most valuable lessons she ever learns.

I'd love the three of us to have some more adventures before the end. Maybe we could discover some new places and things. A lot of it will depend on how sick I am, but I'll tell you one thing. I might be dying, but I'm sure as hell going to have some fun before I do.

Love always,

Claire

Reading her hopes for adventures with us breaks my heart. Time seemed to run out all at once and she was too sick to be able to do much. I also feel a weird sense of comfort. These are her own words and sentiments, written in her distinctive handwriting. I can almost hear her as I read the letter. Her gentle, lilting voice dances across the page, weaving in and out of the words and jumping out at me every so often.

Life is all about finding little pockets of magic and happiness wherever you can.

She's right, although those pockets become more elusive when you lose someone you love. My brain starts to come alive as I dream up all sorts of ideas for my adventure day with Violet. It will be a day of pure magic.

Chapter Fourteen

Excitement bubbles up inside my stomach as I wait for Violet to get up. As per Claire's request, we're going on an adventure. It's taken a couple of days to plan, but I'm ready and can't wait to get going. It's the weekend, which is the perfect time to have a day full of fun. I'm still a little worried about her mysterious bruise, but today is all about letting go and having a good time. I glance up at the clock: just after eight. Should I go and wake her up? No, as the saying goes, let sleeping dogs lie; the same can be said for five-year-olds.

I've made a rough plan for today, but there's plenty of room for spontaneity – it is an adventure day after all. My plan is to start off with the Tim Peake exhibit at the National Museum, then head to a cat café on West Port. I can just picture her face lighting up with joy when she walks into a room full of cats, although I'll probably have to tell her not to pick them up or grab their tails. After that, there's a space workshop for kids at the Royal Observatory. I wondered about factoring in a trip to the cemetery to see Claire's grave, but decided against it. I'll take Violet there one day, but not today.

A little later, my gaze flicks up to the ceiling when I hear soft padding above me. It's slow and a bit uncertain, like she's just stumbled out of bed. I get up and grab her favourite bowl from the cupboard, filling it with Coco Pops, and make myself some more coffee.

When I hear Violet's footsteps on the stairs, a tingle of excitement spreads over my skin. Moments later, she appears in the doorway, clutching her toy rabbit and rubbing her eyes.

'Daddy, can we watch cartoons?' Her voice is heavy with sleep.

I walk over to her and pick her up, balancing her carefully on my hip and kissing her head.

'Actually, baby, we're doing something different today.' A broad grin sweeps across my face when I look at her. 'We're going on an adventure.'

She looks up at me, her large brown eyes widening with excitement. Her smile is a little uncertain though.

It's like she's waiting for me to say I'm joking and our weekend routine will go ahead as planned.

'What kind of adventure? Are we going to the park?'

I shake my head and put her down so she can have her breakfast. 'We're going somewhere even better than the park. But I'm keeping it a surprise. You'll love it though – I promise.'

It's a beautiful morning; the sun's shining but there's a breeze rustling the leaves on the trees so the heat isn't unbearable. Perfect adventure weather. As we sit together, Violet tries every trick in the book to get me to tell her where we're going. She may only be little, but she could teach me a thing or two about subtlety. I almost slip up and give myself away a few times, but catch myself just before I do.

'Off you go and get ready,' I tell her when she's finished her Coco Pops. 'Quick as you can, then we'll get going.'

She heads over to the door then turns back to look at me. The abrupt change of plans has thrown her off a little. She got up expecting to eat cereal and watch *The Magic School Bus* on Netflix, but now she's off on a magical mystery tour. I don't blame her for feeling a bit overwhelmed.

'You're still wearing your pyjamas, Daddy – you can't wear them on an adventure.'

'Don't worry, I'll put some proper clothes on before

we go. I won't embarrass you today. What are you going to wear? Your Halloween costume from last year might be cool.'

Her face drops and she glares at me in disgust. 'I don't want to dress up like a tomato again!'

Oh, God. I thought she'd forgiven me for that, but she clearly hasn't. Dressing your child as a salad ingredient apparently has ramifications for months afterwards.

'I said I was sorry about that, didn't I? I was working and that was all the costume shop had left when I got there.'

What she doesn't know is the shop was closed when I got there, and the tomato costume was the simplest idea I could think of. Red T-shirt, matching jeans, and green knitted beanie hat. She'd refused point blank to go to her nursery Halloween party until Hannah had FaceTimed her and told her she was the most beautiful tomato in the world. Somehow, that was exactly what Violet wanted to hear.

'I wanted to be an astanut.'

'I promise I'll be better organised this year. You'll have the best *astronaut* costume ever. Now, go and get dressed so we can go on our adventure!'

Violet smiles and runs off at full tilt towards the stairs. I resist the temptation to tell her not to go up too fast and to be careful not to fall. Keeping my daughter safe comes a bit too naturally to me sometimes; I need to let go more and enjoy time with her instead of looking out for danger. I breathe in and out, evicting my litany of worries.

Time to go on an adventure.

The Tim Peake exhibit at the National Museum is a pretty breathtaking sight. The Soyuz space capsule that brought him back from the International Space Station is a lot smaller than I imagined it would be. I've got no idea how three grown men could fit in there – it reminds me of a large copper kettle. The lyrics to 'My Favourite Things' circle the periphery of my mind as we wander around the exhibit and I have to fight not to burst into song in the middle of the museum. It's Claire's fault, really; she made me watch that film so many times when she was alive.

'Will they let me try on Tim Peake's spacesuit?' Violet asks.

'I think it might be a bit too big for you right now, so probably not. But it's still cool to look at, isn't it? There's a space-shuttle simulator so you can see what it's like in a real spaceship.'

That piques her interest and she looks up at me with wide, sparkling eyes.

'I can be an astanut?' she whispers.

'Of course you can. We'll take a walk over in a minute; the queue probably won't be too long.'

We fall into a companionable silence as we stare at the exhibit in wonder. A piece of space history is right in front of us, and it's quite humbling to consider.

'How did Tim Peake and the other astanuts fit in there, Daddy? It's not very big,' Violet points out. 'Did an alien do magic on them and make them tiny so they had enough room?'

Once again, I'm treated to a glimpse of Violet's version of the world. It has magical aliens and space adventures and infinite possibilities.

'Maybe they did, baby.' I don't want to ruin the magic that runs through her thoughts. The science and logic behind Tim Peake and two other men fitting inside such a tiny cavity can be discussed another day.

'What other kinds of magic do you think aliens do?' I ask. 'Maybe they can click their fingers and have their favourite food appear in front of them. That'd be cool, wouldn't it? Imagine having pizza or cake whenever you want.'

Violet giggles then pauses for a moment to think of her answer. 'Erm … how about making the floor into a big bouncy castle? Bouncy castles are fun. Why are they so bouncy, Daddy? Are they magic like the aliens?'

'I suppose they are, in a way. They start out all

deflated and sad, but some magic helps them to be bouncy and happy.'

Violet smiles and snuggles in close to me. She stares back at the Soyuz capsule with a look of absolute wonder on her face. I can see her dreams come to life in front of her. Seeing the spacecraft that brought Tim Peake back to Earth sends her a silent message: *you can do this. Other people have seen what it's like up there and you can too.*

'You're bouncy and happy now too. Did you use some bouncy-castle magic?'

I feel my heart do a happy little somersault. I'm glad she's noticed I've been happier recently; she was the main reason I started my Super Dad quest. I haven't had time to think about it, but something has definitely shifted. I've opened up my world and invited people in again: I'm repairing my friendship with Hannah, and I've been on my first date since losing Claire. It's been a strange old time, but it's definitely been good for me.

'You know what, baby, yeah, I did.'

The rest of the museum is a hit, especially the Animal World gallery. I have a hard time explaining to her that the animals are stuffed and have been dead for years, but I manage to talk my way out of it. I tell her the museum made 'special models' of the animals so we could see them, even though they usually live in the wild.

And the Thinking On Your Feet Award goes to…

I decide to let Violet lead me round since this is her day. We see a giant panda, huge dinosaur skeletons and a hippo suspended from the ceiling.

'I didn't know hippos could fly.' She points up to it and frowns. 'Where are their wings?'

'They can't actually fly. The museum just put it up there so we can see it better. Did you know *hippopotamus* means "water horse"?'

Violet giggles and lets go of my hand so she can gallop in a little circle. I watch her, partly in disbelief and partly to stop her from bumping into one of the stuffed animals. For once, she's actually having fun. She's not sticking by my side and observing the museum from a distance.

She's immersing herself in the history, laughing and playing like a kid her age should. Her ironclad grip on rules and structure has loosened a tiny bit, and it's a joy to see.

After we've spent some time at the fashion exhibit, making the most eye-catching designs we can think of, it's time to move on to the next part of our adventure.

'How do you feel about going to a café filled with cats?'

'Yaaaaaaay!' Violet does a little happy dance and claps her hands. 'Cats, cats, cats!'

The cat café doesn't disappoint. There are plenty of felines for Violet to see, although I have to stop her from picking a couple up.

'Can we take one home?' she asks as we sit at a table near the window with glasses of Coke and plates of cake. 'And call him Simon?'

'Simon's a lovely name for a cat, but we can't take any of these guys home. They live here and I don't think they'd be very happy if we took them back to our house.'

Her little shoulders fall as she watches a black-and-white cat curl itself around one of the table legs. She bends down to pet it and I think to myself. We're starting to come out the other side from losing Claire, so maybe a cat wouldn't be such a bad idea.

'Are you having fun?'

'I liked seeing Tim Peake's spacesuit and the shaky thingy that made us feel like we were in a rocket. And the cats are nice too and the cake is yummy.' She stops eating and puts both of her thumbs in the air. 'Two thumbs up and lots out of ten, Daddy.'

A warm feeling rushes through me. We needed this today; we needed a day that isn't about pretending that we don't miss Claire when we do. I've thought about her a lot today, but my chest hasn't constricted like it usually does. Is this what moving on feels like? Does the grief slowly lift off your chest and allow you to live again?

My eyes travel to the mysterious bruise again. Maybe this is a good time to ask her again about how it happened. She might trip herself up or tell me the truth.

'Violet, that bruise on your arm … where did you say it came from?'

She looks up at me, as if she knows she's been found out. 'Um … I can't remember.'

Gotcha. I knew she was lying about bumping it in the book corner. If I tread carefully, maybe I can ease the real cause out of her.

'It only happened this week.' I chuckle, but notice how afraid she suddenly looks. 'You can tell me anything, Violet, you know that, right? If someone hurt you and gave you that bruise, I can stop them from doing it again.'

She's about to say something; I can practically see the words nestled on the tip of her tongue. I hold my breath and wait.

'I hurt it when we did gym. We were playing a running game and I fell.'

I purse my lips and decide not to say anything. There's a reason she's lying to me and I'm going to find out what it is. Today, though, is all about fun and magic, and I don't want anything to ruin that.

'That's right.' I smile, nod and grit my teeth. 'Sorry, I forgot.'

Violet bends down to pet another cat that's come to say hello. 'Can we get a cat called Christopher? He can keep Simon company when I'm at school.'

'Nice try, kid, but we won't be getting a cat for a while. We can come here and see them though. Would you like that?'

She nods and hops off her chair to pet another cat I hear her address as Colin. I've no idea where her animal-naming system comes from, but she seems to like names that sound like they belong to fifty-year-old accountants.

A cancelled space workshop plus a crazy idea of mine is how I find myself in the garden with Violet, preparing to set off homemade bottle rockets. We got two large plastic bottles, filled them with water and put wine corks in the top. I did the tricky bit of making holes in the bottles and connecting the bike pumps to them. Why I have two of them lying around the house when I don't even have a bike is beyond me, but they've come in handy today. A couple of garden forks from the shed make excellent launch pads. While I'm setting this up, Violet's been up and down the stairs half a dozen times, grabbing her toys and making us an audience for our scientific endeavour.

'What do you think?' I step back to survey our handiwork. 'Are we ready?'

Violet takes a minute to assess our rockets and glances over her shoulder at our audience of soft toys.

'Yeah, let's go!'

So I launch our bottle rockets into the sky, one by one, marvelling at the height they achieve. It's hard not to find meaning in the moment of pure joy Violet and I are sharing. We've been struggling through grief since Claire died, but we're rocketing forward into the next part of our lives.

Chapter Fifteen

Dear Claire,

Things are finally starting to get better. The fog of grief is lifting, and Violet and I are happier than we've been in a long time. Your letters have played a huge role in that, so thank you. We needed them more than I ever imagined.

You told me to find little pockets of magic and happiness. Well, darling, I'm glad to tell you, I did. It's as though colour has started slipping back into the world. About bloody time too – being miserable is exhausting. I finally feel like I stand a chance at being Super Dad, or his sidekick at least. I'll include a picture of my costume below. I think you'd like it; it's mostly made of Spandex.

My adventure day with Violet weaves a special kind of magic through the rest of my week. I feel happier, lighter and much more relaxed. The world doesn't seem so terrifying anymore, which makes life in general a lot more pleasant. Our audiobook sessions continue and we learn about space – and each other – together. The bond between us steadily grows and I finally feel like I'm becoming the father I want to be.

I wait for Meghan outside the Edinburgh Dungeons, dodging out of the way as people pour out of Waverley Station. I'm not as nervous as I was for my date with Rachel, which I'm taking as a good sign. At this point, if Meghan is a nice, normal woman who isn't interested in haunted dolls, I'll be happy.

'Hi.'

I turn to see a pretty blonde woman wearing a floral dress and a long pink cardigan standing behind me. Her smile is bright and her blue eyes are sparkling. This is going to be a good date; I can feel it.

'Hi, it's Meghan, right? Nice to meet you – I'm Evan.'

I put out my hand and she shakes it. A pink blush momentarily sweeps across her cheeks. She's obviously nervous and I feel a pang of sympathy for her.

'Nice to meet you too.' Her voice wavers a little. 'Shall we head inside?'

She gestures towards the Dungeons and accidentally drops her clutch bag on the pavement. The contents spill out and people have to veer right to avoid them.

'Oh crap!'

She drops to her knees and scrabbles to collect her things. Instinctively, I bend down to help her and pick up her purse, which has a little pool of change spilling from it since the catch has fallen open. I gather all the coins together and I'm just about to close the flap over when I notice a faded photo tucked into one of the see-through pockets. Meghan and a man are standing on a beach somewhere, looking happy and a little sunburnt.

Meghan takes the purse from me and stuffs it back into her bag, offering only a small smile in return. We gather up the rest of her things in silence until we both reach for her mascara at the same time and our hands touch.

'Um…'

'Yeah…'

I get to my feet and offer her my hand to help her up. She brushes some imaginary dust from the front of her dress and doesn't meet my eyes. I think it has something to do with the photo I found.

'So,' I say in an effort to break the ice, 'let's go and get the crap scared out of us.'

Meghan chuckles weakly and looks up at me. 'Go on then.'

The Dungeons are cheesy, enjoyable fun. The performers put their all into it and really immerse themselves in the stories they're telling. A pang of sadness hits me when I realise they remind me of myself ten years ago: passionate, confident and enthusiastic.

Meghan laces her fingers with mine when someone in the courtroom segment makes her jump and stays close to me the whole way round. I put my arm around her and hold her close as she snuggles in at my side. The only problem is that as we're listening to the performances, we don't have much time to talk. We manage some snippets of small talk here and there, but an immersive history attraction isn't really the best place to get to know each other.

We emerge onto Market Place after a stomach-churning free-fall ride called The Grassmarket Gallows. After being underground for so long, we have to shield our eyes from the sun.

'I don't suppose you fancy going for lunch somewhere?' I suggest. 'There are a couple of nice cafés up the road.'

Meghan nods. 'Yeah, that'd be nice. All that spooky stuff's made me hungry!'

We pick a cosy little café on Grassmarket and make ourselves comfortable at a table by the window. Over tall glasses of lemonade and plates of Victoria sponge, we set about getting to know each other.

'So how did you get into designing Disney merchandise?' I ask.

'Honestly, I saw quite a lot of people doing it on Instagram and fancied giving it a try myself. That's just a side hustle though – my main job is elderly home care.'

'Wow, two jobs! Those must keep you busy.'

'Not quite as busy as leading ghost tours must! Is this your day off?'

I pause for a moment. It's probably better not to discuss my work situation right now. The date's going pretty well and I don't want to sour the mood.

'Yeah, I've got my partner running things today.' What's a little white lie? 'So, have you been on Tinder long?'

Meghan chuckles then suddenly, her expression changes. She turns her head to look out the window and her eyes mist up with tears.

'Sorry,' she whispers, covering her mouth with her hand.

Oh God, I've obviously said something to offend her. Quick, do damage control and maybe the date can still be salvaged. Even if I don't quite know what I've done wrong.

'Have I said something wrong?' I ask. 'Sorry if I've upset you.'

Meghan shakes her head and wipes away some tears. 'This might sound clichéd, but it's not you it's me. I shouldn't be here to be honest – there's no way I'm ready to date yet. My friends convinced me to download Tinder so I decided to give it a go. I didn't think anything would come of it, but then I got talking to you and you seemed really nice and… Oh God, this is a mess.'

She covers her face with her hands and I'm at a loss for what to do next. If it were Hannah sitting opposite me right now, I'd go round to her side of the table and hug her. But this is someone I barely know and the last thing I want to do is make her feel uncomfortable.

'Hey, look … if you want to talk about anything, I'm right here.' I wince as soon as I say it, hoping I didn't come across creepy. 'It might help to talk to a stranger about whatever's bothering you, since I'm kind of removed from it all.'

Note to self: don't apply to join the Samaritans anytime soon.

Meghan sniffles and looks at me. Her nose is red, her eyes are puffy and more tears look like they're about to spill down her cheeks.

'I didn't plan on telling you about this on the first

date… About a year ago, I lost my boyfriend. The guy in the picture you saw? That was Jake. We were together for about four years until he died in a car accident. My whole world fell apart and for the first couple of months, I couldn't get out of bed. If it weren't for my friends, I'd probably still be there now. This whole online dating thing … I guess it was my way of repaying them, if that makes sense? They've been so good to me and they were really keen for me to give it a try, but … I'm not ready. I don't think I will be for a while actually. I'm so sorry I've wasted your time.'

Of all the things I'd been expecting, that was at the bottom of my list. I take a moment to gather my response, hoping the words come out in the right order.

'Don't worry about it.' I smile at her. 'I'm really sorry for your loss. I went through something similar a couple of years ago and, to be honest, I still don't feel ready to do this. Take as much time as you need before you put yourself out there again, and don't let your friends decide for you. It has to be when *you're* ready.'

Meghan manages a sad smile as she dries her eyes with her napkin. 'Thanks, that's really sweet. I thought if I acted how I normally would on a date – holding hands, getting close to you – it might make me feel ready, but it didn't. I still miss Jake. To be honest, I don't think it's hit me that he's gone yet.'

I swallow the lump in my throat and take a deep

breath to keep myself together. 'I know exactly what you mean.'

Near the end of the week, something magical happens: James comes into the office with a sore throat.

'Mate, I don't think I'll be able to do the tour today. I think I've got tonsillitis or something.' He can barely speak and looks like death warmed up. 'I know it's a lot to ask, but do you think you can lead the tour group today? I know you've got the spookathon to plan, but I could stay here and do what you were going to do. If you really don't want to, we'll figure something out but there's no way I can tell ghost stories today.'

Immediately, my heart begins hammering against my chest. This is it; I can prove myself as a great tour host again. I'm ready, raring to go, in fact, until fear swoops in.

'Are … are you sure? Remember what happened when I did the tours last time. I don't want that to happen again.'

James lumbers over to me and pats me on the shoulder. His eyes are heavy and his skin is pale. He really should be at home in bed.

'Mate, you're doing so much better now – you're not

the guy with a face like a constipated squirrel any more. You've got this.'

The words are hoarse but I hear them. He has faith in me and that's all it takes for me to put on my top hat and frock coat.

'How do I look?' I do an awkward little twirl in front of him and await his verdict. 'Do I look like someone who's about to go and scare the living daylights out of some tourists? Or like a total tosser?'

James gives me a thumbs-up as he sits down at my desk. After sitting there myself for so long, dreaming and planning and hoping, it's kind of strange to see him in that spot. For the tiniest moment, I worry I'm a fraud and that I'm stepping on his toes. But I'm doing this out of necessity; we don't want to disappoint our tour group, after all, and I'm the only one who can fill in.

'I'll leave you to the spookathon planning then.' I'm stalling now to avoid heading out the door. 'It's all there – I'm pretty close to pinning down a venue and I've written down some ideas for activities.'

'Go.' James points to the door. 'I'll be fine here, just go out there and do what you do best. Hey, wait a minute, you've got a bloody Ferris wheel written down here. That's a bit extravagant, isn't it?'

I'm out the door before he spots the acrobats and ice sculptures.

I go outside to meet the tour group. My heart is in my mouth and my palms are slick with sweat but I'm ready.

I'm so, so ready for this.

'All right.' I clap my hands. 'Who's ready to see the scary side of Edinburgh?'

My enthusiasm sparks a reaction from the group, who look eager to get going despite it being pretty early in the morning. My heart beats a little faster, though whether that's through terror or excitement I can't tell.

I use all my best stories and get into my character more than I ever thought was possible. For a whole hour, I *am* a Victorian storyteller leading a group of people around Edinburgh's most haunted sites. The group is transfixed, really buying into the locations and the stories that go along with them.

'Is it true people have seen a hunchback on Ramsey Garden?' A tourist near the front of the group puts her hand up to grab my attention.

'It is!' Nobody's asked a question on one of my tours for months, so I get a little overexcited. 'People who've seen him say he's carrying a wooden trunk and dressed in eighteenth-century clothing.'

There's a special feeling when you know you have a group of people eating out of your hand. For so long after Claire died, I lost my connection to the stories I was telling and the people I was in charge of scaring. Today, my special magic is making a welcome return.

James looks like death when I get back, but manages a smile while I babble on about how well the tour went.

'Someone even asked a question, mate! And it wasn't, "Has this got much longer to go because I'm dying of boredom?" People were interested – they bought into what I was saying and I'm pretty sure I ended with a full group. Nobody snuck into a nearby pub or anything.'

'That's great – I'm happy you had fun. I think I've nailed down a venue for the spookathon. What do you think about The Hub? I got some prices off them and their hire cost is quite reasonable.'

My entire body lifts off the ground. The old church on Castlehill with its looming Gothic spire would be a perfect choice for a night of spooky thrills and chills.

'That sounds great to me. We could get a ton of stuff going on in there and I can't think of a better place to start the walking tour. Talking of tours, should I do tomorrow's one if you're still feeling under the weather?'

I'm high on adrenaline and excitement from leading my first tour in what feels like forever and every fibre of me wills him to buy into it too. I *need* him to believe I've changed.

James's smile shrinks by a fraction and he shrugs. 'We'll talk about it tomorrow, OK?'

My heart sinks a little. 'What's there to talk about? I did a really good job today, and I could do it again tomorrow. Things can go back to the way they used to be; me leading the tours and you jumping out and scaring people.'

He stares at me for a moment, as though he's carefully selecting his response. 'I'm glad you had a great time today, mate, but that doesn't mean you're ready to go back full time. Maybe you could do the odd tour here and there, see how things go? I don't want us doing anything hasty.'

I bristle and grit my teeth. I can't decide if I feel unbearably sad or annoyed.

'Anyone would think you don't want to give up leading the tours.' I chuckle to lighten the atmosphere, but it's empty.

'Mate, it's not that, it's just... Well, you want the business to succeed, don't you? I'm not saying you'll never lead the tours again, just not right now. Today's a good start and we'll build on it, OK? I promise.'

I nod as my enthusiasm slowly ebbs away. 'Sure, of course. I'll see you later, hope you feel better tomorrow.'

I turn and head for the door as quickly as I can. I shouldn't have expected James to sign off on me going back to the tours after one good run, but I was hoping he would anyway. My dream of doing the job I love again falls a little further out of reach.

I'm more exhausted than usual by the time Violet and I are slumped on the couch together, listening to more of *Ask an Astronaut.* Robin Ince's voice is so relaxing that my eyes flutter closed a few times until Violet taps my shoulder to check I'm listening. It's been a busy old week and I feel like I've hardly had time to think.

'Will you come to space with me?' she asks. 'You might get sad if you're here by yourself.'

I bring her close to me and kiss the top of her head. 'Of course I will, if they'll have me. Where will we go first? Mars, Jupiter maybe?'

'No, the Moon!'

My phone buzzing breaks me out of my sleepy haze. I frown when I see an email from Miss Thompson, Violet's teacher, on my screen.

FAO: Parent Contributors to St Joseph's Fun Day

Hi guys!

Just a quick roundup email to make sure everyone's still OK to honour their commitments for Sunday's Fun Day in the school hall. Any funds raised will go towards new gym equipment and a trip to The Kelpies for the little ones.

Below is a list of names and what you have signed up to do – just in case you've forgotten, haha!

- *Sharon Smith – bouncy castle*
- *Michelle Wright – face painting*
- *Evan Harper – cupcakes and brownies…*

Wait, *what*?

I scan the list of names again to make sure I've seen it properly. Cupcakes and brownies? Where did Miss Thompson get that idea from? Before I can wonder much longer, the phone rings with an unknown number.

'Hello?'

'Mr Harper, it's Mrs Wilkes here.' Renee's voice is crisp and sharp, and I notice the syrupy sweet tone has vanished. 'I just thought I'd call to discuss your Fun Day commitments. I'm part of the parent teacher association, you see, and I was a little, well, *surprised* to see your name on the list.'

Of course she's on the PTA. Probably runs the bloody thing.

'Really, why?'

'Well…' She trails off and leaves the rest of her words hanging in the air unsaid. 'You don't exactly strike me as a natural baker, that's all. There's obviously been some sort of miscommunication somewhere. Miss Thompson has obviously taken Violet's word for it instead of checking with you. Not to worry – I'm sure one of the other parents will step up instead.'

That sly dig makes my competitive instinct kick in and I sit up a little straighter.

'No need, I've got it covered. Just tell me how much you need of each thing.'

The line falls silent and, for a second, I think she's hung up. I revel in catching her off-guard.

'Three dozen cupcakes and two dozen brownies, please.' The surprise is evident in her voice. 'And a tray of blondies.'

Blondies? What the hell are they?

'All right, that's fine. And when should I bring them to the school?'

Hopefully Renee won't catch on to the fact I had no idea about the Fun Day until I got her email. That's the last thing I need.

'We kick off on Sunday afternoon at twelve, but we're asking all our parent contributors to arrive an hour early to help set up. I hope that's OK?'

She sounds more than a little put out that I've agreed to this and that I'm showing no signs of being ambushed, but I refuse to give her the satisfaction.

'Perfect. See you then.'

When I finish the call, I look at Violet, who's innocently looking around the room listening to *Ask an Astronaut*, and narrow my eyes.

'Violet … is there something you forgot to tell me?'

She looks up at me, her cocoa-brown eyes wide. 'Like what?'

'Like Fun Day at your school this weekend. Did you tell your teacher I'd bake cupcakes and brownies to sell on one of the stalls?'

She flashes me that cheeky grin of hers and nods proudly. 'I said you worked in a cake shop and made nice things all day.'

Oh, great.

I sit forward and rest my head in my hands as it hits me what I've just signed up to. Despite knowing nothing whatsoever about baking, I've agreed to make a bunch of stuff that other people will have to eat. Otherwise, no trip to The Kelpies for the little ones. And if I inadvertently give someone food poisoning, there will be hell to pay.

'What's wrong?' Violet asks, tapping my shoulder.

'Daddy's in trouble, baby. Big, *big* trouble.'

Chapter Sixteen

What the hell have I got myself into?

I ask myself this while I'm sitting in the kitchen at 7am, a cold cup of coffee beside me and a thousand baking-related questions buzzing round my head. I've been up for two hours trying to figure everything out. Why did I have to puff my chest out to Renee and let her digs get to me? I've really done it this time.

Fun Day is tomorrow, I have no recipes or ingredients and everything is going to be a disaster. I leave the kitchen to go upstairs, but as I pass the living room, I see Claire's book sitting on the coffee table. Its shiny purple cover catches the early-morning light and draws me towards it. I'm not even sure why; it's not as if she'll have written a letter specifically for baking.

Oh, wait. She has.

Well, sort of. It's called *Trying New Things Together.* I take it to the kitchen with me and sit down to read it.

Dear Evan,

There's a very real possibility you'll think I'm losing my mind here, but please read this letter all the way to the end. Yes, it's about baking, but it's also about trying new things and embracing experiences. It's all very deep and profound, OK? Just go with me on this.

Baking is one of my favourite things to do with Violet. She's not much help, admittedly, and prefers to make a mess, but I love the time we spend together doing it. Both of us end up covered in flour and in fits of giggles at some point, but we also manage to produce some pretty tasty treats too. Now, I know baking isn't your thing – you're more Paul Daniels than Paul Hollywood – and that's why my challenge in this letter is for you to keep the baking tradition alive with Violet.

You might think I'm winding you up here by asking you to do something we both know you're not good at, but I'm not. Not only do I not want Violet to miss out on something she loves just because I'm not around, but I also want to encourage you to push the limits of what you know is possible. Getting you to bake might not be the most conventional way to achieve this, but I've never done things by halves. When you lose someone, it's easy to get into a rut or bury yourself in your comfort zone, closing the door on new experiences. But I don't want that for you. I want your life to be rich and full and beautiful, and if I have to force you to bake a Victoria sponge to achieve that, then I will. My point is, you currently don't think you can bake anything. And you may well be right. But try. There will be times where you feel completely out of your depth, and that's OK. But remember, you're capable of so much more than you think, even if there's an oven involved.

At the back of this book, I've included some simple recipes for you and Violet to try. Nothing too taxing, just some of my tried-and-tested favourites. Why not give them a go and see how you get on? If nothing else, Violet will love flinging flour and icing sugar everywhere. And keep pushing yourself to try new things – you never know what could happen.

Love always,

Claire

I turn to the back of the book and find some homemade recipe cards stuck to the back cover with a strip of Sellotape. There are recipes for cupcakes, chocolate fudge cake and red velvet cake, which was always Claire's favourite, and – my heart leaps – brownies and blondies! It's the best start I could hope for. At first, I wonder what she would say if she could see me now, about to unleash my inner baker for the first time and worrying about making a fool of myself.

I smile because I know exactly what she'd say: *don't worry about getting things wrong, you daft sod, just get on with the baking. And if you burn my red kitchen units, I'll never forgive you.*

After a quick trip to raid the baking aisle at the local supermarket for ingredients, I empty my kitchen cupboards and pick out anything I think might be a baking utensil. Luckily, since it was her favourite hobby, Claire had a pretty good supply already. From here I can see: a selection of different-sized bowls, a whisk and a strange-looking device that I think might be a melon baller. It'll come in handy for something.

'Can we make space cakes?' Violet asks as she rummages in a cupboard. 'We could make them look like planets.'

I raise an eyebrow at her. 'I think we've got enough to do without adding more to our list, kiddo. Why did you tell Miss Thompson I work in a cake shop?'

She shrugs. 'I thought it was funny.'

The doorbell rings and I head down the hall to answer it. Hannah is standing on the other side, holding a supermarket carrier bag that looks like it's about to burst. She flashes me a smile that lights up her whole face and makes her eyes sparkle.

'Hey, thanks for coming,' I say, standing to one side. 'Come on in.'

'What kind of best friend would I be if I let you bake alone?' she asks. 'I stopped off at the supermarket to pick up some stuff in case we either get it completely wrong and have to start again or get into it and fancy making more.'

She looks up at me and we exchange smiles. A rush of warmth sweeps through me and I'm not sure why.

'Ready to get started?' she asks.

I grimace. 'I'm not so sure about that. I asked Violet what she was playing at, signing me up for this, and she said she thought it was funny.'

Hannah chuckles and we go into the kitchen where Violet is standing, looking more excited than I've ever seen her. I hand out the aprons and we're ready to start.

Until I notice the strange looks I'm getting.

'Come on, guys, we've got a lot of baking to do.'

Hannah purses her lips as though she's trying not to laugh. 'Um, Evan…'

She points at my apron and I look down. Instead of a plain white one, I've managed to pick up one that says,

Don't like my cooking? EAT ASS. It was a Valentine's Day present from Claire a few years ago.

'Daddy, *ass* is a bad word!' Violet shoots me a disapproving glare. 'You say we're not supposed to say bad words because they're not nice. No cake for you.'

I whip the apron off and throw it in the washing machine, trying to laugh the whole thing off. Hannah is hiding her face behind her hand and turns away to let out a giggle.

'OK, let's get started, shall we?'

Claire wasn't lying in her letter; I really am terrible at baking.

Our first lot of cupcakes burns to a pile of cinders because I accidentally grill them instead of putting them in the oven. Our second don't rise and look more like Yorkshire puddings. So, we have to make another batch. Luckily, we have enough ingredients to launch our own commercial bakery.

'Just so you know, most people bake in the *oven* rather than under the grill,' Hannah jokes as we whip up new batter together. 'I could be wrong, but I don't think you *quite* know your way around a kitchen.'

She glances at me and our eyes meet for a moment.

The atmosphere in the kitchen grows heavy for a moment until I hear Violet clattering around behind us.

'And there was me thinking a great baker was lurking underneath that art-boy exterior,' she says when things return to normal. 'I think I'll hold off on sending in that *Bake Off* application for you.'

'Very funny.' I narrow my eyes at her and smile. 'I *do* know my way round a kitchen, I just … got distracted, that's all.'

Hannah moves to the other end of the counter to open another bag of sugar and I watch her for a second. I'm struck by the way she moves – elegant and graceful, almost balletic. Why have I never noticed this before? She catches me staring and meets my gaze with a confident smile that stretches all the way up to her eyes. The amber and gold hues are more noticeable today.

Is she blushing or am I imagining things?

'Violet, how are the decorations coming along?' I ask, giving myself a shake and breaking eye contact with Hannah.

She holds up two of the tubs of sprinkles and shakes them. 'There're a lot of nice ones! We just need some cupcakes to decorate now.'

'Coming right up,' Hannah says, 'unless your daddy opens the wrong door again.'

'Hey!' I flick some flour at her. 'Give me a break – I'm under a lot of pressure.'

Flour hits my cheek. 'Oh yeah?' she says. 'Or what? You'll take me for another awkward lunch at Cosmo?'

More flour comes my way, this time landing on my shirt.

'Yeah, maybe I will.' I retaliate by throwing flour into her hair. 'And if you thought last time was awkward, you ain't seen nothin' yet.'

Hannah grins mischievously, readying her next attack. 'Bring it on – I've got some tricks up my sleeve I've been meaning to show you. Haunted Doll Lady will look like a walk in the park compared to what I've got planned.'

'That's it. This is war.'

Our grown-up, sophisticated baking session turns into an all-out flour fight. Violet soon joins in and we're on the floor before we know it, covered from head to toe and laughing.

'Hey,' Hannah says, 'have we actually put any cakes in the oven yet?'

We look at one another and time slows down to a stop. Flour is peppered across her skin and hair and there are creases at the corner of her eyes from smiling so much. She looks so happy and content and…

'*Flour bomb!*' Violet yells, throwing more white powder on top of us. We burst out laughing once again and the flour fight continues for another few minutes.

The kitchen looks like it's been caught in a snowstorm and we're seriously behind on baking.

But I'm happy. I'd almost forgotten what it felt like until today. There's flour in my hair, a wide smile on my face and a lightness in my heart that I haven't felt for the longest time.

It's a small miracle, but we manage to get everything baked: three dozen cupcakes, two dozen brownies and a tray of blondies that I'm sure Renee just added in for the hell of it. From the few bites I sample, I can tell we've done a really good job. The three of us eat pizza to celebrate while I tell the best kid-friendly ghost stories I can come up with.

All too soon, though, it's over.

'Well, that was fun,' Hannah says with a smile as she leans against the counter. 'I think there's hope for your culinary skills yet, Harper.'

I laugh as I pile more dishes into the sink. 'Thanks, I think! But today's been a really good laugh. I don't usually get to do stuff like this at weekends.'

She edges a little closer to me. 'Well, maybe you should. I'm always on the lookout for a sous chef and, with a bit of training, you could be the one.'

I feel her eyes on me and stop what I'm doing to look

at her. It's just the two of us standing here; Violet is in the living room playing a very complex, boisterous game.

'I'll have to get practising then,' I reply. 'Have you got time for a coffee?'

'I've got time.'

I brew two cups of coffee and we take them over to the table by the window. The pale afternoon sunlight drapes her in a golden glow. She looks almost ethereal.

'So, you seem happier lately,' she says, steepling her fingers and resting her chin on them. 'It's nice to see.'

'Thanks, it's actually kind of fun not being a miserable bastard for once.' I chuckle softly. 'I think it's down to a lot of things: getting back out there, being a better dad to Violet … having you back. It's been great seeing you again.'

Hannah tilts her head to one side and smiles. 'Bit soppy, but I'll let it slide. Just this once though.'

That heavy feeling comes back and settles on the room as we study one another. She catches her bottom lip between her teeth and raises her eyebrows, as though we're sharing a secret moment in a room full of people.

'Thanks for today,' I say to her. 'I had a really good time.'

She smiles. 'So did I. Those recipes were amazing – where did you get them?'

I pause for a moment, my gaze dropping to the coffee

cup and my fingers drumming on the sides. 'They were Claire's,' I say softly. 'She was a great baker.'

Hannah screws her eyes shut and drops her head into her upturned palm. 'I'm sorry, I completely forgot. She did the best lemon drizzle, didn't she?'

Her voice is gentle and kind. I lift my gaze to her and manage a smile.

'Yeah … yeah, she did. She used to bake with Violet all the time, but she probably doesn't remember. She was too little to really help, but she liked making a mess with the icing sugar.'

Hannah's attention turns to the Handbook, which I left on the kitchen table after reading the *Trying New Things Together* letter. Her fingers skim the glossy purple cover and my heart twists in my chest. She's probably the only other person in the world who knows what the book means to me.

'She loved the both of you so much,' she says. 'This book was so important to her. I remember her showing it to me one day when I came to visit. It was back when she was still having treatment and we thought she might … might be OK. I told her not to be silly, that you guys would never need this book and…'

She trails off and I see tears in her eyes. Her pain and loss are visceral, sewn into every fibre of her. We are together in that moment, bonded by the person missing from both our lives. I go over and wrap her in my arms, just as I've done countless times in the years we've known each other. She leans against my chest and sobs for a moment before pulling back. For a brief second, she stares at me, her mouth slightly open, as though she's just noticed a detail on my face that she's overlooked for years. Her expression is a mixture of subtle fascination and curiosity.

'Everything OK?' I ask.

Hannah nods and her body jerks slightly, as though she's banishing whatever thoughts were running through her head.

'Of course, everything's fine.' That smile is back, but it doesn't quite reach her eyes this time.

I return to my seat, deciding that putting some space between us is a good idea. Where has this weird atmosphere come from? We've always been comfortable in each other's company, but today something has changed. Suddenly and without warning, Hannah reaches over the table and gingerly brushes my fingers with hers. I'm not sure what to do at first, but I take her hand and give it a gentle squeeze.

'Listen,' she says. 'I know this might sound weird, but I'm really proud of you. Starting all over again when you lose someone you love is one of the hardest things in the world, but you've done it. I know how painful it was for me to say goodbye to her – I can't imagine how it must have been for you.'

I didn't say goodbye, or tell her I loved her one last time. While she was taking her final breaths, I was waiting for my coffee.

A lump forms in my throat, but I manage to swallow it down with a smile. I can't tell Hannah what really happened the day Claire died: that she died surrounded by strangers because I couldn't wait a few more minutes for my morning coffee.

I look into Hannah's deep hazel eyes, aware that I'm still holding her hand. She has such a kind, open face and the sunniest smile I've ever seen. Why have I never noticed these things before?

My eyes are drawn to the half-finished mug of coffee in front of her and memories begin to stir. I fight as hard as I can to push them back into the box at the back of my mind. This is a moment for thinking about Claire and what she meant to us, not losing myself in a whirlwind moment that happened a million years ago.

She smiles warmly. 'What's on your mind?' she asks. 'You look like you're a million miles away.'

I look down at our laced fingers, thinking I'll find my answer there.

'Well, I—'

A car horn blaring outside ruins the moment. Hannah and I drop hands and look everywhere except at each other. Moments later, there's a knock at the door. When I answer it, I find a tall dark-haired man standing on the other side.

'Hey, man, nice to meet you. I'm Alex.' He smiles and puts a hand out for me to shake. 'Is Hannah ready?'

Who on earth is this guy?

I'm momentarily blindsided at this total stranger's appearance on my doorstep, so all I can do is stand there, nod and smile as I shake his hand.

'Sorry, who are you?' I ask.

Alex's face takes on a smile I'm not sure I like. It falls somewhere between mischievous and knowing.

'I'm … a friend,' he says, leaving the hidden meaning lurking in the air. 'She asked me to pick her up about four-ish, but I finished work early and thought I'd drop round.'

Picking her up an hour early? Good job, chief. I study him for a second, taking in his well-built frame, thick crop of hair, blue eyes and goatee. He looks like Hannah's usual type: athletic with a limited emotional capacity. My heart sinks to my boots, but I can't work out why.

'Uh, sorry… Yeah, I'll just let Hannah know you're here. I'm Evan, by the way. Come on in. Sorry, she didn't say she was expecting anyone.'

Alex steps over the threshold and casts an appraising eye round the hallway. I do everything I can to hide my discomfort and the feeling that he's judging more than just the décor.

'Nice place you've got here, mate,' he says. 'Have you lived here long?'

'Thanks, about ten years, I think. Time flies when you're having fun!'

What the hell am I saying and why do I sound like I should be on children's TV with a glove-puppet sidekick? Hannah comes out into the hall and greets Alex with a warm smile, but her demeanour changes when she realises I'm there too. She shoves her hands in her pockets and looks awkwardly between the two of us while she shifts from foot to foot.

'What are you doing here?' She chuckles nervously and glances at Alex. 'I thought we said four?'

He gives an affable, nice-guy shrug that gets right under my skin. 'I got off work early so thought I'd pop round to see if you were ready. If you've still got some baking to do, maybe I could lend a hand?'

Oh, bugger off. Whatever you've come round for, it wasn't to help make cupcakes.

Two pops of colour appear in Hannah's cheeks and she giggles. I look between them for a moment, my arms folded across my chest, feeling like the third wheel.

'Bit keen, aren't you?' She tucks a stray lock of hair behind her ear and her smile widens. 'We've just finished up here – I'll go and grab my jacket.'

She disappears into the living room, leaving Alex and

me in the hall together. Silence falls as we look at each other, nudging slightly into discomfort.

'So, how do you know Hannah?' I ask.

'Tinder.' Alex flashes me a smile straight out of Hollywood. 'Matched a couple of days ago. She's really great.'

My lip begins to curl, but I stop it just in time. Reducing all of Hannah's qualities to two pretty insipid words doesn't mark this guy out as a winner in my book.

'Oh, cool. I'm happy for you.'

Silence falls again and Alex decides to break it this time.

'Hannah told me about the mess your kid landed you in,' he says. 'They can be little sods at times, can't they?'

My mood sours in an instant. Who is he to call Violet a 'little sod'? 'My daughter's very well-behaved, actually. And she didn't land me in a mess – I volunteered.'

Alex frowns. 'That's not what Hannah said.'

'Well, that's what happened. I volunteered and she came round to help.'

Why I'm continuing with this daft lie – and why I even started it in the first place – is a total mystery to me, but I've committed now so I have to see it through. Nobody calls my kid a 'little sod' and gets away with it.

'Oh.' He doesn't look convinced, but I couldn't care less. 'I wish I'd known sooner – I could've lent a hand.'

'Bake much, do you?' My voice is laced with bitterness.

'You could say that. I'm a professional pastry chef.'

Of course you bloody are. A smug smile spreads across his face and my stomach drops. Part of me wants to knock him to the floor and the other part wants to ask if my brownies are up to scratch.

Before we can snipe at each other again, Hannah emerges with her coat and bag.

'Right, we'll be off,' she says. 'Thanks for today – it was a really good laugh.'

'Thank *you* for all your help,' I reply. 'I don't know what I'd have done without you. Alex, nice to meet you.' I reach over and shake his hand again. 'Hannah, I'll see you at Fun Day tomorrow if you can make it? It starts at twelve, but I'll be there a bit earlier to help set up.'

'I'd love to go. Count me in.' She holds my gaze for a fraction too long. We say our goodbyes and I watch her and Alex walk out the door. There's an ease and warmth between them, yet I can't forget the moment Hannah and I had in the kitchen…

Violet tugs at my jeans to get my attention. 'Daddy, can we listen to Tim Peake now? I want to hear about astanuts.'

I scoop her into my arms and balance her on my hip. 'Of course we can. We still don't know if you can drink a cup of tea in space.'

Chapter Seventeen

St Joseph's School Fun Day is a lot busier than I thought it would be.

I got here with Violet and Hannah a little after eleven thirty to set up our stall and since things kicked off half an hour later, it's been packed. Renee and the other yummy mummies have their own stall, decorated with bunting and covered in stacks of cakes and treats that I could swear were shop-bought.

Alex is here too, for some reason, and he's only gone and baked his own stuff. It doesn't matter that he's not one of the parents, since Renee saw what he brought, she's been treating him like a gift from God. The whole lot looks straight out of a French patisserie and I hate myself for feeling even the tiniest bit jealous. Mine were 'adequate', apparently.

'He's a pastry chef,' Hannah reminds me when she catches me looking at his display. 'This is his thing, so he had a bit of an unfair advantage. I don't know if you've noticed, but your brownies have been more popular than his.'

She's right, a lot of people have stopped by our stall and the brownies have sold like hot cakes, for want of a better expression. I laugh and shrug it off as best I can, trying to look nonchalant about the whole thing. I still haven't figured out why I'm so curious about Hannah and Alex anyway, but that can wait until Fun Day is over.

'It's not a competition,' I say. 'It's about the kids.'

Hannah laughs, narrowing her eyes at me. 'That's very noble of you, but you look like you're about to sprinkle pepper over someone's lemon drizzle cake.'

'Don't be silly, I wouldn't sink to that level. I mean I *might* buy some chilli jam to smear over the other brownies, but that's called giving yourself an edge over the competition.'

'I thought you said it wasn't a competition?' She arches an eyebrow. 'All about the kids, you said.'

We hold each other's gaze for a second too long, before Alex interrupts us.

'Hey, Han, are you going to help me over here or fraternise with the enemy all day? Just kidding, man.' He raises a hand to me and flashes that Cheshire Cat grin. 'Save me a cupcake, yeah?'

Why does he have to be so bloody nice? And why do I care so much anyway? It's none of my business that he and Hannah are seeing each other. When she goes over to him and playfully nudges his arm, my heart drops to my boots.

'Instead of standing here mooning over her, why don't you ask her out on a date?'

I turn to my right and see Michelle, one of the other parents, standing beside me with her head cocked to one side in a classic don't-argue-with-me pose. We're on nodding and smiling terms at pick-up and drop-off, but definitely haven't reached the sharing-unsolicited-life-advice stage yet.

'I don't know what you're talking about. Now, if you'll excuse me, I have cakes to sell.'

I busy myself straightening up my remaining wares, even though they're perfectly neat already. Judging by the way Michelle's eyes are burning into the side of my head, I'm not out of her crosshairs yet.

'Listen, tell me to mind my own bloody business if you want, but I've seen the way you look at her. I don't know the pair of you from Adam, but I can see you're into each other. Go over to her, see what the story is with her and that guy, and if the coast is clear, ask her out.'

She throws me a challenging look, arms folded across

her chest and daring me to defy her. I scramble to find words; while most male-female friendships are subject to scrutiny, people tend to leave Hannah and me alone. Michelle's observation has thrown me for a loop.

'What, me and Hannah?' I burst out into a fit of incredulous laughter. 'We've been friends for years and nothing's ever happened between us. Well … almost nothing, anyway. If we were supposed to be more than friends, I think the universe would've tried to push us together by now. Sh-she's like a sister to me, if anything.'

Michelle rolls her eyes. 'Don't start with all that sign-from-the-universe rubbish. What's the worst that could happen? She says no. Big bloody deal. At least you'd know. You can say what you like, but I know what it looks like when two people fancy each other.'

I stare at her in disbelief. 'I don't know where you're getting this from, but you couldn't be more wrong. We get on well, but that's as far as it goes. She's a great friend to me and even if I did have feelings for her – which I absolutely don't – I wouldn't want to put what we already have at risk. Besides, she's over there with that Alex guy, whoever he is. They matched on Tinder, apparently.'

I look over at them just in time to see Alex take Hannah in his arms and kiss her.

Bollocks.

Michelle puts her hands on my shoulders and I worry

for a minute that we're about to launch into an impromptu yoga display. She's a qualified instructor and has a free taster session starting in one of the classrooms soon. Maybe she needs a partner to demonstrate some moves, but I'm not a great candidate. My downward dog needs work and don't get me started on sun salutations.

'You don't get it, do you? I was listening in and she only went over there because he asked for her help. If she'd had it her way, she'd have been over here with you, giving *you* long, sultry looks.'

I snort. 'Come on!'

She shakes her head a little, as though trying to get the conversation back to factory settings. 'Take it from a casual observer who doesn't know you very well: there's something between the two of you and you'd be silly not to at least think about it. If you could see the way you two are around each other, you'd see where I'm coming from. So, go over there and do something about it before that other guy does.'

My brain tries to process what I'm hearing. Someone who's no more than an acquaintance is telling me I've got feelings for one of my best friends, someone who's been a part of my life for so long and was part of Claire's too. That's another thing: what would Claire make of this wild assumption? That's all this is: a person who doesn't know me or Hannah getting the wrong end of the stick. There isn't an ounce of truth in what she's saying.

'You're barking up the wrong tree,' I say. 'There's no way there's anything going on with me and Hannah. Even if there was, it would be way too complicated to do anything about. She's a great friend and godmother to my daughter, but that's really all there is to it. We're a great team, but not in that way.'

I look over at where Hannah is standing. Alex is talking to her and gesturing with his hands; he has her full attention. A moment later, she bursts out laughing. Her eyes sparkle as she tangles her hands in her hair and she purses her lips to keep more laughter from escaping. My heart begins to race and my stomach somersaults.

What does moving on look like? Maybe it's in all the big moments and decisions you make that keep you propelling forward. Maybe it happens slowly and in tiny little steps that we barely even register. Or maybe it looks different to everyone who has to do it.

One thing is for certain: it can't involve falling for your best friend.

Beloved Wife

My heart wrenches as I read the inscription on Claire's grave. She was *my* beloved wife and when she was alive,

I loved her with every fibre of my being. Guilt stabs somewhere deep inside me.

My mind travels back to the day she died. I haven't thought about the exact order of events for a long time; I'm not even sure if I remember them properly. Maybe my brain, in an act of self-preservation, has changed certain details to take some of the pain away.

'I love you.'

Her voice is small and hoarse, but still ripples with the same trademark warmth. She looks tired now. So, so tired, yet still utterly beautiful. Forever has gone from an infinite number of days to just a few weeks at most. We're almost at the end now and buried underneath the layers of grief and sadness is a deep-seated anger. Why my family, why my wife? What did she ever do to anyone?

And yet there is also love. The most beautiful and perfect love I've ever known. I love Claire for everything she is and isn't and for all she has ever been. An A.A. Milne quote springs to mind: 'how lucky I am to have something that makes saying goodbye so hard.'

I smile at her as her eyes flutter closed. I realise I haven't said it back, lost in my own thoughts, and now she's fast asleep. I'll make sure to tell her when she wakes; for now I'll take this moment to grab a coffee from the café on the other side of the hospital. The stuff from the vending machine on this floor tastes like warmed-up soil.

There wasn't time.

While I waited for a cup of coffee, Claire drew her final breaths. I wasn't there to hold her or tell her everything would be OK. I was in a queue waiting for my flat white.

She died without hearing the three words that meant so much to her and it's all my fault.

I blow air out through my cheeks and run my fingers through my hair. As much as I hate the quiet moments in my brain, when bad thoughts can spring up at any moment, I also hate when I'm so overloaded that I can't think straight.

After Claire's funeral, Mum said I should see a therapist, thinking I had some sort of PTSD, but this is the only therapy I need.

'I miss you,' I whisper.

'Great minds think alike.'

My first thought is Claire has risen from the dead, but I look up and see Hannah walking towards the headstone.

'Yeah, I just needed some thinking time.'

My eyes travel to the latest bouquet of violets. I've relocated them to a grave just across from Claire's, the vivid purple a stark contrast to the dull grey stone.

'Hey, have you ever found a bunch of violets at Claire's grave?' I ask. 'No note to say who they're from, just a bunch of flowers sitting here?'

Hannah scrunches her nose up, the rapid change in

topic throwing her off a little. 'Now you come to mention it, yeah, I have a couple of times. I just assumed they were from you since they were her favourites.'

I shake my head and my frown deepens. 'No, I sometimes bring them but not all the time. I've found a lot of bouquets lying at her grave since she died, but I don't know who they're from.'

I pull myself out of my thoughts for a second to look at her. There's a faraway expression on her face and she doesn't look settled. 'Are things a bit heavy today? Is that why you came to visit Claire?'

Hannah nods, sitting down beside me and hugging her knees to her chest. 'You could say that.'

'Are you OK?' I ask gently. 'You can tell me if something's bothering you.'

'I'm not sure about applying for the art-therapy course anymore. I looked at the entry requirements and ... I'd be up against people with so much more experience than me, and if I didn't get it, I don't know what my next move would be. I've always had a plan, but this time I don't. Everything seems so messed up. Maybe I should just go back to midwifery instead of retraining.'

She looks at me, her eyes heavy and glossy with tears.

'You hated the job before you left, so what's made you consider going back? Apart from money, obviously.'

Hannah shrugs helplessly and rakes her hands

through her hair. 'I don't know. I've been thinking a lot about things lately and I honestly can't remember why I wanted to be a midwife in the first place. Well, actually, I can, but it's not a great reason.'

'You can tell me, even if it's the worst reason in the world. You know I won't judge.'

'Promise not to laugh?'

'Scout's honour.'

'You weren't a Scout.'

'OK, well, Evan's honour then.'

I watch her for a moment as she psyches herself up. It takes a moment, but her gaze finally lands upon me.

'I picked it on the spot.' Her gaze drops to the grass at her feet. 'Everyone seemed to know what they wanted to be when they left school and I didn't. One day, a mate of mine asked what I was planning on studying at uni and I said the first subject that popped into my head. I'd been watching a documentary about a maternity ward and it must have been floating around my mind somewhere. I just… Everyone had these huge dreams, you know, things they wanted to achieve and I … I wanted a bit of that for myself. I loved the idea of living this wild, creative life: making art, travelling the world, dancing on a beach somewhere. My parents flipped when I suggested a gap year. So I picked midwifery and ran with it because I liked the idea of helping people. Then when Claire died, I realised I'd spent the last decade doing a job I wasn't sure about because I'd never taken the time to figure out what I really wanted out of life. Claire was… She was amazing. You could tell she was made to be a doctor – it was in her bones. It was never like that with me and midwifery, and, before she died, Claire told me to find what made me happy. That's why I went travelling: I wanted to get away from all the memories of her and find out who I really was. Turns out I still don't really know.'

My heart hurts for her. I had no idea she'd been feeling so lost and confused, probably because my mind's been too wrapped up in dating and the Super Dad quest.

'You've always said that anything's possible if you put your mind to it, and I think that's true. If you want to stick around and retrain as an art therapist, you're more than capable of making it happen.'

Hannah looks up at me and I notice for the first time how tired she looks. Her eyes are heavy and her skin is pale.

'I just want to belong somewhere.' Her voice is shaking. 'This is probably going to sound silly, but I don't think I know how to be *me.* I feel like I'm this collection of cherry-picked traits that I think people will like, instead of a real person who knows who they are and what they want.'

I shake my head as guilt prickles across my skin. It's

so easy to assume that Hannah's one of those people for whom things just seem to fall into place. Her carefully curated Instagram feed and sunny smile give that impression. But she has insecurities too, just like everyone else.

'You belong here,' I tell her. 'It might not always feel like it, but you do. Stay and I'll help you work it all out.'

Hannah's shoulders relax, as though a giant weight has just been lifted off them. She wipes her face with her hands and even manages a small smile.

'I thought Claire might know what to do,' she says with a sigh. 'She had her shit together when I never did.'

I get to my feet, wincing as my knees protest at being stuck in the same position for so long.

'You don't give yourself nearly enough credit. How many people do you know who *really* have their shit together anyway? We're all putting on an act and pretending we've got life sussed, even me.'

Hannah gets up and brushes the grass from her jeans. 'You talk a lot of sense, Harper. Let me know what happens with Tinder, eh?'

I smile. 'Cheers, I'll keep you posted.'

I think about asking what's happening with Alex and instantly hate myself for it. A cemetery is a place for sober reflection, not for asking about my best friend's love life. We walk towards the gates and out onto the street, our steps heavy with grief and sorrow.

'So...' I shove my hands deep in my pockets as we meander towards who knows where. 'Alex.'

That's it? That's how you're approaching the subject? Good one, Evan.

Hannah's face breaks into a beaming smile and my insides twist. What the hell is wrong with me?

'Alex,' she repeats, a dreamy quality to her voice. 'He's really lovely. It's early days, but I don't know... I think there's potential there. It's all down to you, really.'

'Me? What did I do?'

She looks at me for a second, her fingers delicately tracing along the stone wall separating us from the cemetery.

'You inspired me! I thought, "If Evan can start dating again after everything he's been through, what's stopping me?" So, after I gave you that Tinder crash course, I downloaded it myself and matched with Alex.'

My heart plummets and I have to remind myself to smile.

'Well, that's great,' I say, cringing at using the same word Alex used to describe her. 'Really, I'm pleased for you.'

I'm not. But why not?

We reach the corner of the street, where we have to go our separate ways. For a moment, we stand there, exchanging awkward smiles while people move around us and grumble at the inconvenience.

'Evan? I meant to tell you at the time, but remember that day we did the baking for Fun Day? It might be my imagination, but there were moments Violet seemed ... I don't know, not herself. Quieter and more withdrawn, you know? I caught her looking sad a couple of times when she thought no one was looking. And I could've sworn I saw a bruise on her arm too.'

Every muscle in my body tenses and my stomach twists. Is this something else I've been too busy to notice? I remember seeing a bruise on one of her arms before and not buying her explanation of how it happened, but to my knowledge she didn't seem to be acting that differently; I thought she was happier, if anything.

'Thanks for telling me,' I say, desperately trying to keep the panic from my voice. 'I'll check it out.'

Chapter Eighteen

Dear Claire,

Before you died, you made me promise that I'd look after Violet and stop anything from happening to her. I've done that to the best of my ability, but now it looks like something is seriously wrong. I wish you were here; you'd know what to do.

Someone is hurting her, I'm sure of it. I don't know who, but when I find out, there'll be trouble. I've gone a bit Liam Neeson – you always said I looked a bit like him, actually. There's nothing I hate more than the thought of someone making our little girl miserable. She's so kind and sweet and friendly to everyone. Leave it with me, though; I'll sort it out.

When I find out who it is, feel free to make some cupboard doors bang around their house.

I watch Violet like a hawk that night, looking for any of the signs Hannah told me about. If I've skimmed over this because of all the other things going on at the moment, I'll never forgive myself.

As has become our tradition, we cuddle up on the sofa and listen to Robin Ince tell us all about outer space. I sneak quick glances at Violet to see if I can spot the bruise Hannah mentioned, and it's there on her right arm, just under the cap of her sleeve. The first one I saw was on her left arm, so this is definitely a new one.

'When can I go to space?' she asks. 'Tomorrow?'

I chuckle and ruffle her hair. 'You'll have to wait until you're a bit older, I'm afraid. But you'll get there one day, I promise.'

She sighs and picks at a loose thread on her trousers. Now that it's in my head, I notice she has been a little withdrawn. Usually when we listen to *Ask an Astronaut*, she's full of questions and loves learning more about what it's like to go to space. Tonight though, she's been different.

'Violet…' I trail off as the rest of my words crumble away. What is the best way to say this without alienating her? If I go in all guns blazing, she'll clam up and deny everything.

She looks up at me, her hands still busying themselves with the thread. 'What is it, Daddy?'

'Is everything OK? You know, at school and here? There's nothing bothering you or making you sad, is there?'

Her brow creases a little and she frowns. For the briefest second, her eyes drop away from me, but she looks back before I can say anything.

'No, I'm OK. Nothing's making me sad.'

'You know that if you ever need to talk to me about something, I'm here, right? I know things have been pretty busy lately, but you'll always be the most important person in my life.'

Gently, I move my hand to her sleeve and lift it up to reveal the new dark bruise.

'How did this happen, Violet?' I ask. 'And please don't tell me you bumped it in the book corner or hurt yourself playing a game. Someone did this, didn't they?'

Violet yanks her arm away and puts her hand over the bruise.

'No! I hurt it when we were doing art.' There are tears brimming in her eyes now.

'You can tell me what happened, I won't be angry.'

She jumps off the couch and runs upstairs. I'm sure I can hear her crying as she disappears off to her room. Why won't she tell me what's going on? There's something I'm missing here, but I'm not sure what it is.

I flick through Claire's book, hoping there's a letter than can help me. However, there isn't one called *When Something's Wrong and You Don't Know What.* There are some scenarios she just couldn't account for. There is another one called *Bullying* though, so I decide to read that one. Although I'm not 100 per cent sure that's what I'm dealing with, I'm sure her insights will help.

Dear Evan,

I hope you never have to read this letter. If you are, it means Violet is either being bullied, or you suspect she is. This is every parent's worst nightmare and it hurts me to even think about it, but I'll do my best so I can write this letter.

Trust your instincts. If you think there's something wrong, you're probably right. Talk to her, get her to open up to you and let you help. You've always been so good at putting people at ease. Don't worry about seeming intrusive; if you think she's in trouble, ask as many questions as you need to in order to find out what's going on.

If it turns out someone is bullying her, please don't fly off the handle. Easier said than done, I know, but Violet will need your most calm and rational self instead of your angriest. If you keep a cool head, she'll be more likely to tell you things that will help you to help her. If the member of staff you speak to is an absolute twatbag, feel free to tell them exactly what you think. Oh, and make sure you know the anti-bullying policy back to front. That way, you'll have it to refer to during any meetings with the school.

God, I hope this never happens to her. The thought of anyone bullying our sweet, loveable little girl brings tears to my eyes. Unfortunately, sometimes these things happen and they're beyond our control. If it does, all you can do is make sure she knows you're on her side, give her all the support she needs and make sure the school plays its part too. Give her a squishy cuddle from me if she needs it, eh?

Love always,

Claire

OK, so according to Claire, I should keep calm and talk to Violet. That way, she'll open up to me and tell me if anything's going on.

I hope to God there isn't.

I'm so deep in thought while I'm dropping Violet off that I almost don't notice Miss Thompson walking into the playground. It's only when I hear the heavy door to the school building slam that I realise she's there. I walk up to her, my heart in my mouth as I prepare to discuss such a sensitive subject.

'Hello, Mr Harper,' she says as I approach. 'Is everything OK?'

'How do you know when your kid's being bullied?'

Her body language becomes a little defensive: arms folded across her body, chin slightly raised. 'Why do you ask?'

I tell her about the bruises I found on Violet's arms, along with what Hannah told me at Claire's graveside. Miss Thompson twists her hands together as she considers what I've said.

'And she's said everything's fine?' She waits for me to nod. 'Right. OK, thanks for bringing this to my attention. I'll certainly keep an eye on the situation and see if I notice anything amiss. In the meantime, try to coax as much as you can out of Violet. She might just need a bit of time before she's ready to tell you what's going on.'

My mind eases a little, and I smile. 'Thanks, I barely slept last night worrying about her. I hate the thought of her being too scared to tell me that someone's hurting her.'

The bell rings and I go to head back to the car. There's

nothing else I can do today; I've spoken to Violet's teacher and the situation is in her hands now. Hopefully, these were a couple of one-off incidents and not part of a pattern. I take out my phone and open up Instagram. Right at the top of my feed is a picture of Hannah and Alex, looking blissfully happy. He's kissing her cheek and she's laughing, her head angled slightly away from the camera and her hand on his chest. She looks so alive, so … so beautiful.

I swallow hard and banish those thoughts instantly. Where the hell did they come from? Ever since that moment in the kitchen and seeing Hannah with Alex, my head has been a mess. I tap out a comment – *Looking good, guys!* – and even add a tongue-out emoji for good measure. Then, I look at the picture again and my heart does a somersault.

I shake myself, trying to recalibrate my thoughts until they're back to normal. This isn't like me; I don't think of Hannah like this. I come out of Instagram and switch back to Tinder. I have three new messages and ten new matches to sift through. That should keep me busy and hopefully halt the crazy thoughts I'm having about my best friend.

James is on hand to dispense some priceless advice when I ask him to help me sort through Tinder.

'I haven't really looked at it since I went on that date with Meghan the merchandise designer,' I admit. 'Ten new matches, mate! How the hell did that happen?'

If I'm being honest, I haven't missed the dating app all that much, and I'm glad James is here to help me get started again.

James jumps down from sitting on the desk and puts his hands on my shoulders.

'You're a good guy,' he says, 'and that makes you a bloody rare beast in the wonderful world of online dating. You wouldn't catfish or ghost or breadcrumb anyone – you probably don't even know what those words mean! Let me have a look at your phone – I bet you ten quid you end up with a date for tonight.'

I snort. James might be an online-dating whizz, but there's no way I – a rank amateur who downloaded Tinder less than a month ago – could pull off a feat like that.

I'm proven wrong later that night.

With the help of some pointers James gave me in between tours, I've somehow managed to get a date for this evening. Danielle is a yoga instructor who lives in the city and has her own studio. We're currently sitting in a nice Italian restaurant on George Street, smiling at each other over hearty bowls of pasta and soft candlelight. This is what I thought dating would be like: no haunted dolls, no unexpected sharing of mutual traumas. Just nice food and good conversation.

'Have you ever wanted to try yoga?' she asks. 'You look quite supple to me.'

I laugh. 'No, I can't say I have! My balance is a bit iffy – I'd probably end up causing a domino effect and knocking everyone over.'

Danielle shakes her head. 'Maybe you should book a one-on-one session then? Can't bang into anyone if you're the only one in the studio.'

'Good point,' I reply, raising my fork in agreement. 'Tell you what, one day, I'll let you teach me everything you know. How does that sound?'

Her grin widens and I get a funny feeling in my stomach. This date is going a lot better than I thought it would.

'Sounds good to me. I think I could teach you a few things you might not find in your average yoga class.'

She looks up at me from beneath her eyelashes and my cheeks begin to burn. I hope the light between us is dim enough for it not to show.

'So what else do you teach?' I ask, clearing my throat. 'You strike me as a woman of many talents.'

Where are these lines coming from? What happened to the awkward guy who had no idea what to do on a date?

'Now that you mention it…' She pauses to flip her black hair over her shoulder. 'I teach ballet, some cardio classes and I do personal training sometimes as well. Only for a select few though.'

Our eyes meet and I wonder if she considers me one of the 'select few'. Do I want her to?

'Are the ballet classes for kids? My five-year-old would love that.'

'Oh! You have a kid. That's amazing.'

I'm not sure if I'm imagining it, but I could swear I see Danielle's smile shrink by a fraction. James had assured me that mentioning Violet in a casual way was OK, despite my initial reservations.

'I do. I have a daughter. Her name's Violet and she's just started school.'

'She must keep you really busy.' Danielle chuckles. 'Five is a great age though, isn't it? They're so curious about the world around them.'

Something about her bright, cheerful tone seems a little off, but I ignore it. Finding out your date has a child is a pretty big revelation to be landed with.

'Do you have nieces or nephews that age?' I ask.

She nods. 'My sister has two boys and they're amazing. I love taking them to the park and spending time with them, but it's nice to give them back too!'

The conversation is swiftly changed to other areas of our lives – food, music, films, art – and we don't revisit the subject of kids for the rest of the night. Hannah pops into my thoughts more than once, but I try my best not to think about her. It's not fair to Danielle, after all.

The date goes well and ends with a kiss goodnight before Danielle gets in her taxi home. She even puts her number in my phone so I can call her about a one-on-one yoga session. Can't be too bad, right?

When I get home and thank my mum for looking after Violet, I get my phone out and decide to call Danielle to make sure she got home safe. That would be a nice thing to do, wouldn't it? Shows I care and was thinking about her even after we parted company. Yes, it's little touches like that that turn a good date into a great one. I dial her number and prepare my cool, smooth greeting in advance.

'Hi there, thank you for donating five pounds to the Happy Paws Sanctuary, where furry friends are our favourites! For more information on adoption, please visit our website. Thank you!'

I frown at the phone, wondering what the hell I've just heard. I've obviously dialled the wrong number, so I try it again.

'Hi there, thank you for donating five pounds to the…'

Ah. Not a wrong dial on my part, but a completely wrong number on Danielle's. I'm now ten quid down – twenty if you count the tenner I had to give James – and in no doubt that Danielle and I won't be going on a second date.

Chapter Nineteen

When I drop Violet off at school, I make a point of locating Miss Thompson to get an update on the suspected bullying situation. Ever since I spoke to her about it last week, I've been keeping tabs on it when Violet isn't looking.

'She seems fine, in all honesty,' she says, her voice weary, like a teacher who's dealt with tons of overprotective parents. 'Her work's good, she's made some friends and she seems happy. It *is* quite hard to keep an eye on one child when you have a class of thirty, Mr Harper.'

This latest response is a variation on a theme. Miss Thompson has said much the same thing since I brought up the matter with her.

'I understand,' I reply, 'I'm just worried. There's

something different about her – she's quieter and more withdrawn at home than usual, and then there are the bruises I've found on her arms…'

I trail off as my insides twist with sorrow and guilt. The fact that Hannah had to point out my own daughter's change in mood as well as the bruises makes me feel terrible. What kind of parent misses those things?

'Anyway…' I pause for a moment to gather myself. 'If you could just look out for her as best you can, I'd really appreciate it. Maybe you could ask her if there's anything going on? I've tried, but she won't tell me anything.'

Miss Thompson gives a wan smile and nods. I can tell what she's thinking: *he's overreacting and looking for problems where there are none.* And maybe that's true, but those bruises didn't come out of nowhere. I let her head back to her classroom to get set up before the bell rings and walk across the playground. There's still a few minutes to go until school starts, but as Violet's off playing with her new best friend Theo, I decide to head off. Being a helicopter parent will probably only lead to trouble.

I check Tinder as soon as I get home. I've got another date tonight; I haven't let the Danielle/Happy Paws fiasco put me off. My date, Lara, is a veterinary nurse from Newcastle and moved to the city for a job six months ago. She seems nice, but previous experiences have taught me to exercise caution. Before I hoof it into the office, I decide to pick out my date clothes. Usually, I'm a throw-on-whatever-works kind of guy, but this Super Dad dating quest has turned me into someone who plans outfits.

I'm not sure how to feel about this.

When I've pulled on my first outfit – pale blue shirt, dark jeans, nice shoes – I take a picture and send it to Hannah.

What do you think of this? I want to wear something that says, 'Please don't show me your haunted doll or give me an animal charity's phone number instead of your own.' Apparently, I've donated enough to Happy Paws to feed two dogs for a month.

Three little dots appear on the screen, letting me know Hannah is typing out her response. For some reason, I feel nervous as I wait to see what she'll say.

Hmm, I'm not sure. You look cute, but there's still something that says 'unwitting animal patron' about this outfit. Maybe it's the shirt. Try another one.

A smile spreads across my face and a funny sensation brews in my stomach. I catch my reflection in the mirror and shudder. I look like a lovestruck teenager in the throes of their first crush. Clearly, my nerves over this date are getting to me. I look at the screen and wonder about asking Hannah to elaborate on the 'you look cute' comment. But, of course, I don't, because I'd make myself look like a massive tit.

Cute isn't really what I'm going for; I was hoping for devilishly handsome. OK, how about this? Bear in mind, I'm a single dad on a budget. Charitable giving is good for the soul, but a man's got to have a limit. Be brutally honest.

I message her a picture of me in a casual grey T-shirt instead, deciding to abandon collared shirts altogether. The dots appear and the butterflies in my stomach start their gymnastics routine.

Ding, ding, ding, WE HAVE A WINNER. You've hit the devilishly handsome jackpot. Tan France would be proud. Or he will be if you wear that T-shirt with the black blazer you got about a million years ago. And check out that smile! A burst of sunshine if ever I saw one. Have fun – Lara's a lucky girl.

A warm, fuzzy feeling spreads through me, but I halt it in its tracks. The last thing I need is to let whatever's going on with me and Hannah ruin my date with Lara. This is one date that I am hoping will be blissfully … normal.

Violet is surprisingly receptive when I tell her about my date with Lara while we're at Mum's house. When she found out I was going out this evening, I thought about making up an excuse but didn't fancy lying to her again. Until now, I've made excuses like I'm going to work or seeing friends, but she hasn't fully believed me, so I've decided to be honest.

'Is Lara your new friend?' she asks. 'I hope she knows lots of good games.'

I ruffle her hair. 'She might be, yeah. I'll ask her about games when I see her, OK?'

Violet nods, chuffed that she's had some input into my dating endeavours. I'm glad to see her so animated, especially since I've been so worried about her. She's been almost back to her old self this afternoon.

My gaze falls on Mum, who's sitting quietly in the corner sipping her tea with a small, knowing smile on her face. A quirk of her lips lets me know she wants to talk to me about something.

'Violet, why don't you go and see if you can find where Gran keeps the biscuits?' I suggest. 'If you're really quick, you can have two.'

Her face lights up and she slaps her hands to her cheeks. The change in her since I stopped being a miserable bastard is remarkable. If I'd said this to her a couple of months ago, she'd have been worried about spoiling her tea. But now she's like any other five-year-old being told they can have a treat.

'Yay!' She jumps up and down on the spot. 'Can we have sausage rolls for tea?'

I nod my head. 'Oh, I think Gran can do that if you ask her really nicely. Now, go and find the biscuits. You might find those pink wafers you like.'

She gasps and tears off towards the kitchen to find them. They're her favourites and if she thinks Mum might have some in her biscuit tin, that's all the incentive she needs.

'She's a great kid, isn't she?' I smile after her. 'I was worried about her overthinking things and missing out on all the fun of being a kid, but she's been doing so well recently. Especially since I started making some changes.'

Mum nods and sets her cup down on the table. 'She's been like a different kid lately, and it's lovely to see. She gets it from you, you know. The overthinking.'

'Touché. Now what was that face for? You look like you want to say something.'

Mum folds her hands in her lap. 'Oh nothing, sweetheart, I just want to know about the marvellous Lara that I've heard almost nothing about. I won't be around forever – we should have these discussions while we still can.'

I roll my eyes. 'For God's sake, you're sixty. Stop

being so bloody morbid! Lara, she's... Well, she's awesome. We've been talking on Tinder for a few days and we're meeting up for dinner tonight. I think you'd like her. In fact, I should thank you for all of this; I'd probably never have tried online dating if you hadn't suggested it.'

She regards me for a moment, one leg crossed over the other and a quizzical expression on her face. 'Would I indeed? You haven't said that about anyone since Claire.'

I frown. 'That's because we were together for twelve years. I couldn't say that about anyone else because there was no one else. Just her.'

And look how you treated her at the very end, when she needed you most.

I ignore the stab of guilt and compose myself before my mum realises there's anything wrong. She thinks I was there with Claire during her final moments. I don't know what she'd say if she found out I wasn't.

'Can I ask you something?'

Mum's tone is neutral, but there's something hiding behind it. I allow myself a small, uncertain smile as I look at her. A small part of me is still terrified she's going to bring up the subject of Violet coming to live with her, even though things are better now.

I swallow down the lump of fear in my throat. 'Go for it.'

She purses her lips for a moment, twisting her face

into shapes I've never seen before. 'How can I say this without sounding like an interfering old bat? OK, I've got it. How many women are you going to meet off Tinder before you realise you have feelings for Hannah?'

My gaze snaps upwards to meet Mum's. She's looking very pleased with herself. She has the air of someone who's been waiting to say something a bit spicy for ages and has finally got it off her chest.

'Ugh, not you too.' I tip my head forward into my hands. 'This mum at Violet's school Fun Day said the same thing, and I've no idea where she got it from. She said she could tell by the way we looked at each other or some crap like that. Hannah and me, we're … we're best friends and I love what we have. I'd never want to risk that to see if we could be more.'

Mum smirks at me and I'm taken aback. She *never* smirks; she's got that sweet middle-aged-lady smile that reminds people of old-fashioned sweet shops with bells above the door.

'I don't know if you noticed this, son, but for all your objections, you didn't deny having feelings for her.'

Bollocks. First, I'm outsmarted by my five-year-old in a soft-play car park and now by my own mother. I need to up my game. When I open my mouth to say that I categorically *don't* have a crush on my best friend, the words don't come. I try again and the same thing happens.

Mum walks over to me and puts her hand on my shoulder. 'Sometimes, Evan, you've just got to feel the fear and do it anyway.'

She's been on Instagram looking at inspirational quotes again. Great, just what I need. She goes back to her seat and picks up her magazine and pen so she can do the crossword. We exchange a look heavy with unspoken implications.

'I'm proud of you, you know. It looks like you're finally starting to move on.'

I can't hide my smile. She might be completely wrong about my feelings for Hannah, but it feels like she approves of the new life I've cobbled together and that I'm finally the person she thought I was capable of being. A weight lifts off my heart.

'I'd better go and see where Violet is with the biscuits. She's been gone a long time.'

When I get to the kitchen, I find her sitting on the floor with the biscuit tin open and the contents half strewn around her.

'Hey.' I smile at her from the doorway. 'Mind if I join you?'

She shakes her head and hands me a Penguin as a welcome gift when I take a seat next to her.

I take it from her and peel the wrapper off. 'Thanks, how did you know these are my favourites?'

She looks up at me, abandoning whatever she's doing with the biscuits in front of her. 'You eat lots of them when you have a cup of tea. Miss Thompson says we shouldn't eat chocolate because it's bad and that we should have carrots instead. I think she's a poopyhead.'

I laugh and pass her a pink wafer she hasn't noticed in the tin. 'We should eat stuff that's good for us, but sometimes it's nice to eat stuff that makes us happy too, isn't it?'

'Daddy, why do you have lots of special friends? You said you only wanted one to spend time with and do nice things with. Some of them might get upset if you say they're your special friend but you have other ones too.'

Well, this has knocked me for six.

'And what about Mummy?' she continues. 'She wouldn't be very happy with you either. She'd make you sit on the naughty step and not give you any biscuits.'

I make a half-arsed job of explaining that I don't *actually* have any special friends at the moment and that I've been getting to know lots of different people recently. Somehow, she buys it.

'If you're not OK with me having a special friend just now, that's fine. You don't need to be scared to tell me.'

'No, that's OK, Daddy. You need someone to keep you company when I'm in space, remember?'

I lift her onto my lap for a cuddle.

'You're right. Mummy wouldn't want us to be unhappy forever, would she? She'd want us to meet nice new people and do fun things. She liked doing fun things, do you remember?'

This is pretty much the first time I've brought up the subject of Claire on my own since she died. If we've spoken about her before now, it's been Violet who's initiated it.

'She liked to bake cakes with me. They were yummy. I liked the lemon one best and she said I was a good helper because I put special sugar on top. It looked like snow and we made a big mess.'

I feel tears sting my eyes and my throat tightens. But I'm not sad this time, I'm happy. I was so worried that Violet didn't have any special memories of Claire to hold on to, but I've been proven wrong in the loveliest way possible. I think back to Claire's letter, *Trying New Things Together,* and of how fondly she talked about her baking sessions with Violet. I'm so glad our daughter remembers them.

'I've been thinking about what you said about getting a cat,' I grin at her. 'Maybe it wouldn't be such a bad idea. What do you think?'

Her head snaps to attention and she throws her arms around my neck. 'Yay, Daddy! Can we call him Barry? Or Nigel?'

Here we go with the fifty-year-old accountant names again. Her next suggestions will probably be Jeremy or Martin.

'How about we go with a space-themed name instead? See what cool names you can come up with.'

She heads off towards the living room to tell Mum the good news. My heart lurches as I catch sight of the bruise on her arm again. It's an angry purple colour and I'm still no closer to finding out where it came from.

What *is* going on with her?

Chapter Twenty

The hours before my date with Lara pass so much quicker than I thought they would and a renewed sense of panic makes my stomach churn. I thought I'd stopped worrying about dating, but I was so wrong.

We're having dinner at The Glasshouse next to the Omni Centre at 6pm. I was originally going to suggest eight, but realised I'd probably fall asleep on the sofa before I made it out of the door. Plus, it worked out better for childcare. I haven't told Lara I have a kid yet; I've learned my lesson from what happened with Danielle. When she asked why it was so early, I told her I had to be up early for work the following morning.

After we brought Mum back here from hers, I head upstairs to get changed. Although I picked my outfit earlier with Hannah's help, Violet appoints herself as my style adviser and disagrees with every choice I've made.

'Do you want Lara to be your special friend?' she asks, reaching for a pink shirt in my wardrobe. 'She has a nice name.'

I chuckle and shake my head. 'Thank you for your seal of approval, but we're just going out for dinner to have a nice time. Now…' I trail off as I lift her into my arms. 'I know you don't like the grey T-shirt, but what do you think of this?'

I pull my black blazer on over the T-shirt and wait for Violet's response. She turns her head this way and that, appraising me.

'Yes, Daddy, that looks better. But take your glasses off, you look weird. Like Peppa Pig's dad.'

There's that comment again. You can always trust a five-year-old to be honest.

'Don't sugar-coat it, say what you think.' I smile and slip my glasses off.

After a word of encouragement from Mum ('Don't do anything I wouldn't do') and Violet's insistence that I bring her hippo along for good luck, I head out to meet Lara. My nerves escalate as I get closer to the city centre and I run through everything I've learned about her so far. She's thirty, a veterinary nurse, and is originally from Newcastle. Her hair is long and blonde, her eyes are blue and she's a couple of inches shorter than me. Bit by bit, my heart rate slows down and I remind myself that everything will be fine. I've come a long way since that first date with Rachel.

I'm walking along Waverley Bridge when my phone buzzes. When I pull it out of my pocket, my heart somersaults when I see there's a text from Hannah.

Good luck for tonight – I hope you remembered that blazer! Really proud of you, dude. If this goes well, maybe you and Lara can double-date with me and Alex one night?

So, Alex is still on the scene. I'm not entirely sure what to make of that. She's probably over at his flat right now and it won't be long before he whips out his croquembouche…

'Hi, it's Evan, right?'

The voice pulls me out of my thoughts and I stuff the phone back in my pocket. I look up to see a vaguely familiar-looking woman approaching me, a shaky smile on her face.

'That's me,' I say as I go to meet her. 'And you must be Lara?'

She nods and we shake hands. I notice her palm is

slightly clammy and her gaze shifts from me to the pavement and back.

'Feeling a bit nervous?' I flash her what I hope is a reassuring smile. 'Don't worry, I'm not some weirdo serial killer! Just a normal guy.'

All colour drains from Lara's face and her eyes widen. 'Um… OK, that's good to know, I guess.'

Brilliant. Instead of putting her at her ease, I've deepened her suspicions that she'll end up on *Buried in the Backyard*.

'Anyway,' I say, chuckling nervously, 'shall we?'

The Glasshouse Hotel is a beautiful old building, attached to the Omni Centre and lying just up the road from the Edinburgh Playhouse. It has a rooftop garden that takes you away from the buzz of the city, and you can see Calton Hill from the restaurant window.

Lara and I walk down the road, past the huge metal giraffes that guard the Omni Centre, talking about what kind of week we've had. The awkwardness between us is slowly dissipating and we're finding our comfort with one another. Probably because I haven't made any more references to serial killers. I can't wait until we're sitting down to dinner. We'll have plenty of time to talk and get to know each other.

We walk through the glass double doors into a sweeping entrance hall with a marble floor. To our left is a curved staircase and straight ahead is a reception desk. Lara hangs back and looks at her surroundings while I approach and ask where the restaurant is.

'It's just up there, sir,' the receptionist replies, gesturing to the staircase. 'One of the waiting staff will show you to a table. Have a nice evening.'

Lara and I head through to an area called the Snug Lounge, a long room with a huge communal firepit in the middle and cosy lighting. Bottles of whisky line the walls, shut away behind barred glass. We're shown to a table for two in a slightly quieter part of the restaurant and given menus.

'Can I get you anything to drink?' the waitress asks. 'We've got a selection of speciality whiskies if you're interested.'

I opt for a Glenlivet, while Lara chooses a lime and soda. Moments later, we're left alone.

'So you're a vet nurse?' I say, lifting my glass and taking a sip. 'That must be a pretty great job.'

'It is.' She smiles, but then her eyes cloud for a moment, as though she's reliving a sad memory. Within seconds, she's back in the room. 'I mean, it's really tough at times as well, but I've always loved animals. The feeling you get when you're able to make someone's pet better or even just give them more time—'

The rest of her sentence is sheared off when her phone buzzes. Her face is unreadable as she looks at the screen. There's a slight frown to her brow, but her eyes dance with delight. Whoever's texting her, she's glad to hear from them, even if she won't admit it.

'Everything OK?' I ask.

'Sure, it's just Domino's offering me a buy one, get one free on their large pizzas.'

The white lie trips off her tongue with ease and I fight to hold back a smile when her phone buzzes again. Seconds later, it rings with an incoming call.

'That's what you call aggressive marketing,' I say with a chuckle. 'They'll be offering you a free tub of Ben and Jerry's next.'

Lara gives an absent-minded smile and rejects the call before shoving her phone back in her handbag.

'Sorry about that,' she says. 'Anyway, tell me about your job. Scaring people every day must be fun.'

I feel a stab of pain somewhere, but style it out with my sunniest grin. 'You could say that! It's not what I planned to use my history degree for, but I really love it. Just me and my business partner, telling stories and shouting "Boo!" for a living. So, have you been on Tinder long?'

Lara pulls a face and chuckles. 'Too bloody long, probably! A couple of my mates said it might be fun, so I downloaded it. How about you?'

'I-I…' I decide not to tell her I was put up to it by my mum. Might ruin the ambience. 'I was the same – a friend of mine talked me into it and here I am. Not a bad place to be, I'd say.'

Our eyes meet across the table and we exchange shy smiles. My stomach flips and tightens with anticipation. This date is going really well. We haven't even ordered food yet, but I'm sensing a connection between us. If the last couple of minutes are anything to go by, we're in for a good date.

Just then, Lara's phone rings again. She pulls it back out of her handbag and looks at the screen, sighs and shoots me an apologetic glance.

'I should take this,' she says. 'Do you mind? I'll only be five minutes.'

I shake my head. 'No, of course not. Do what you need to do. I hope everything's OK.'

She smiles. 'Thanks, I'll have the beef Wellington if the waitress comes back.'

I sit at the table and watch Lara cross the dining room until she's well out of earshot. The next few moments play out like a silent movie: sharp, jerky movements and a tense facial expression, then a pause, followed by a gradual softening. I can practically see her muscles relax, one by one. Whatever the person she's speaking to has said, it's struck a chord.

'Have you decided?' The waitress approaches again, notepad and pen at the ready.

I don't reply right away because I'm too preoccupied looking at Lara. She's only across the room, but she may as well be on the other side of the world, judging by the serene smile on her face.

'Sorry, I'll, um, have the duck please and my … dining companion will have the beef Wellington.'

My unintended pause makes it sound like Lara and I are up to something nefarious that doesn't involve having dinner together. The waitress shoots me a glance then heads off back to the kitchen. Lara returns to the table seconds later, as though she'd never been away. Except, of course, she has and I don't think she's fully come back.

'Are you OK? That phone call wasn't something wrong, was it? There's not a cat in danger somewhere that you need to save with emergency surgery?'

She chuckles and her hands, which were previously occupied with the cutlery, come to an abrupt halt on the table-top. There's a silence before she speaks again.

'That was my ex-boyfriend, Adam,' she replies with a wistful smile. 'He wants us to get back together.'

From that moment, the date as we know it is over. Instead, Lara and I spend a nice evening together, eating delicious food and talking about lost love.

'I shouldn't have even been on a dating app,' she

says, shaking her head. 'I don't know what I was thinking.'

That seems to be a common theme among my Tinder matches, but I don't tell her this. Instead, I offer a comforting smile as I browse the dessert menu.

'Sometimes, you can think you're ready for something like this, then when you actually go out with someone who isn't your ex, you realise you're not. Don't beat yourself up about it. What happened with you and him, anyway?'

We've skirted around the details all evening, talking about how raw and lonely and painful it is to be without the one you love, but avoiding specifics. Until now, that is. My nosiness has once again got the better of me.

Lara looks down at her empty plate and allows herself a secret smile. 'You'll laugh when I tell you.'

I hold my hands up. 'I promise I won't. Scout's honour.'

Or Evan's honour. Hannah pops into my head for a second, but I force myself back to the present.

'We were work colleagues – he was the head vet and I was one of the nurses. Things were great for a while until we disagreed about whether this one cat had worms or not. I said it did, but he said it was something more serious and that the cat would need surgery. Anyway, it turned out I was right, the cat got better and the owner saved loads of money. Adam didn't like that

I'd questioned his professional opinion and he dumped me.'

I screw up my face. 'But you were right and the cat ended up getting the treatment it needed. Why end a relationship just because you were right and he was wrong? Doesn't seem like much of a reason to me.'

Lara shrugs and drinks the last of her lime and soda. 'You know those arguments that start off being about one thing and end up on a totally different topic? That argument was one of those. One minute, we were arguing about surgery versus worming tablets, the next he was telling me how needy I was and that I always had to be right. I gave as good as I got though – I shouted at him about his superiority complex and called him an arrogant dick.'

She stops for a moment, her fingers delicately tracing the glass. 'He's an arsehole at times, but … I love him. Can't help who you fall for, right? Bloody wish I could.'

Right at that moment, my phone buzzes with a text from Hannah. It's a video of her waving to the camera and wishing me good luck. Just before it cuts out, she blows a kiss and gives me a glimpse of the most wonderful smile.

'Judging by the look on your face,' Lara says with a knowing grin, 'you wish you could help it too.'

'Oh, um…' I trail off and wave a hand, hoping to bat the moment away. 'It-it's nothing like that. My best friend just sent me a video, wishing me luck for tonight. That's all, there's nothing else to it.'

I don't need to see my reflection to know that two pops of colour have appeared in my cheeks. Lara's expression says it all.

'Take it from someone who knows,' she says. 'Losing the one you love is shit, especially if it's over something stupid like a cat needing worming tablets. But loving someone and never telling them, *then* having to watch them fall in love with someone else ... that's a whole different kind of pain.'

I open and close my mouth a few times, totally lost for words. My eyes move from my phone to Lara and back again, before I make a strangled snorting sound.

'You're not the first person to assume I have feelings for Hannah,' I tell her. 'But honestly, you're wrong. Our relationship ... well, it's just not *like that*. If you want to call Adam back and tell him you still love him, go for it, but I... It's too complicated to explain, but even if I wanted to, I can't.'

The stare she fixes me with makes my stomach lurch. It's a knowing glance that looks eerily like my mum's. Probably best not to mention that though – might stick me in Norman Bates territory.

'You know what's interesting? You said your relationship with this girl "isn't like that", but you didn't say you didn't have feelings for her.'

I cover my face with my hands and groan. 'Oh God, not you as well!'

She gets up from the table and walks over to my side. 'Thanks for a great night, but I'm going to go and tell Adam how I feel before it's too late. I suggest you do the same.'

She hands me a twenty-pound note and leaves me alone at the table. Most of the other diners are shooting me looks of pity, thinking I've been ditched. I feel oddly exposed. This is what it must feel like being one of those reality-show cast members.

I nod at everyone and manage a smile. 'Nothing to see here, folks. Everything's fine,' I mutter to myself.

Chapter Twenty-One

I should go home.

I should walk through the door, thank my mum for babysitting Violet as I embarked on yet another failed romantic venture, and sink into my favourite armchair.

But I don't.

I climb into the driver's seat of my car and check my phone. Seven o'clock. Hannah isn't seeing Alex tonight, is she? I'm sure she mentioned something about him having a boys' night out. I could pop over and see her for a while; it wouldn't do any harm.

It's not too late, is it?

Before I can talk myself out of it, I start the engine and drive over to her house, which is on the opposite side of Holyrood Park from mine. It stands out from the crowd, just like its owner, with its garden full of wildflowers and ivy coiled lovingly around a wooden trellis.

Hannah comes to the door as I make my way up the path. She's wearing an oversized jersey, a pair of checked pyjamas bottoms and her thick, black glasses. As she stands in the open doorway, the light from inside the house surrounds her like a halo. I stop midway and just look at her, taking her in. My heart skips a beat and I scramble to gather my thoughts.

'Hey, you,' she says with a lazy smile. 'What are you doing here?'

Good question.

I open my mouth to answer, hoping some sensible words will arrange themselves in the right order.

'I ... wanted to see if you were free to go on an adventure.'

Fuck. Judging by the look Hannah's giving me, that's not what she expected to hear.

'An adventure?' she repeats, raising an eyebrow at me. 'Don't take this the wrong way, but you're not usually an adventurous kind of guy.'

I shrug. 'Well, tonight I am. What do you say?'

She doesn't reply right away, just crosses her arms over her chest while she looks at me. For a moment, I think she'll say 'Thanks, but no thanks,' and wander back inside.

But she doesn't.

'All right then. Let's do it.'

Walking up Calton Hill in the dark always seems like a good idea until you actually do it. It's a fair old trek in the daytime, but when light isn't on your side, it can be a treacherous journey too.

I take Hannah's hand as we make our way to the top. At least if we fall, we'll go down together. Once we reach the summit, we settle on a spot near the Dugald Stewart monument. The city below is picked out in fairy lights and it's a breathtaking sight.

'I forgot how beautiful it was up here,' Hannah says as she pulls her jumper sleeves over her hands. She didn't change before I whisked her off on this adventure and I kind of love her for it.

She breathes a sigh of contentment and I sneak a glance to catch that smile of hers. It really is wonderful.

'So, how many meaningful looks do I need to give you before you tell me what happened with Lara? I thought you were looking forward to seeing her,' she says, turning to me before returning to gaze at the skyline.

I take a deep breath in, blow air out through my cheeks, and tell her the whole thing from start to finish.

'She's probably having a romantic reunion with her

ex as we speak,' I say with a smile. 'I hope they remember to thank me in one of their wedding speeches. I'd like to think I played a crucial role in their love story.'

Thinking of love stories sets my brain down a path that I desperately try to pull back from. One that involves a cup of terrible coffee, the unexpected event that followed and all the things that could've happened next, if only we'd been a bit braver.

It's starting to get chilly so I drape my jacket over her shoulders and wrap my arms around her to protect her from the cold. In a companionable, contented silence, we watch as the city carries on as normal below us.

'Do you remember that time you kissed me?' The words are out of my mouth before I can stop them. 'It was just after I made you that crappy coffee.'

Hannah's gaze snaps from the city lights to my face in one swift movement. Her expression is unreadable, but her eyes are shining.

'Of course I do,' she whispers. 'I didn't think you did though. I thought you'd have forgotten about it by now. What's made you bring that up?'

I pause and shrug. 'I don't know, I just … I've been thinking about it a lot lately for some reason.'

She looks surprised, like my confession has caught her off-guard. For a moment, she looks at me as though she's searching for some minute detail in my face. Then she turns her attention to the grass and picks at a tuft of it.

'We just … forgot about it, didn't we?' she says with a wistful smile. 'Because of everything that was happening with my dad.'

There's more she wants to say, I can tell, but I don't push her. Years of friendship have taught me that she'll talk when she's ready. Looking at her now, I think of the day we met: a sunny August morning when we were lined up for our first day at school. Hannah looked at me, her eyes full of tears because she was nervous. I was anxious about what lay ahead too, so I took her hand in mine and told her it would be OK.

We've been taking care of each other ever since.

'I thought about it too, you know,' she admits. 'Not after you met Claire because I could tell that was it for you. She was the one. But before … I wondered what would've happened if things had been different. Maybe we could've … I don't know…'

She shakes her head as though she's trying to dislodge some unwanted thoughts.

'Maybe we could've what?'

I have a fair idea of what she means, but for some reason, I need to hear her say it. To confirm it's not just some crazy collection of thoughts that have taken root in my brain.

'We could've … seen what happened, maybe. I don't

know, Evan.' Hannah groans and drops her head into her hands. 'Why are we talking about this anyway? I have a boyfriend. Well, I have an Alex.'

The atmosphere between us has clouded and I need to find a way to bring back the magic we had earlier, when I showed up at her house and whisked her off on an adventure to look at the city we've loved our whole lives.

'I'm sorry,' I say, shooting her an apologetic smile. 'You're right, I shouldn't have brought it up. It's just … well…'

I stop to choose my next words carefully. If I'm going to say what's on my mind, it has to be now. She can tell me how ridiculous it all is and then we can move on.

'A couple of people have said that they think we have feelings for each other. I mean, it's crazy, right? There's never been anything between us apart from that one kiss a million years ago that didn't lead to anything.'

Hannah doesn't respond immediately and won't meet my eyes. She's focusing all her attention on the tuft of grass between her fingers like it's the most important thing in the world. The silence grows and so does the urge to say something – *anything* – that will break the tension.

'Do you want me to tell you what you want to hear, or would you rather know the truth?'

The words are so small and faint that the slight breeze

almost carries them away. My heart is in my mouth and my palms are slick with sweat, despite the chill in the air.

'Tell me the truth.'

After another pause, Hannah continues. 'I've loved you for as long as I can remember, Evan Harper. Since the day we met, you've been everything to me and I've never known how to say it. But there's a problem. You're the love of my life, but I'm not the love of yours. When you came bounding into my room the night after your first date with Claire, I knew nothing would ever happen between us. The way you talked about her… I'd never seen you like that with anyone before. And I was so pleased for you. That probably sounds insincere, but it's true. All I've ever wanted is for you to be happy and when you met Claire, you were. It almost didn't matter that you had no idea how crazy I was about you. Watching you fall in love with her made me realise I had to let you go. You'd found your person and somewhere along the way, I realised I deserve something like that for myself. I want someone to love me the way you loved Claire, but it can't be you because … you can't love someone that way twice. For you, it's never going to be me and I know that. I helped you start dating again so you could maybe find someone to make you happy. But it's time for me to have my once-in-a-lifetime love, just like you had yours.'

There are tears running down her face and it takes all

I have not to reach forward and brush them away. I stare at her, my mouth slightly slack, wondering how on earth I could've missed it all these years. This great, unheard love story was happening right under my nose and I had no idea. Probably because I was too busy living my own.

'Hannah, I…' I swallow down the lump in my throat. 'I didn't know.'

She shrugs, as if that will make the last few minutes go away. 'It's not a big deal, it just is what it is. I loved you and you loved Claire. Look, can we just … can we just pretend I didn't say anything? Please? You can pretend you don't know anything about this and we can just be normal?'

She looks at me, begging me to forget it, but somehow, I know I never will.

'Please,' she whispers.

Slowly, I nod my head and relief spreads across her face. She throws her arms around my neck and I bury my face into her hair for one tiny, perfect moment. The smell of springtime ensnares my senses and it pains me to let her go.

'Sure,' I agree. 'We never have to talk about this again.'

Hannah smiles and I can see what this means to her. After over twenty years of unrequited, unspoken love, she can finally move on and find the love she so deeply deserves. She's told me how she feels and there's nothing more to do or say. My insides ache with all the things I'd like to tell her, but I don't. She has a chance to be happy with Alex and I don't want to rip it away from her.

'Thank you,' she says.

We walk down the hill in a companionable but slightly tense silence. I have no idea what to say or think or do. The absence of conversation allows guilt and shame to slither across my skin as emotions I never wanted to feel begin to rush through me.

What would Claire think of this? Of me?

'Hannah, I—'

Before I can launch into an incredibly difficult conversation, I get a message from Mum:

Violet's been sick, are you on your way home?

Chapter Twenty-Two

Dear Claire,

I'm sorry. I'm so, so sorry for leaving you that day. Please forgive me. You deserved so much better than that.

I thought I'd only be gone about ten minutes. The line was longer than I thought it would be and the barista seemed to take an age to make my flat white. While I waited, I thought of all the things I wanted to say to you, what I wanted you to know before the end. I knew we were running out of time, but I thought I'd at least have the chance to tell you I loved you one more time. When I came back and saw you were gone, something broke inside me.

I thought I was ready to move on and meet someone else, but I'm not. I never will be. No one will ever be you.

What the bloody hell was I playing at?

I ask myself this over and over again after I head back home to see Violet. She's in bed by the time I get in, but I pop my head round the door to make sure she's OK.

'She seems fine,' I say when I'm back downstairs.

Mum shakes her head and rolls her eyes. 'I don't know how she managed to get into the ice-cream tub – I put it back in the freezer. She told me she was going to the toilet and I only realised she was in the kitchen when I heard some weird rustling. How was your date?'

The mention of the word *date* sends tingles of dread down my spine. I keep replaying my conversation with Hannah over and over, hearing every raw, beautiful word she said and the cracks at their edges. The heartbreak laced within them takes my breath away and I put my hand on the wall to steady myself.

'It was fine,' I say, deciding to keep the details to a minimum.

A funny look briefly crosses Mum's face, just long enough for me to notice it.

'Well, as long as you had a good time.' She looks away from me and knots her fingers in her lap for a moment. 'I've, er, got some news actually.'

I look at her, searching for clues to what she's about to say. After the emotional rollercoaster I've been on tonight, I'm not sure I can take any more surprises.

'Oh?'

'A little while ago, just after I suggested you download Tinder, I decided to give it a go myself. I thought, "Why not? I've still got my own teeth and if Rosemary and her dodgy hip can get a match, maybe I can too". And ... well, I *did*. His name's Rod; he used to be a children's magician until the arthritis kicked in. Now, he potters around in his garden and does line dancing.'

Her face lights up with a smile as she talks about him. I swallow down the lump in my throat and put my mess of a love life to one side. I can deal with it later.

'Wow, Rod sounds like an impressive guy,' I say with a smile as we walk into the living room. 'Have you been on a date with him yet?'

Mum blushes and the grin on her face makes my battered, bruised heart soar.

'Once or twice,' she says coyly. 'Just for a coffee or a bite to eat, you know. Early days and all that, but he's nice. I think you'll like him.'

'That's great, Mum,' I say, my voice thick with emotion. 'I'm really happy for you. When can I meet him? I'll have to give him the once-over, ask him what his intentions are, that sort of thing.'

She chuckles and shakes her head, taking my face in her hands for a moment. 'You'll do nothing of the kind, mister! A couple of minutes of being interrogated by you, the poor man will be running for the hills. We're just getting to know each other, but once I've figured him out a bit more, you'll meet him. He's coming round to my place for Netflix and chill one night next week.'

I look at her in wonder. 'Who are you and what have you done with my mum? And please don't say "Netflix and chill"; I guarantee it doesn't mean what you think it does.'

Mum gives my arm a playful swat then stops to look at me. In an instant, I feel exposed, all of my protective layers unravelled. While everyone else sees what I want them to see – a collection of worries and sadness masquerading as a functioning human – I've never been able to fool my mum. She sees me exactly as I am.

'Really? I heard it on Channel 4 a few nights ago. Sounded innocent enough to me. Anyway, I'll get going,' she says, getting up from the sofa and grabbing her coat. 'Let me know tomorrow that Violet's OK.'

She pats me on the arm and gives me a smile. Part of me wants to tell her everything that happened tonight, but I don't know where to begin. I say goodbye to Mum and lock the door behind her. I'm tempted to just slide down to the floor and stay there for the night. I definitely won't be sleeping after the events of this evening, that's for sure. But Violet might get a bit freaked out if she finds me here in the morning though, so it's probably best to move myself to the living room. I collapse onto the sofa and push the heels of my palms into my tired eyes.

Hannah is in love with me.

Or at least she was, before she decided to let me go and find someone who could love her in the way she deserved.

Why didn't I see it before? Now she's said it, it seems so obvious.

I wouldn't change a second of what Claire and I had together or do things differently – Violet wouldn't be here otherwise. But the idea of Hannah being painfully in love with me for all these years breaks my heart. I don't know how to think or how to feel.

Except I do, but I haven't been able to face it until now.

I have feelings for my best friend.

Admitting it to myself doesn't make me feel any better. In fact, I feel like the worst person in the world. What would Claire make of the situation we've found ourselves in? Would she be crushed or think I'd harboured feelings for Hannah while we were together? Although I know in my heart these feelings have only developed recently, I still feel awful for having them.

And now, just as I've acknowledged how I feel about Hannah, I have to let her go. She has the chance to be happy with Alex and I don't want to ruin that. Even if I could tell her how I feel, I'm not strong enough, not ready enough, not healed enough to be with her.

Just not enough.

I look in on Violet again to make sure she's OK, then head back downstairs and pull out Claire's book of letters. It's become my refuge from the world, a sanctuary when everything around me seems crazy and unpredictable. I don't know exactly which letter I'd like to read tonight or which set of words will speak to me the most, so I open it at a random page. The Post-it attached to it says *When You're Afraid to be Happy* and this seems too much of a coincidence to ignore.

Dear Evan,

Though you may be in the depths of despair right now, there will come a time where you feel more like Pooh and less like Eeyore. Bad analogy, but I've just finished reading that book to Violet, so I'm using it. I wonder how many more stories I'll be able to read to her…

Wait. Let's not dwell on that. I'm supposed to be writing about why it's OK for you to feel happy again. Damn brain.

I'd blame the tamoxifen if it weren't doing such a spiffing job of keeping me alive.

Anyway. If you're on a Caribbean cruise while reading this letter, feel free to skip past it. You've clearly already embraced happiness if you're on deck, sipping cocktails and hanging out by the pool. Then again, you might still be in the worst stages of grief, but hopefully things are starting to feel normal without me. If you're at the worst stage, the cocktails will happen eventually. Having time to prepare for my death won't have made things easier or have sped up the process, so don't beat yourself up if it's taking longer than you'd like. But if you are starting to see little shards of light poking through the gloom, please do not feel guilty. You'll probably worry that being happy is a betrayal to me.

Well, my love, it isn't. I might be dead, but that doesn't mean you have to stop living. Do it for Violet or your mum or our favourite Domino's delivery person if you can't do it for yourself at first. The point is to live. Do things that make you happy, laugh at the silliest things, be spontaneous. I know you're not so good at the last part, but please try. You might find you like it! Being happy without me isn't wrong. Phil and Grant might be fucking things up for us, and a life without me may not be what we had planned, but it's still a life that has to be lived.

I've asked a lot of you in my letters, but my challenge in this one is simple: I want you to live for a day. In case you're furrowing your brow right now, let me explain what I mean. I want you, for just one day, to be you. Not a grieving widower and single dad, but wonderful, funny, amazing you. Get as far away from your feelings as possible or just break your routine and do something different. Anything that gives you a break from being sad is fine by me. If you decide to keep being a miserable shit, you may find the lights flickering and doors banging at odd hours. Just saying.

Sometimes you might find the grief gets too much and you can't find happiness no matter how hard you try. If that does happen, just know that I'm there for you. I'm in every word and page of this book. All you have to do is find me.

Love always,

Claire

Grief sneaks up on me from nowhere, reminding me the woman I love is gone. She created this legacy for Violet and me in case the worst happened, and it did. She says I was the strong one during it all, but I wasn't. I didn't feel it, at least. Inside, I was crumbling because the idea of losing her was unthinkable. And despite what her letters say, I wasn't perfect. I didn't always ask the right questions or know what to feel and when to feel it. We argued too: huge, blazing rows because I didn't want to accept the reality of our situation and neither did Claire. Always so independent, she hated not being able to do everything she used to and hugely resented me having to take care of her. I did the best I could, but ultimately, I let her down.

Because of me, she died alone.

If I'd waited just a few minutes longer, I could've held her hand and told her how much I loved her as she passed away. The pain and guilt I feel over that will probably never leave me.

She wants me to put my grief aside and live for a day, find humour in all the pain and loss. I want to honour her wishes, but it'll be easier said than done. I've missed her for so long, I'm not sure I know how to do anything else.

Maybe I should just say fuck it and read all the remaining letters now. Claire wouldn't mind; she never was one for convention.

First stop is *First Date*. I'm quite intrigued to see what advice she's written down for Violet to follow. It must have been weird, thinking of her as a young woman making her own way in the world, while she was still a toddler.

But the letter isn't for Violet. It's for me.

Dear Evan,

I rang the chemo bell after my final treatment today and it got me thinking. One day, you will go out with a woman who isn't me. You might think this is me warning you off the idea with threats of haunting you, but it isn't. It's me letting you go and telling you it's OK.

I suppose that's what I've been doing with this book. Each letter I write lets you go a little more and prepares you for a life without me.

This one is probably the hardest to write because, truth be told, I hate the idea of you being with someone else. I want to scratch the metaphorical woman's eyes out and stake my claim on you so no one else will dare. Except I can't, can I? Soon it'll be someone else's turn to make you happy. After all, you can't grieve me forever.

Jesus, that was morbid, wasn't it? Quick change of tone is called for, I think. So, a date. I know this isn't your strong suit and it probably won't enter your head for a while. Or maybe that's wishful thinking on my part and you're reading this after marrying a Pilates instructor in Las Vegas. Moving on can happen in big or small steps, Evan, but it has to happen. Here's a selection of sage advice to get you started.

Tip No. 1: Give yourself a chance

You have so much to offer, darling, even if the idea of dating scares the hell out of you. Don't write yourself off, and take things at your pace. Gradually, your confidence will grow and it'll start to feel normal. Well, as normal as going out with complete strangers can feel! Don't let a rocky start put you off. A little fear is natural and healthy, especially when you're doing something scary like dating. But keep going, eh? Things will get easier.

Tip No. 2: Be yourself

You are a funny, kind, intelligent man and you don't need to be anyone other than who you are. I hope this gives you a kick up the arse or counteracts any bad advice that James, Dave, Lorna or Hannah might have given you. If someone doesn't like or accept you for who you are, fuck them. They aren't worth your time.

Tip No.3: Don't look for me

Don't look for someone who's exactly like me. If you do, you'll wind up disappointed. Not because I'm a one-off – although I am – but because it's impossible to replace someone you've lost. You love everyone differently and that's OK. The way you love me is unique and can't be replicated.

What you'll have with the one you love after me will be beautiful in entirely new ways. So don't look for me. Look for someone who can help you start again.

Love always,

Claire

I don't sleep that night. In fact, I don't even go to bed. As the sun rises over Edinburgh the next morning, I'm still exactly where I was eight hours ago: curled up on the sofa, clutching the book of letters. Somewhere in the back of my mind, I'm willing myself to move and get the morning started. Violet has to get to school, I have to get to work and life has to go on the way it always does.

Not even the sound of Violet's footsteps on the upstairs landing brings me out of my daze. She'll be down any moment, expecting cuddles, cereal and some cartoons before school, but I physically can't provide any of that.

What am I going to do?

Before I have time to think, Violet comes into the living room. When she sees me, her eyes widen and a look of panic crosses her face.

'Daddy, are you OK?' she asks. 'Was someone not very nice to you?'

I wipe my tear-stained face with the heels of my palms. 'No, nobody's been horrible to me, baby, I just … I'm just tired, that's all.'

That's as close to the truth as I can get without resorting to downright lies. Violet climbs up on my lap and wraps her arms around my neck. I pull her close for a hug and have to stop more tears from falling. There's no way I deserve a kid as amazing as her.

'Why don't you go for a nap?' she suggests. 'You can have my rabbit to cuddle if you want. Or my hippo.'

'That's really nice of you, but I'm fine, I promise. Anyway, I don't have time to go for a nap right now – I have to get you to school, don't I?'

The thought of pulling fresh clothes on and driving her to school makes my head spin. She needs me to be normal for her and for things to run as they usually do. Her life has been marked by so much chaos and she needs this bit of consistency in her day. But I don't know how to pull it off. I can't think or do anything except hold her on my lap and quietly panic.

'Could I stay home with you?' she asks. 'I don't want to go to school if you're sad.'

I shake my head and smooth her wild hair back from her face. The last thing she needs is to be around Dad the

Miserable Bastard today. At least at school, she'll be learning and having fun with her friends.

School.

'Is everything OK at school?' I venture. 'You like it and you have lots of friends, right?'

I wait for her to go off on some excited tangent, but she doesn't. Her gaze drops to the floor and I could swear she's about to start crying.

'What's wrong?' I draw her closer to me so her head's resting against my chest. 'Come on, baby, you can tell me.'

She shakes her head. 'I don't want to make you more sad.'

My battered, broken heart splinters even more. 'You can talk to me any time you want, and I'm sorry if I've ever made you feel like you can't. Is there something you want to tell me about school? Why don't you want to go in today?'

She adjusts herself so she's sitting more comfortably in my arms. It looks like she's finally ready to open up about what's going on with her and where those two mysterious bruises came from.

'I don't like school very much. Miss Thompson's not very nice and they don't have any space books in the book corner. And you're sad and we don't have a cat yet.'

Great, another brick wall, just what I need.

'Those are all very valid reasons to stay home, but I'm

afraid you still have to go. You've got a big old brain inside that head of yours, and you need to fill it with all kinds of knowledge about books and numbers and the world. We'll get a cat soon, I promise, and you don't need to worry about me. I'm OK, really.'

I'm going to have a fight on my hands to get her out the door this morning. Reluctantly, she jumps down off my lap and lands on the floor with a soft thud.

'I'm not going to school,' she tells me, folding her arms to emphasise her point. 'I'm staying with you and I want ice cream for breakfast.'

Oh fuck, she's not in a good mood.

'Violet, it's not up for discussion. You're going in today and that's that.'

To my utter astonishment, my sweet-natured little girl stomps her feet, lets out a piercing scream of frustration and storms off towards her bedroom. I follow as quickly as I can, but by the time I get to her bedroom door she's blocked it, probably with her toy box.

'Open the door and let me in.' I try desperately not to panic about what could happen to her in there. 'You're going to be late for school.'

Not the greatest bargaining chip I could have used considering she doesn't like it there, but I'm exhausted and grief-stricken. This standoff takes me back to her first day at school. I thought things had changed, and maybe they did for a while. But now, we've arrived back at square one.

'Go away!' Her voice is muffled, but her anger comes through loud and clear.

'Violet Isabelle Harper, open this door right now! Do you want me to take the Tim Peake audiobook back to the shop?'

'It's in my room, so you can't!'

Damn, she's got me there.

'Baby, I know you don't like school and you want to stay home with me because you're worried, but honestly, you don't need to be. You know how you feel sad sometimes?'

I wait for the muffled 'Uh-huh', a sign that she's listening to what I'm saying instead of pretending she's on Mars. When it comes, I take it as my cue to continue.

'Well, adults sometimes feel sad too, for lots of different reasons. I know it's not very nice for you to see, and I'm sorry I scared you, but I'm going to be OK. And if you tell me what's wrong at school, I can make that OK too.'

Silence falls, and I wonder if I've finally said the right thing.

'No. I want to stay home,' Violet whispers through the door.

Time to call in reinforcements.

Chapter Twenty-Three

It's days like today that make me realise how lucky I am to have Dave and Lorna in my life. After my desperate phone call pleading for help, they're straight round to take control of the situation. Lorna wrangles Violet into her school uniform, Dave gives her breakfast, and she's out the door in less than ten minutes. It's one of the world's greatest phenomena.

'Thank you so much,' I croak as I see them out the front door. 'I'm ... I'm not feeling my best today.'

Lorna looks at me with concern and bites her lip. 'Yeah, I can see that. Is everything OK?'

I wave a hand as if that will get rid of all my problems and worries. 'It will be, don't worry. And thanks for not telling my mum – if she saw me like this, she'd go bananas.'

Dave pauses for longer than I'm comfortable with. 'Um…'

I look past him to the front street and see my mum coming up the path. Her face is unreadable and her eyes are blank. Whatever she's here for, it's not good.

'Thanks a lot, guys.'

I head back inside, closely followed by Mum. The door slams shut behind her.

'Well.' She takes a seat at the kitchen table and looks at me with a mixture of concern and caution. 'What's going on?'

Under normal circumstances, the creative side of my brain would craft a more palatable version of the truth. I would work hard to keep my deep, dark secret locked away in case it destroyed everything I have. Today, I'm tired, miserable and completely incapable of thinking outside the box. So I decide to climb inside the box, fold the flaps down and tape it shut. At least I can hide from the world in there.

It's time to finally be honest.

'Mum … everything's gone to shit. I've done some terrible things and you need to know what they are…'

Her eyes widen and her hands shake a little as she clenches them into fists.

'OK… Why don't you tell me *exactly* what happened then we'll see what we're dealing with?'

I laugh and shake my head, allowing it to fall into my

cupped hands. 'Mum, it's OK – you don't need to help me shift a dead body or anything. It's … it's about the day Claire died. I did something and I've never told anyone about it.'

Understandably, this doesn't do anything to ease Mum's panic. If anything, she looks even more terrified, but she's trying not to show it. Admitting it out loud feels weirdly freeing, like a weight is slowly being lifted from my chest.

'I don't understand. What do you mean? She died from cancer; you didn't have anything to do with that.'

I tell her what those last few months were like. I start with all the things I didn't tell her before – the arguments we had, the difficulties of caring for her, how resentful we could both be on our worst days – and then I get to what happened the day she died. I can't remember when I started to cry; in fact, I don't even notice the tears until they make my voice tremble and body shiver.

'It's all my fault,' I manage to say through great, heaving sobs. 'Before I left the room, she told me she loved me and I was going to say it back, but she was falling asleep so I decided to tell her after I'd been to the café. She died surrounded by a bunch of strangers without knowing how much I loved her and it's all my fault.'

Mum's face softens. She rushes to my side and pulls me in for a tight hug as I crumble.

'Listen to me, Evan. Claire was in no doubt about your love for her. You showed her in so many different ways, before she was ill and after. You couldn't have known she'd pass away when you left the room – you'd only have been gone for, what, twenty minutes at the most? She was so ill that it could've happened at any time, so please don't beat yourself up.'

'If I'd just stayed a little longer, I'd have been there. I promised her I'd be right by her side until the end and I failed. This is all on me, Mum.'

Now that I'm talking to someone about it and not hiding it away, I wonder how I've managed to survive the last two years. Keeping the events of Claire's death to myself has damn near killed me. Now, I can breathe again. Mum's still here, she hasn't disowned me or told me how awful I am.

Hannah's confession comes spinning out next, before I can stop it. Mum listens and nods but doesn't look surprised once.

'How did I miss it, Mum? Why did I never see it?'

She shrugs and places a hand on mine. 'You didn't want to. Or you were too close to it. And then you met Claire and everyone could see how much you loved her.'

Claire. The guilt over my feelings for Hannah hits me all over again and I screw my eyes tightly shut, hoping it'll go away.

'I think I have feelings for Hannah too,' I admit,

taking a second to see how those words hang in the air before continuing. 'I know it's crazy and I shouldn't, but I do. Since she came back from travelling, I … I don't know, I've started to look at her differently. But it's too late and there are a million reasons why it shouldn't happen.'

Mum squeezes my hand and I manage a smile. She really is wonderful. I'm not sure what to make of the odd expression on her face right now though.

'Darling, you're not going to like this, but … I think Violet should come and stay with me. Just for a few days before you go off on one like you usually do. You need a break. I've known for long enough you haven't been coping with losing Claire, but I thought things were starting to get better. Maybe if you had some time to yourself, it would do you the world of good.'

My heartbeat quickens. No amount of objections spoken through gritted teeth or ice-cold glares is going to stop her this time. She looks serious about taking Violet away.

'Please, Mum, don't do this.' My words are shaky as I try to keep more tears from falling. 'She's everything to me – I don't know what I'd do without her. Please let her stay with me – I can be a good dad to her, I swear.'

Mum stands up, her eyes heavy with sadness, and strokes my cheek.

'Oh, Evan, I know you can. You *are* a good dad, but

you have too much grief and pain you haven't dealt with yet. I'm not doing this to hurt you, I'm doing it because I think it's best for you and Violet. We'll start off with a few days, just to give you a bit of a break, then see where we are. How does that sound?'

I feel utterly broken and powerless. There's nothing I can do to stop her; she's taking Violet whether I like it or not. I've run out of chances to prove to her that I'm handling my grief and moving on with my life. Without saying a word, I follow her upstairs to Violet's room and help her gather some clothes together.

'You'd better take these too.' I pick up her hippo and rabbit from her bed. 'She can't sleep without them.'

Mum looks as if she's about to cry when she takes them from me. Part of me wants to hold on to them and not let go, but the other part of me knows I've lost.

'Oh, and her Tim Peake CD.' I whirl around in a clumsy circle until I find it. This time, I can't stop the tears as I pick it up. It's a reminder of just how much I've screwed up. I've failed at being the dad Violet needs. I sit down on the bed, still holding the CD in my trembling hands.

'Please, Mum,' I whisper. 'I love her, please don't take her away.'

She crouches down so she's at my level and cups my face with her hands. 'I know you do. This is only temporary, I promise. I'm doing it for you, son.'

She takes the Tim Peake CD from me, promises to listen to it with Violet as much as possible and walks to the bedroom door. I don't follow her this time.

'I'll pick her up from school,' she says, her voice small and quiet. 'It will make it seem like a big adventure. Look after yourself, Evan, and for God's sake, try to forgive yourself, eh? You've beaten yourself up long enough.'

It's official: my mum is taking Violet. I can't believe I let this happen. Just what kind of father am I? No matter what else has been going on, I've always tried to be the best father I can, but it looks like I've failed. It will be good for Violet though; some time away from the grief and sadness that have seeped into every part of our lives will really benefit her.

My phone rings. It's Violet's school.

'Mr Harper, can you come into the school as soon as possible, please? We need to discuss a very serious matter.'

My daughter is a bully.

At least that's what the head teacher, Mrs Sullivan, tells me while Mum and I sit in her airless, overheated office. A fan does its best to circulate hot air and the acrid stench of stale sweat. She reels off a list of apparent incidents that Violet has been involved in: kicking, name-calling, pushing. They've all involved the same kid, Arabella, and haven't come to light until now because she's been too scared to tell any adults after Violet threatened her. Each incident has also taken place with no witnesses. Funny, that. We're here to discuss today's confrontation; apparently, she's graduated to hitting. Arabella and her mum – none other than Renee of the yummy mummies group – sit in stony silence in two plush-looking seats.

'Pardon my language, Mrs Sullivan, but this is bullshit,' I declare when she's finished. 'I know you've probably heard this a hundred times, but my daughter isn't a bully.'

'Are you calling my daughter a liar?' Renee snaps.

'Calm down, Mrs Wilkes, we'll get to the bottom of this.' Mrs Sullivan's beady eyes turn to me. 'Mr Harper, as you know, we have to take all accusations of bullying very seriously. From what I can gather, your daughter has been tormenting Arabella for quite some time.'

In the moments of silence that follow, my clapped-out brain starts knitting together a theory. The bruises on Violet's arms, how sad she's seemed lately… I look at her. I know her better than anyone and she's not a bully. Any parent would probably say the same, but it's just not in her nature. She's not wearing her cardigan so I can see the bruises as clear as day. When she sees me looking, she tries to cover them.

'I don't suppose you've noticed whether Arabella's come home with any marks on her? Scratches maybe, or bruises?' I ask Renee. 'Has she seemed herself to you lately?'

She narrows her eyes. 'What's that got to do with anything?'

'It's a simple enough question.'

Her cheeks flush scarlet. 'If you must know, I haven't noticed anything, and she's seemed fine. But that doesn't mean your daughter isn't a bully! She pushed Arabella into a ball pool, as well you know.'

'She said nasty things to me and pushed me down a slide!' Violet yells. 'She said it was my fault I don't have a mummy anymore and that I was horrible and smelled funny.'

Ah-ha. Now, it all makes sense.

How did I not notice this?

I straighten in my seat and present Mrs Sullivan with all the facts at my disposal. Atticus Finch has nothing on me as I make my case for Arabella being the real bully out of the two girls. Renee looks horrified and screeches about taking this further, but the look of resignation on Arabella's face provides me with all the proof I need.

Checkmate.

Mrs Sullivan asks for each girl's side of the story. Violet is a little superhero as she gives her account. Moving one of the girls to another class is on the table for a minute, but Arabella doesn't want to be separated from her friends and Violet doesn't like the idea of going to a new class either. So, a fragile peace is brokered between them. They'll never be best friends, but at least Violet won't have to worry about being bullied every day. When we step outside Mrs Sullivan's office, I pull Violet aside.

'Listen, baby.' I crouch down to her level and take her hands in mine with no idea how I'm going to get through the next few minutes. 'Since you've been such a brave girl today, Grandma wants you to go on a special sleepover to her house for a few days. How cool is that? You'll get loads of treats and as many pink wafers as you can eat.'

Most kids would be excited about this, but not Violet. She looks from me to Mum and back again, her little face etched with confusion and worry. She knows something is wrong.

'I want to stay with you,' she says. 'You were smiley and listened to Tim Peake with me.'

'You're going to have a great time,' I tell her as my voice wavers. 'You love spending time with Grandma, don't you?'

I exchange a look with Mum, hoping that seeing Violet's reaction to the idea will put her off. She stands there in silence and looks away from me, before crouching next to Violet.

'Why don't we go for some ice cream, eh? You've had quite a day of it, missy.'

'Can Daddy come?'

'Um ... Daddy's busy just now,' Mum replies. 'Another time though.'

I watch them walk away and my heart splinters in my chest. How did I let things get this bad?

Chapter Twenty-Four

When I walk up the path to my house after leaving Violet's school, Hannah is waiting for me outside, arms folded and a stormy expression on her face. I really hope she doesn't want to go over what she said last night; I simply don't have the energy.

'I know last night ended on a weird note,' I say as I put my key in the door. 'But can we talk about it some other time? I've had a bitch of a day.'

Hannah puts her hands on the door, just in case I was thinking of closing it behind me, and follows me inside.

'Do you want to tell me why I've just had a phone call from your mum, telling me that if I want to see Violet in the next few days, I'll have to pick her up from her house instead of yours?'

I turn around and look at her square on. This is the very last thing I'm in the mood for.

'Not really, no. Unless you fancy explaining why the hell you waited twenty years to tell me you're in love with me?'

Hannah's face darkens and her head tilts a fraction to one side.

'Evan.'

A shiver runs down my spine and I swallow hard. Judging by the ice running through her voice, I'm in deep trouble.

'All right, you really want to know?' I spread my arms wide. 'I screwed up, Hannah – I tried my best, but I couldn't be the dad that Claire wanted me to be. The dad *I* wanted to be. I was so close, so *fucking* close…'

I trail off and let my head fall into my cupped hands for a moment. A couple of deep breaths help me to gather myself, so I tell Hannah everything.

'Now Mum's taken Violet to stay at hers to "give me a break",' I say. 'I'm so scared, Hannah – what if I don't get her back? What if she prefers it at Mum's and wants to stay there instead of coming home? I don't know what I'd do without her.'

Hannah wraps her arms around me and I pull her close, burying my head in her shoulder as I cry, telling her about Claire's last day. She holds my shaking body and tenderly strokes my scalp while she shushes me.

That beautiful smell of springtime, of new beginnings and flowers and rainstorms, takes me back to Calton Hill for a single glorious moment. I'd give anything to be back there right now.

'You need to find a way to move on,' she says eventually. 'Because this – what you're doing now – is killing you. I wasn't in the room when she died either, and yes, I feel guilty about not being there, but I can't change it. Neither can you, so stop being so angry with yourself and everyone else. There's only so many times people can tell you that you deserve to be happy again – you have to listen to them. And, you know … I love you, you miserable shit.'

There's a moment between us when everything stops. I reach out and gently brush my fingers against her cheek. She leans into it for just a second, then moves away. I want more, I ache for more, but now isn't the right time. Maybe it will never be. And then, just like that, the moment passes. She opens her arms and we hug. When we pull apart, I wipe my eyes and heave a weary sigh.

'So…' I chuckle. 'Now all I've got to do is sort my entire life out. Easy stuff, eh?'

Hannah chuckles. 'Oh yeah, piece of cake. Where are you going to start?'

A small smile kicks up the corners of my mouth. 'I've heard the beginning is a pretty good place.'

Claire's book seems like the ideal point to begin. I flip to the letter called *Things I Want You to Know*.

Dear Evan,

Before I depart this mortal coil – God, how dramatic does that sound? – there are some things I want you to know.

Bins are collected on Wednesdays. Make sure the mortgage and council tax payments are up to date. We have direct debits set up for these, but you know what banks are like. The life insurance documents are in the bedside table, second drawer down. I don't remember how much I'm insured for, but probably not enough to make bumping me off early worth your while. Just bide your time, eh? Violet won't eat peas, but she does like sweetcorn. Don't give in to her demands and let her have chocolate pudding for every meal or you'll end up facing the Shit-pocalypse. She gets picked up from nursery at twelve, and her favourite story is The Tiger Who Came to Tea.

OK, that's the practical stuff out of the way. Now for the stuff I really want you to know. I bloody love you, Evan Harper. More than I'll likely ever be able to show you. When I met you that day a million Septembers ago, I had no idea how things would unfold between us. You offered to carry my boxes into my dorm and I fell in love with you right then and there. We've crammed so much into our twelve years together, yet it doesn't feel like enough. It never will. I'll always want more of us. A house full of kids, some dogs and cats. Maybe we could move to the Highlands and open up a B&B. You could scare everyone with your ghost stories and I could make sure the guest towels are extra fluffy. Nice dream, isn't it? Just one of many that Phil and Grant insist on ripping away from us.

I don't want to leave you. Before all this, we were having the time of our lives. OK, we were knackered, thanks to Violet, but life was pretty sweet. We had time and possibilities and endless dreams and plans. Now all we have is a countdown until the end. How unfair is that?

I want you to be happy again after I'm gone. Moping doesn't suit you, for one thing. You have a face that suits smiling much more than frowning. All jokes aside, you've been my rock through all this cancer shit and you deserve some happiness when it's all over. Since I was diagnosed, you've been the strong one, always looking for silver linings. I'm so sorry you couldn't find any, darling.

I have a job for you. Do something that makes you smile. The sillier and more embarrassing the better. In fact … I've just had a brainwave. Do you remember you wanted to do stand-up comedy at uni, but you came down with food poisoning thanks to that dodgy burrito? This is the perfect chance to make up for it! Call a comedy club and book a slot. Find some humour in this shitstorm we've landed in. If you don't laugh, you cry, right?

Love always,

Claire

PS My mum used to say that holding grudges made you look old before your time; I'm not sure how true that is, but I do know you can hold a grudge like no one else. Try letting some stuff go. Don't hold it all in and let it hurt you. And if people want to help, let them. There's strength in numbers.

Find humour in the shitstorm? Easier said than done. I've never done stand-up comedy in my life and the idea to do it at uni came one drunken night when I thought I was Edinburgh's answer to Mickey Flanagan. A bad chicken burrito halted that idea in its tracks and I haven't considered it since.

Until now, that is.

'What do you reckon?' I ask Hannah, who's reading the letter over my shoulder. 'In another letter, she said she wanted me to live for a day and do something that makes me happy. This could be it.'

She sits down beside me on the couch, her brow furrowed in thought. 'Do you think you're ready for something like that? Getting up on stage and talking about your dead wife is a pretty big step, especially considering you were in the depths of despair this morning. Don't look at me like that, I'm just repeating what your mum said.'

I don't say anything because, whether I like it or not, Mum was just telling the truth. I still hate the fact she has my daughter, but we'll deal with one thing at a time.

'Maybe this is what I need,' I reply. 'Claire's death has always been this dark, scary thing looming over me, so maybe talking about it in a way that makes a bunch of strangers laugh will help me to put it behind me.'

I think about the *First Date* letter and my promise to make things right again. Stand-up comedy could be the thing to set me on the right path.

Hannah puts her hand on my shoulder. 'It's a great idea, but don't do anything you're not comfortable with. Maybe this should wait until you're feeling a bit better.'

I shake my head. 'No, this has to happen now. I need to do whatever it takes to make things right, and if that means making a twat of myself on stage, so be it.'

Hannah holds her hands up and tells me she can't argue with that. I kind of wish she would; I'm bricking it.

I can do this.

People do it all the time. Some even do it for a living.

So why can't I even step over the door of the Monkey Barrel Comedy Club? They're having a lunchtime open mic session and all I have to do to take part is go inside.

'I don't mean to rush you, but the session finishes at three.' Hannah says. 'So sometime in the next three hours, you'll have to either crap or get off the pot.'

I take a deep breath and run my hands through my hair. 'Well, pardon me for being a bit nervous about going into a club full of strangers and talking about my wife's death.'

Hannah smiles and raises an eyebrow. 'I thought it didn't matter? And I did tell you to rehearse before we came here, but you wouldn't listen. You said you wanted it to come from the heart or some bollocks to that effect.'

I groan and screw my eyes shut for a second. 'You're right. God, I'm an idiot, aren't I?'

'It'll be fine. Just get in there and do your stuff. Sorting your life out starts right here.'

I walk towards the door until I realise Hannah isn't following behind me.

'Aren't you coming in?'

'Give me a sec – I had some plans for today that I

need to shuffle around. Go on in, I'll be right behind you.'

Were her plans with Alex? If they were, why is she moving them around for me?

I make my way inside and after discovering there are no escape routes available besides the front door, I give my name to a woman with a clipboard and tell her I want to take part in the open mic session.

'Excellent,' she says. Her smile fades when she looks up and takes in my dishevelled appearance and eyes that are red from crying. 'Anything special you want us to say in your introduction? What's your material about?'

'Death. Well, death and some other stuff. I'm not really sure yet.'

She nods slowly and scribbles down what I've just said. 'OK… Why don't you take a seat? We'll call you when it's your turn.'

I find a free seat near the back and make myself comfortable. As I watch a young blonde woman take to the stage and get ready to perform, a tiny ray of hope cuts through all the pain and loss from today. Even by sitting here right now, I've done something I didn't think was possible. I've made it here and signed up to do a comedy slot, just as Claire's letter said. And if I can do that, who knows what else I'm capable of?

I'm not the only one who's chosen to make fun of something tragic. Divorces, car accidents, deaths of loved ones: nothing is off limits in this open mic session. It makes me feel better and gives me a sharp reminder that I'm not the only one to have their world turned to shit by something awful.

Then it's my turn.

As I approach the stage, I begin to wish I'd taken Hannah's advice and rehearsed what I was going to say. 'Speaking from the heart' seems an awfully bad idea when I get up there and see everyone looking at me. The door opens and some more people file in, but I can't see who they are. I wait until they sit down near Hannah before I begin.

'Hi, everyone. I'm Evan and as you can probably tell, I'm woefully under-prepared for something like this. My best friend suggested I practise a little first, but I decided to improvise, so please accept my sincere apologies.'

Some people laugh and I take that as a good sign. I find Hannah's face in the crowd and we exchange smiles. That's enough to tell me to keep going.

'I run ghost tours around the Old Town. Maybe some of you have been on one before? In case you haven't heard of us, I'm the guy that online reviews say has a face like a constipated squirrel. Oh well, you can't please everyone, right?'

More laughter. This is going better than I thought.

'Everybody has a story, don't they? Every single person who steps up on this stage has something they want to tell you. Well, here is mine. Two years ago, I lost my wife and everything went to shit.'

Silence, but that's not surprising. I do see a few intrigued expressions though, so I'm motivated to continue.

'When you lose someone you love, it's like a tornado rips through the centre of your life. There's no pain like it, trust me. I read a lot of grief books just after my wife died, trying to understand what the hell was going on, but there were some things I wasn't prepared for. Like the sheer volume of people knocking on my door with casserole dishes that were *always* filled with lasagne. And the sympathetic head tilt – can't forget that one. I'm not sure what it's supposed to achieve other than giving the person doing it neck cramp, but there you go. Oh, and my favourite: the exaggerated whisper. You know the one – it's a whisper, but may as well not be because it's so loud.' I do the best imitation of it I can. 'People would say, "How are you doing? You know, SINCE YOUR WIFE DIED." As if there was a chance I'd forgotten!'

I pause to let the laughter settle down. I can't believe I'm doing this or how good it feels. I'm talking about the worst experience of my life and finding little pieces of humour amidst all the gloom. I'm starting to feel comfortable up here. Even though I have no clue what

I'm going to say next, it's fun to see which direction my brain will take.

'I recently started dating again, on the advice of my friends,' I continue. 'And let's just say the results have been mixed. One woman brought a haunted doll named Sally with her as a plus one. Believe me, I wish I were making this up! This doll was the kind of thing you'd expect to see in your worst nightmares. Another woman gave me her number after we went out and when I called her, I ended up donating money to the Happy Paws Sanctuary. Twice.'

Laughter ripples through the room and the grin on my face widens. I continue telling stories for another ten minutes until it's time for me to step off the stage. Adrenaline rushes through me and I feel happier and lighter than I have in a long time. It feels like I've finally found the right place to channel my grief. I walk over to Hannah and see Dave and Lorna have arrived too. The three of them stand to greet me and we end up in a group hug.

'You were great up there, buddy!' Dave slaps me on the back and pulls me in for a hug-headlock. 'Well done.'

'Thanks! Why are you guys here?' I ask.

'Hannah called us,' Lorna explains. 'She said you needed us to come down to Monkey Barrel, so here we are.'

Dave puts a hand on my shoulder. 'We heard what

happened with Violet. I'm so sorry, mate. Maybe it'll be good to have a few days to yourself? You can ... well, you know, relax and get some things sorted out...'

He trails off and shrugs; he knows there's nothing positive about your child not staying with you.

'Yeah,' I reply. 'It'll be good for Violet too – she's had a lot to deal with the last couple of years. It's just for a little while, until I'm back on my feet.'

I can't keep the anger and sadness from my voice, but I don't break down. That won't help anything. I'm not the victim here – this is a mess entirely of my own making.

'Good job up there, mate.'

I look over to see Alex approaching us with a tray of drinks. He's wearing the same friendly smile I saw on the first day I met him. When he sets the tray down on a nearby table and puts his arm around Hannah, my heart sinks.

'Thanks,' I say, 'it was tough to start with, but I really enjoyed myself towards the end. Maybe you should give it a go?'

He holds up a hand and shakes his head. 'I'll leave the stand-up routine to the experts, I think. I've got enough to keep me busy right here.'

Was that a dig? It felt like one. The look in his eyes when he meets my gaze confirms my suspicions. He looks down at Hannah with that nice-guy smile of his and I murmur, 'Smug bastard,' under my breath. I'm sure no one hears me until I catch Lorna giving me a pointed stare.

'Well, it's up to you,' I say, avoiding Lorna's gaze. 'Oh, and while I've got you all here at the same time … thank you, all three of you. If you guys hadn't encouraged me to get out there again, I'd still be in the house listening to Claire's favourite songs on Spotify. I'm going to be a better friend to you from now on – no more Mr Miserable Bastard.'

They all smile and say variations on 'glad to hear it', but their faces tell a different story. They've heard me promise to turn things around before and I haven't followed through. This time will be different though.

It has to be.

Chapter Twenty-Five

My next stop is Mum's. The idea of Violet not being with me is unthinkable and I will do whatever it takes to get her back. So I park up outside the cosy Victorian semi and knock on the door.

Mum answers. 'Evan, what are you doing here?'

'I'm here for Violet. Look, I know you think you're helping the both of us by having her stay with you, but you're not. We're a team, Mum, just like you and I were when Dad left. We need each other and I know I haven't done a great job, but that's all going to change. I went to Monkey Barrel today and got up in front of everyone to talk about Claire's death. And they laughed! It felt so good and I know I can—'

She holds up a hand and her grave expression makes my stomach drop to my shoes.

'I'm glad you've had a nice day, darling, but that doesn't mean you're ready to have Violet back. You have a lot to deal with and need some time to yourself.'

I shake my head. 'No. I'm sorry, Mum, I love you but you're wrong. I mean, you're right that I haven't dealt with everything to do with Claire's death, but I don't need time to myself. I need my little girl. She's everything to me and if I'm not her dad, I'm nothing. So please, let me take her home. I've got this, I promise.'

I look at her, pleading with her to listen to me. I wouldn't blame her if she didn't, given what a mess I was this morning, but I hope she gives me another chance.

'Evan, you've got no idea what it's been like, watching you fall apart these last two years. There's nothing worse than seeing your child suffer, you know that. You've been so lost for so long that I was scared you'd never find your way back. Lately, it seemed like you were, but when I saw you today… It was like you'd gone right back to the day Claire died and it scared the life out of me.'

My insides twist with guilt.

'I know, and I'm sorry – I didn't mean to scare you. Last night was … well, I had a lot on my mind, put it that way. I know I still have a long way to go before I deal with it all, but please, Mum. Violet is safe with me, I swear – just let me take her home. I promised her we could get a cat and she'll never forgive me if we don't.'

Mum considers me for a moment, her brow furrowed in thought. I should probably be insulted that she's taking so long to decide whether to let my own child come home with me, but I'm not. Things haven't been easy for her since Claire died either. Who wants to watch their son lose himself in grief, knowing there's no way they can help?

'I've promised her we can have a *Madagascar* movie marathon tonight,' she says. 'So how about you pick her up tomorrow? That way you've got the rest of today to do whatever you like.'

My whole body slumps with barely concealed relief. I almost throw myself on my knees, but stop myself just in time. The last thing I need is one of the neighbours phoning the police about the 'strange man on Nora Harper's doorstep'.

'Thank you,' I whisper. 'And I promise I won't let you or Violet down. I'm going to be better from now on.'

Mum pulls me in for a quick hug and kisses my cheek.

'Just be my boy again, eh? I've missed him.'

I'm not alone in the cemetery this time.

I've wanted to catch Claire's phantom flower-giver in the act for weeks now and, as it turns out, I'm in luck.

I spot them when I walk through the gates, but I can only see the back of them. They're wearing a cream jacket, jeans and have long blonde hair. I hang back for a moment and observe them, not wanting to be noticed just yet. The person stands in front of Claire's headstone then kneels down for a moment, as if they might be conducting a conversation with her. It's more than a little eerie to see an echo of myself before my eyes. On any other day, this would be me, having a private moment at my wife's graveside. My stomach does a flip, but I can't tell if it's joy or nerves I feel. I'm about to unmask whoever it is that's leaving these flowers, but it could be the start of a whole new mystery. How does Claire know this person? Maybe they're part of a secret area of her life that I never got to see?

My imagination's running away with me again.

I take a few tentative steps forward, my breath hitching in my chest. I don't know what I'll say to this person; I don't want to go in mob-handed and make them feel unwelcome. I just want to know who they are.

'Hi.'

The mystery flower-giver gets up and turns round. She looks to be around twenty years old with fair skin and bright blue eyes.

'Um … hi.' She lifts a hand in an awkward greeting.

'I'm Evan. I was Claire's husband. Did you know her well?'

The woman nods and stares wistfully at the headstone, heaving a sigh. 'You could say that. She saved my life. My name's Alice. I had leukaemia about six years ago and Claire – Dr Harper – looked after me. If it weren't for her, I wouldn't be here now. I was really sad to hear she died.'

My heart swells with pride and I smile. Remembering her doesn't hurt this time.

'She was a great doctor, wasn't she?' I look down at the purple flowers next to her grave. 'Always went the extra mile for her patients.'

'She was the best. I gave the doctors a really hard time because I was so angry about having cancer, but Dr Harper saw through all my bullshit. She could see how scared I was and that I really wanted to get better. So she talked to me, told me to cut the crap and to stop shouting at everyone when they were just trying to help. It took a while and quite a lot of treatment, but I had my five years all-clear last year. Because of her and the impact she had on me, I decided to go to university to study medicine. I want to make a difference to people like she did.'

I look up at Alice and I'm suddenly struck by how much she reminds me of Claire. They're made of the same stuff, I can tell: that burning desire to help people in any way they can and make a difference on their lives.

'Well, I'm sure you will. Claire would be really happy to know she inspired you. Have you been visiting her grave long? I wondered who was leaving the violets for her.'

Alice's cheeks pink up and she shifts from foot to foot. There's no doubt in my mind that she's the person behind the rest of the bouquets, not just today's. It does my battered, bruised heart a lot of good to know that Claire had such a long-lasting effect on someone. But of course she did, because that was who she was. She inspired people without knowing it.

'I visit as much as I can while I'm in the city for uni. I'm from Perthshire originally, so I can't really come when I'm at home. It works out quite well though. Violets are a winter flower, and I'm in Edinburgh from autumn to early spring, except at Christmas. I know somewhere you can get them from about late August too. The florist manages to grow them themselves a bit earlier than usual.'

And just like that, the final piece falls into place. Lots of bouquets being left from August until mid-December, none over Christmas and summer, and a few in spring. The dates of the flowers being left fit into a typical university year.

'Anyway, I'd better be going – I've got lots of studying to do. It was really nice to meet you, Evan.'

I wave to Alice as she walks towards the cemetery

gates. Now I'm alone, I take my usual position in front of Claire's grave.

'It's funny, I thought I knew what I was going to say when I got here, but now I'm sitting here in front of you … it's all gone. I can't remember how many times I've told you I'm going to start being the person I should be – surely it must be around a thousand by now? I think I'm finally ready to start forgiving myself. It's taken me two years to realise I can be happy, but I reckon you'd be proud of me for getting there in the end. I haven't made a very good job of moving on so far, but I promise that's going to change. Violet deserves better, and so do I. Your letter about meeting someone else made me understand I need to change and stop being a miserable shit. So that's what I'm going to do, or try to at least. I've got a lot to sort out, but I'll get there.'

I pause and steady myself for what I'm about to say. 'I … I actually *have* met someone. God, it sounds crazy saying that out loud. This next bit will sound even crazier, but I'm just going to come out and say it. I have feelings for Hannah. I spent so long being angry because she left me when I needed her, but … since she's come back, things have changed. I'm seeing her in a way I've never seen her before. She isn't a replacement for you – nobody could ever do that, and it wouldn't be fair to ask anyone to either. Who wants to be treated as a substitute for someone else anyway? I just… She makes me happy and she feels a little like home. Things are messy and complicated and I'm not sure anything will ever happen between us, but that's OK. It doesn't matter how she's in my life, just as long as she is. I've got a lot of making up to do first, but that's next on my list after visiting you. Oh, Violet and I are getting a cat tomorrow. I'm way more excited about that than I should be.'

I get up, my body protesting at being folded in on itself for so long. Maybe this is the start of getting old.

'I'll always love you, Claire, and nothing will ever change that. It's just … I think I have to let someone else into my life now too. Not right now and I won't love them in the way I loved you because you can never love two people the same way.'

I take a step backwards, being mindful of not disturbing the graves directly behind me, and look at the headstone.

Beloved Wife, Daughter and Mother

I get a Tinder notification as soon as I walk through the door, but I ignore it. I even consider deleting the app, but I decide to leave it for now. Inviting someone else into my life isn't a good idea at the moment, but it has been instrumental in helping me make changes. First, I have to find a way to get over Hannah.

Get over her.

And just how the hell am I supposed to do that? I wonder as I make my way to the kitchen. I've only just realised what she means to me and now I have to let her go. Since we had that moment on Calton Hill, I've thought of almost nothing else. The love I had with Claire was perfect and I never dreamt that someone might feel that way for me again, or that I might reciprocate in some way. There might not have been a movie-style happy ending waiting for us, but there was the possibility that we could have made each other happy. I won't make those mistakes again. The next time someone amazing comes into my life, I'll be ready. I'll fling open my heart, even if it's slightly rusty by then, and invite them in and love them with everything I have.

Only after a thorough vetting process, of course – I'm not completely stupid.

For now though, I have to let things unfold how they may. It may not be what my friends had in mind, but happy endings take lots of different forms. I've started to forgive myself and deal with my grief. I've learned that my heart – beaten and bruised though it may be – still works. I'm still capable of opening up and connecting with people.

There's just one more thing I have to do to draw a line under it completely.

I grab one of Violet's notebooks from the living room, curl up on the sofa and write like my life depends on it.

Dear Claire,

This might be my last letter for a while. I want to try this living-in-the-moment thing I've heard so much about. Your wonderful letters have helped in ways I can't even begin to explain and a part of me will always belong to you.

I will never, ever forget you and I'll make sure Violet knows all about you. We've made the memory book – complete with bright pink feathers – so she can look at it whenever she wants, but I'll also tell her about your dreams and talents, your kind heart, your adventurous spirit. And one day, when the time is right, I'll tell her about us. How we met, how we fell in love, everything.

Thank you so much for making The Single Dad's Handbook. It has helped me in more ways than you could ever know. For a long time after you died, I tried to pretend that I was handling things, but I wasn't. You knew I'd need something to help me move on, so you made the book: a beautiful collection of words to refer to whenever I need them. And bloody hell, I needed them more than I realised.

I'm better now, or getting there, anyway. Grief doesn't go away overnight and there are always elements that stay with you for the rest of your life. But I'm going to be a better dad, son, friend and business partner. I have some great people in my life, and I want to repay them for everything they've done for me.

It's time to let you go now. I will always love you.

Evan

I turn over the page and begin a new letter. For a brief second, I almost trace the sweeping, elegant curls of 'Claire', which has always felt so familiar, but I take a different direction instead. New name, new letters. It feels sharp and different, but exciting and new. It is, at least, a start.

Dear Hannah…

The next morning, I pick Violet up from Mum's and we head to the Happy Paws Sanctuary to choose a cat. I've donated money to them, so it's the perfect place. It's sad to think there are lots of cats out there in need of a good home, but we're finally at the stage where we can include one as part of our family.

'Can we have two? Or three? They might get lonely when I'm at school.'

I narrow my eyes. 'We're getting *one* cat and one cat only. Now, which one do you like the best?'

Asking a kid to choose which animal they think is the cutest is a futile exercise, but after a lot of deliberation, Violet picks a two-year-old black-and-white cat.

'Can we call her Luna, Daddy?'

I lift her into my arms and kiss the top of her head. 'We can call her whatever you want. As long as it's not Brian or Geoff.'

She reaches her little hand out and touches my face. 'Are you Smiley Daddy again?'

I stroke her hair and smile. 'Yeah, baby, I am. I'm sorry about yesterday – you shouldn't have had to see me like that. Things have been tough since we lost Mummy, haven't they?'

She nods and I see that all-too-familiar sadness creep back into her face. I put her back on the ground and take her hand so we can go and sort out the adoption paperwork.

'Everything's going to be OK, I promise. From today, Smiley Daddy is going to be around a lot more. We're going to have fun and adventures and make lots of great memories. We'll never forget Mummy, but it's time for us to be happy again.'

Violet looks up at me. 'Does that mean we can get two cats so Luna has a friend?'

'Nice try, kiddo.'

Chapter Twenty-Six

I step back and look at the jardinière, tilting my head to appraise my work.

Are there enough flowers?

Did I choose the right colours?

I reach forward and adjust a bright pink peony that's slightly off-centre and allow myself a smile.

'What do you think?' I say to the empty hallway. 'Do they look OK to you?'

There's no answer, of course, but the house feels lighter somehow. It's as though the brightly coloured flowers and all the changes I've made the past two weeks have helped it shed some of its grief. I run my hands through my hair and stretch. My bones still ache with exhaustion, but I've started sleeping better. Facing up to my grief over Claire's death has given me a peace that seemed so far away before.

I hear a low, steady murmuring in the kitchen: the pot of pasta is boiling away nicely on the hob and the vegetables in the oven smell delicious. Violet is in her bedroom, preoccupied with her Tim Peake audiobook and has no idea I'm making her favourite for tea. But, just to be on the safe side, I've put new batteries in the smoke alarm.

There's just one piece of unfinished business: Hannah. The letter I wrote her is hidden in the living-room bookcase, wedged between my copies of *This is Going to Hurt* and *The Seven Deaths of Evelyn Hardcastle*. I couldn't bring myself to send it; she's happy with Alex and I didn't want to put her in an awkward position.

Just as I'm checking the vegetables, my phone buzzes in my pocket. I fish it out, expecting to see a text telling me that my e-bill is ready to view.

It isn't.

Can I come over? I have something to tell you.

My heart leaps. I haven't seen Hannah much since my attempt at stand-up at the Monkey Barrel; what could she possibly have to tell me?

As my imagination starts to run away with itself,

Luna, our new cat, comes into the kitchen and rubs against my leg. I bend down and pick her up for a cuddle, which lasts all of two seconds before she decides I'm not worthy.

'What do you think?' I ask her as she looks up at me, waiting for her dinner. 'Why does Hannah want to come over?'

All I get in return is an insistent meow, followed by an ominous hiss.

Hannah arrives at the door fifteen minutes later. As soon as I see her, I can tell she's been crying.

'Hey, what's wrong?' I step aside and let her walk into the hallway. 'Are you OK?'

She wipes her eyes and looks at me. I can see pain and hurt etched all over her face. My heart drops to my shoes. Gently, I lead her into the living room so she can sit down.

'Sorry I haven't been around much.' Her voice wavers and it sounds like she's about to burst into tears again. 'I feel like I haven't seen you or Violet for ages.'

I shake my head and place my hand on her shoulder. 'Don't worry about that. What's happened?'

Hannah covers her face with her hands and starts to

sob. Her body shakes and folds in on itself, as though she's trying to shield herself from any more pain.

'I had a fight with Alex,' she whispers. 'I think we broke up.'

'What?' I rear back a little, surprised at this turn of events. 'I thought things were going great with you two.'

She lifts her head and pushes some hair out of her face. When she looks at me, her eyes red and puffy, I can't help but wrap her in my arms.

'I thought they were too.' Her voice is strangled and small. 'But his ex-girlfriend is back on the scene and he wants to give things another go with her. Apparently he likes me but that's not enough. She's his once-in-a-lifetime love.'

I think of the way I saw Alex look at Hannah that day at Monkey Barrel. It seems unthinkable that he could just ditch her for someone else, even if he does have history with this other woman.

'I'm sorry,' I say. 'You deserve so much better than that. If Alex can't see how amazing you are, that's his loss.'

She sits up and wipes her eyes again, though I can see more tears are about to stream down her face. Seeing her so upset kills me.

'It's always like this,' she says. 'I'm always second choice. Every guy I meet has found their once-in-a-lifetime love and I'm just a substitute or a stopgap or a distraction until they can be with whom they really want. Even if there's no way it can happen.'

Our eyes meet and I feel a stab of pain. She's talking about me.

'I've spent the last couple of days going over everything in my head,' she continues, 'wondering how the hell I could've missed it and let myself like Alex when he was clearly still in love with someone else.'

I frown. 'You've been dealing with this for two days? You should've come over, I would've…'

I trail off, unable to finish the sentence. What would I have done? Taken care of her? Made her feel safe and loved and appreciated? Wrapped her up in my arms? Listened while she poured out the contents of her broken heart? She doesn't need to hear that right now.

Luckily, Hannah doesn't press me for answers and just shakes her head. 'I didn't want to bother you.'

'That doesn't mean you should give up on finding someone. One day, probably when you least expect it, you'll meet a guy who can't believe how lucky he is to be with you. And until then, you have so much going on in your life. You've got great friends and new career plans – you've seen the world and made memories you'll remember forever. You don't need anybody else to complete you, Hannah. Who you are will always be more than enough.'

There's a short pause and for a second, I'm not sure

Hannah even heard me. Her gaze is firmly fixed on the living room carpet and she looks a million miles away.

'Talking of seeing the world…' She trails off as she gets up and wanders to the other side of the room. 'I've been thinking about travelling again.'

My gaze snaps up to meet hers. 'What do you mean?'

'There are still places I'd like to see, things I'd like to do…' Her voice cracks. 'I've looked at maybe backpacking around South America or going to New Zealand.'

I walk over to her. 'Because of what happened with Alex? Don't let him derail your plans! You've been so happy to be back here and what about your plans to go back to uni?'

Hannah folds her arms and takes a few steps away from me. 'I can still do that. Applications aren't due in for months and I'll be back in Edinburgh way before then. I just … I just want one more adventure, you know? I'll go away, get Alex out of my system, then come back and swear off men for good.'

She heads towards the bookcase and a note of panic strikes in my heart. The letter is well hidden, but all she has to do is pick up one of the books it's wedged between.

'Staying could be fun,' I offer. 'Violet and I are always up for adventures and they're always better with three people.'

Hannah stops just short of the bookcase and turns round to look at me, a weak smile on her face.

'When I come back, we'll have plenty of adventures, I promise. I won't be gone long; just a few months or so.' She looks at the shelves full of books and runs her fingers along the spines. 'Do you mind if I borrow a few of these? I'll need something good to read on the beach.'

I take a step forward, but it's too late. She's picked up *The Seven Deaths of Evelyn Hardcastle* and dislodged the letter. It flutters to the ground and she picks it up, frowning.

'Since when do you hide letters in your bookcase?'

She shakes her head at me, but her easy smile vanishes when she unfolds it and begins to read. The room grows deathly silent and I scramble for what I should do next. Should I start my explanation before she reaches the end, try to make light of it or just do nothing?

I go for option three.

In the quiet, Hannah's body language becomes even more pronounced. Every blink, gasp and frown is magnified in super-high definition.

'Tell me this is a fucking joke.'

She looks up at me, her mouth slightly open and her eyes shining. I swallow hard and look around the room, as if that will reverse the last thirty seconds.

'Look, Hannah—'

'No, no excuses, not this time. What the fuck is this? I

thought after the whole thing on Calton Hill – you know, where I embarrassed myself by telling you how I felt – that we agreed never to think about it again? And now you're writing me a fucking letter?'

My cheeks burn and I finally pluck up the courage to meet her gaze. 'I'm really sorry. You were never supposed to see it. I wrote it a couple of weeks ago to kind of … I don't know, draw a line under how I feel for you. I know I should've ripped it up and thrown it away, or maybe I shouldn't have written it at all, but I did and I can't take it back. This is probably the worst time for you to see something like that, and I'm sorry if it's put you in a terrible position.'

Tears stream down Hannah's face as she looks at the letter again. Right now, I'd give anything to go back and never pick up the pen.

'You're bloody right it has! I bet you had to stop yourself from doing a happy dance when I told you about me and Alex. I sat there, pouring my heart out to you about how much I liked him, and all the time you're there with your … with your *feelings*!'

She turns away, embarrassed, and I get the impression that last part didn't come out quite as she intended.

'It wasn't like that at all, I swear!' I take a tentative step towards her. 'I mean, yes I have feelings for you, but

I'm your friend first. If someone hurts you, I don't sit there wondering if it's an opportunity to make a move on you.'

Hannah shakes her head in disgust, throws the letter at me and heads for the living room door.

'You have no new messages.'

'Thanks for that, voicemail,' I mumble under my breath. 'Really fucking helpful.'

I've tried calling Hannah umpteen times since our argument, but she hasn't answered. No responses to my text messages either. All I want to do is explain the letter to her, maybe even try to articulate how I feel, but I can't do that if she won't pick up the phone.

'All right, mate?' James breezes in from his latest tour and shrugs off the frock coat. 'How's the spookathon coming?'

Shit. I style out my lack of productivity with a bright smile and a totally unnecessary thumbs-up.

'Great, everything's coming together. Just a few last-minute things to do and we'll be ready for next week.'

James walks over and perches himself on the edge of the rickety desk, flashing me a knowing smile.

'I'm going to take that to mean you've done

absolutely nothing because you're too busy thinking about Hannah?'

I screw my eyes shut. Damn, I knew I shouldn't have confided in him.

'I wish I'd never written that stupid letter.' I let my head sink onto the desktop. 'Feels like I've really screwed it up this time. She'd just split up with Alex, she came round because she needed a friend and ended up finding my emotional spaffathon.'

James has the good grace to try to mask a chuckle, but ends up laughing anyway.

'OK, so maybe the timing wasn't *great*,' he concedes, 'but everything will be fine, I promise. Just give her some time, eh? And in the meantime, get organising this spookathon. It was your idea! Oh, and about the walking tour … I think you should lead it.'

I stare at him, my eyes widening in shock. My head feels light, as though I'm in a dream but can't wake up.

'Are … are you sure?' I allow myself a small, uncertain smile. 'I mean I'd love to, but—'

My business partner holds up a hand and shakes his head. 'Yes, I'm sure. You're ready for this. The last little while, you've become more like the old you again. I don't think anyone will say you've got a face like a bunged-up squirrel now.'

I chuckle. 'Thanks, mate, I won't let you down.'

When he goes to get ready for the next tour – yes,

we're actually taking multiple groups a day now – I open the desk drawer and sneak a glance at the glossy purple book that started all of this. Without the beautiful words on its pages, I wouldn't have found my way back to myself.

'Thank you,' I whisper.

Chapter Twenty-Seven

This is it.

All the planning, worrying and dreaming has come down to tonight: the Monsters, Murders and Magic Tours Spookathon. Everything is in place – apple bobbing, scary-movie corner, prizes for the costume contest – and we're ready to go. The Hub looks deliciously spooky. It's shrouded in shadows with pockets of neon light here and there to help guide our guests around the venue. There's still a little while to go before things kick off, so I give myself one final look in the mirror to check my costume. I've gone for a classic vampire this year and it's turned out very well, if I do say so myself. My skin is sallow and my eyes are sunken. It took more makeup to achieve this than I thought it would because I've started sleeping better.

'Daddy, can I have some sweets?' Violet runs over to me, dressed as an astronaut and looking ridiculously adorable. 'I'm hungry.'

'Later, baby, we'll start giving the sweets out when everybody gets here. How's Luna?'

We look over to the little corner we've created for Luna, complete with basket, water bowl and toys. I thought about leaving her at home in the peace and quiet, but Happy Paws said she didn't like being alone and Violet wouldn't hear of leaving her. She's curled up in her basket, looking happy and relaxed.

'Will you let me win the prize for nicest costume?' Violet looks up at me with a cheeky smile. 'The big bottle of pink stuff looks yummy.'

I scoop her up into my arms. 'That's a drink for grown-ups, baby – I don't think you'd like it very much. Why don't you go and see if the apple bobbing has been set up properly?'

When I put her down, she runs off with reckless abandon. It's great to see her having so much fun and the night hasn't even begun yet. I take a moment to sit down while James is outside getting the signs ready. We've done away with some of my more ludicrous ideas, such as the ice sculptures, and kept it simple. We're going to throw a fun, spooktastic evening and let everyone know Monsters, Murders and Magic Tours is back in the game. Now that I have a minute to think, I grab my messenger bag and pull out my phone. I haven't heard it buzz to notify me of any messages, but part of me can't help wondering…

No.

It's been three weeks since Hannah found the letter telling her I love her, and I haven't heard anything. She hasn't called, texted or even written a letter back. It's not totally unexpected. I hope she comes around soon; Violet's starting to wonder where she is. I've managed to make excuses so far, but I'm fast running out of ideas. Next, I turn my attention to Claire's book, which I've brought along for moral support.

'You would've loved this,' I whisper. 'This was your kind of thing.'

I gently run my fingers over the neon Post-it notes until I come to the final letter: *Read me Last*. I can't resist taking a peek. She won't mind, will she?

Dear Evan,

Well, here it is: my final letter to you. I don't have much energy now; most of my time is spent either sleeping or watching snippets of One Tree Hill. There are brief moments where I talk to you about something other than my impending demise or read a story to Violet, but those are becoming rarer by the day. God, I'll miss you both. My little team.

It was never meant to be like this, was it? I was never meant to get ill and you were never meant to be my carer instead of my husband. Violet wasn't supposed to have a mum who was too weak to get out of bed and who would die before her first day of school. Yet here we are, this is our life. If Phil and Grant have taught me anything, it's that the tiniest moments are the most precious. The ones you don't see coming or are too busy to notice: they're what really matter. I've been thinking of our moments lately. Not our wedding or when we bought this house or even the day Violet was born, but the lazy Sundays we spent drinking coffee together in bed while rain pelted off the window. Or when we were too skint to buy a bed, so you made us a tent in the living room out of a tablecloth and some chairs. Or when you tried to cook me a romantic dinner, burnt it and gave me spaghetti hoops instead. Those are the moments I'll hold on to until the very end. The beautiful ones we created together without even trying.

I love you so, so much. I could write it a million times over on every piece of paper in the world and it wouldn't be enough. Taking care of me hasn't exactly been a walk in the park, has it? I've refused to accept my newly imposed limitations, shouted at you when you've tried to help me and tried to be the old me when it was painfully clear I couldn't. I'm sorry for giving you such a hard time. Cancer really is a bitch. Through it all though, you never made me feel any less than myself. You always treated me like the woman you loved, even when I didn't feel like it. Oh, and thank you for shaving my head that time. You did a bang-up job – I looked like Natalie Portman from V for Vendetta. I do think that not taking you up on your kind offer to shave your head too was the right decision though. You wouldn't have suited it the way I did.

If you're reading this letter, that can only mean one thing: it's time to let go now, darling. You have the rest of your life to live, so please don't let grief hold you back. Be happy, embrace each moment and only look back with fondness. Moving on doesn't mean forgetting; it means allowing yourself to live again. I'm trusting you to create a beautiful life for you and Violet after I'm gone. Make it something colourful and worth remembering. Chase your dreams, get a tattoo, fall in love again: whatever makes you happy. Know that I loved you with all my heart and never wanted to leave you or Violet. During my darker moments, I'd sit and make plans. The life I would live if I could. I'd sky dive and have another baby and we'd take off round the world, taking short-term jobs to fund our travels. We'd settle down somewhere in the country or in a beautiful, vibrant city that buzzes with possibilities. We'd grow old together and live out our days by the sea, holding hands as we walk along the pier and kissing like teenagers. Maybe you'd even win me a toy on one of those grabber machines.

But living's your job now, sweetheart; dying is mine. So let me go now, eh? It's time.

Love always,

Claire

I wipe a couple of stray tears from my face and tuck the book back in my bag. She's right, as always; it's time to let her go now. A part of me will always love her, but it's time to live life for Violet and myself now. Dating isn't my main priority at the moment. I've met a couple more women off Tinder, but nothing happened, mostly because of my feelings for Hannah. I wonder what she's doing for Halloween and if she's made any travel plans? Whatever she's up to, I hope she has a great time.

There's a knock at the door and I assume some guests have arrived early and don't want to wait outside. I don't blame them; it's not a nice night. I'll get soaked when I lead the walking tour later.

'Hey, come in. We're just about to get started.' I open the door and step to the side. 'It's horrible out there, isn't it?'

A group of people files in and spreads out around the room, taking in all the things James and I have spent all day setting up. From the impressed murmurs and expressions of wonder, I'd say we've done pretty well. I leave the door slightly ajar and watch as more people come in. It isn't long before we have quite a crowd gathering. So *this* is what happens when you remember to mail out the flyers.

Mum flashes me a smile from across the room. Things between us are as good as they've ever been, especially now that I'm back on track. She's here with Rod tonight and they look great together. I've given him the once-over and he's a nice guy: uncomplicated with a good sense of humour. They've even matched costumes: she's Wilma Flintstone and he's Fred.

A snippet of Claire's letter whispers to me: *the tiniest moments are the most precious. The ones you don't see coming or are too busy to notice.*

I certainly didn't see my feelings for Hannah coming. Falling for my best friend was the last thing on my mind just a short while ago. Now look what's happened.

'Hey, nice costume,' James takes off his werewolf mask and smiles at me. 'Are you ready for the walking tour in a bit? I thought we could kick that off in about an hour. If you're still up for it, that is?'

There's mischief in his grin and I match it with one of my own.

'As if I'd ever turn down a chance to scare people shitless.'

James heads off to mingle with the guests. I go to do the same when my phone buzzing interrupts me. I pray to whoever might be listening that it's not a problem with one of the suppliers.

It isn't.

It's Hannah.

Good luck for tonight. Sorry I couldn't be there, but I think it's for the best that I'm not. I hope I haven't interrupted your walking tour – I just didn't want to leave without saying goodbye.

Leave without saying goodbye.

What does she mean by that?

I try to call her, but it goes straight to voicemail. Rather than waste time trying again, I pull up Facebook to see if she's told anyone where she might be going. All I can find is a cryptic post saying, *The adventure starts here…*

'Shit,' I murmur.

I scroll down the comments, hoping to God there's a clue somewhere. Near the bottom, I hit the jackpot: she's getting the train from Edinburgh to Glasgow so she can fly to New Zealand. In a fit of panic, I dash off to find James.

'Listen, I'm really sorry but something's come up. Can you handle things here until I get back? I shouldn't be more than half an hour.'

He frowns. 'Everything OK? Nothing's wrong with Violet, is it?'

'No, nothing like that. I just … Hannah's leaving for New Zealand and I need to talk to her before it's too late. I know I'm the worst business partner in the world, but I—'

'Say no more.' James holds up a hand to stop me. 'Go. Everything will be fine here.'

I thank him and rush to get Violet, who's only too happy to accompany me when I tell her we're going to see Hannah. She makes Mum and Rod promise to look after Luna first, though. She has her priorities straight.

Violet and I barrel into Waverley Station a few minutes later, weaving in and out of crowds as we try to spot Hannah on one of the platforms. Holding Violet's hand is murder on my back, so I lift her into my arms and run as fast as I can. I get my fair share of strange looks. It's not every day you see a vampire and astronaut pinballing through the busiest station in the city.

'Wheeeee! This is fun,' she says, clapping her hands with joy.

I smile at her, glad she has no idea about the sense of urgency we're facing. For all I know, Hannah could have left already, but I have to try. I have to talk to her and explain everything.

'Will you do me a favour? If you see Hannah before I do, will you tell me? We're going to give her a big hug and say happy Halloween.'

Violet frowns. 'Why is she here, where all the trains are? Is she going on holiday?'

I shrug and say yes, my brain too frantic to think of a better explanation. My head darts from side to side as I run across the main concourse, past WHSmith and Boots, hoping to catch the faintest glimpse of her.

'Daddy, look!'

I follow Violet's gaze to the waiting room and ticket office. Hannah is just coming out of the M&S Food Hall, a large rucksack slung on her shoulder. She looks over, locks eyes with me and freezes on the spot. I do too, for a moment, until Violet taps me on the shoulder.

'Come on, we have to wish her happy Halloween!' she reminds me impatiently.

I snap out of my daze and put her down so she can run to her favourite human. I follow, keeping a few steps behind her.

'Hi, you!' Hannah heaves her rucksack to the floor and scoops Violet up in her arms. 'Great costume! Although I think I prefer last year's tomato.'

My little girl erupts into a fit of giggles and my heart

fills with joy. Hannah looks at me and for a moment, everything around us melts away.

'What are you doing here?' she asks, putting Violet down and walking towards me. 'How did you find me?'

'Detective work,' I reply with a soft chuckle. 'Don't worry, I didn't pull a Joe Goldberg or anything. I just wanted to talk before you left, that's all. There are a lot of things I need to say.'

She folds her arms across her chest and gives me a guarded stare. 'Such as?'

'Such as … I'm sorry about the letter. That was the last thing you needed to see after what happened with Alex. I'm not sorry about the things I said because I meant every word. I just… You didn't deserve to find out like that. If I could go back and do it all again, I would.'

I expect her to look angry or tell me to piss off so she can catch her train, but she doesn't. She looks sad. So unutterably sad.

'Evan, we talked about this on Calton Hill. You've had your once-in-a-lifetime love. No one else will ever measure up to Claire. Yeah, you'll love whoever comes next, but it won't be the same. I don't want to be anybody's second choice, especially not yours. Do you know how long it took me to make myself believe I didn't love you anymore?'

I take a step closer to her, but she backs away. I take that as a sign to stay right where I am.

'You're right – you don't deserve to be anybody's second choice. And I'm not asking you to be mine. I'm asking…' I pause for a second to collect myself. 'I'm asking if you'll let me love you, exactly as you are.'

Hannah puts a hand to her mouth and her eyes shine with tears. I tread carefully into the moment, hoping to God I don't ruin it. This is so important.

'You're my best friend,' I tell her. 'And I might have only recently realised how deeply, ridiculously and heartbreakingly in love with you I am, but *I am*, Hannah. You're right that Claire was the first love of my life and she always will be. Nobody can ever replace her, and I'd never ask them to. But I think you might be wrong about this once-in-a-lifetime thing. See, I don't think we just get one shot at falling in love. I think it happens over and over again, in a million different ways. You can fall in love with a person, a city, a friendship… And sometimes it sneaks up on you when you're not looking.'

Hannah is in tears now. She doesn't look like she's about to say anything, which worries me, but I hold back and wait.

Violet comes up to me and tugs at my hand. 'Is Hannah OK? She looks sad.'

'I hope so,' I whisper. 'Let's give her a few seconds.'

She shakes her head and wipes her eyes. 'No, I'm fine, don't worry! Why don't you have a look in my bag and see if you can find my train tickets? I can't remember where I put them.'

Violet jumps at the chance and busies herself opening the rucksack's various compartments. My heart sinks; she's still set on leaving, but I can't say I blame her. Hannah steps closer to me and reaches for my hands, but pulls back at the last second.

'I waited for you for so long,' she says. 'And after you met Claire, I just … accepted that you'd never love me the way I love you. And now you do and you're saying all these things that I've always wanted to hear and … I don't know, it's a lot to take in. I-I … I should go, my train leaves in fifteen minutes and this place is like a bloody maze since they rejigged the layout.'

She whirls round to grab the rucksack, but turns back to me instead, as though she's forgotten she has to be somewhere else.

'Please don't go,' I whisper. 'I'll … I'll miss you. I mean, *Violet* will miss you… N-not that I won't too, I just…'

I'm making a mess of this. It feels like a really big moment and because I'm aware of that, I'm tripping over my words.

'Finding your letter really threw me, Evan. It was the last thing I expected after what happened between us on Calton Hill. What made you write it?'

I wasn't prepared for a question, but she's looking at

me expectantly so I need to come up with something quickly.

'I thought it might help me come to terms with how I feel about you. Like I said in the letter, it wasn't to pressure you to feel one way or another. The last thing I wanted was to confuse you or mess with your head, so I'm sorry if I did. I just … I just wanted to say it, if that makes sense? I wanted to write it all down, then draw a line under the whole thing. I love you, Hannah, and I don't think I can stop. I've tried, but you're not easy to forget.'

Hannah's eyes are glossy with tears. I must've said something to upset her. My panic increases when the tears begin to spill down her cheeks.

'Oh God, I'm sorry. I-I didn't mean to upset you. Forget what I said before – I was being selfish. Go to New Zealand, have your adventure and we can figure everything out when you come back.'

She shakes her head and walks towards me, bringing my apology to an abrupt halt. She stands on her tiptoes, puts a hand on the back of my neck and draws me close for a slow, soft kiss. It takes me a moment to gather myself, but I place my hands on either side of her face and hold her like she's the most precious thing in the world to me. Her lips are warm and soft and having her body pressed against mine sends shockwaves of delight cartwheeling through my veins. I feel dozens of pairs of eyes on us and realise why. I'm dressed as a vampire and telling a woman I'm in love with her.

'I love you too,' she whispers, leaning her forehead against mine when we break apart. 'And if you still want to, I'd love to see where this goes.'

'Of course I would.' My voice cracks and breaks, but the words slip out with ease. I don't feel guilty or as though I'm betraying Claire any more. 'And I'm sorry about what happened before. I promise I've got my shit together now, or I'm getting there anyway.'

'I should bloody well hope so too.' She laughs and shakes her head before pulling me in for another kiss. I hear footsteps and see Violet running towards us, tell-tale smears of chocolate around her mouth. She's obviously found Hannah's not-so-secret stash.

'Are you not going on holiday anymore?'

'Nope, I'm staying here to have fun with you instead.' She lifts Violet into her arms and kisses her forehead. 'Have you been on lots of space adventures since I've been gone? Can I come on the next one?'

Violet nods. 'Yes! I've been to the moon and Mars! Can I tell you about them after the party? Will you come? Oh, and we've got a cat. Her name's Luna and she likes to sleep a lot. Do you want to meet her?'

Hannah looks at me for confirmation and I nod.

'Of course you can – I'd love to hear your stories and

come and meet Luna. We could have a go at the apple bobbing too, if you want, to see if you can beat me?'

'Yay! Did you know aliens are the best at apple bobbing? I think they cheat though.'

'That's a new one on me!'

'Why don't we all head back to the spookathon? There's a lot of fun stuff going on and we don't want to miss it,' I say.

Violet claps her hands with glee and goes dancing around in circles. I pull Hannah in for another kiss.

'Do you think she'll be OK? With us, I mean.' She jerks her head towards Violet. 'I know I can't replace Claire and I wouldn't want to try either.'

I place a kiss on her forehead and stroke her cheek. 'Everything's going to be fine. We'll work it out as we go along.'

'I'm a bit worried about turning up to this spookathon without a costume,' she says with a smile. 'Will everyone judge me?'

'We'll find you something.'

I check my watch. Soon, it'll be time for me to lead the ghost walk. The three of us head back to The Hub, holding hands and taking in the ethereal beauty of Edinburgh at night.

I grab Hannah a spare witch's hat when we return and plonk it on her head. She does a little twirl and I laugh. We head over to Mum and Rod.

'It's about bloody time,' Mum mutters when she thinks nobody else is listening. 'I'll leave the "I told you so" until later though.'

Before I know it, my big moment arrives. The crowd gathers in the middle of the hall. There are more people than I expected, and for a second my nerves overtake me. Will I be able to perform the walking tour? Will I be compared to any woodland creatures with bowel problems?

Hannah squeezes my arm. 'You've got this.'

James gives me a thumbs-up. We've come so far in a short space of time. Our business still isn't where we need it to be, and I don't know what's going to happen after tonight. Things might stay the way they are, with him doing the tours and me in the office looking after everything else. Or we might decide to put things back to normal. Either way, I know now that we'll be OK.

I step forward to greet everyone. 'Good evening and thank you all for coming. It's time for our walking tour to begin, so if you'll follow me, I'll show you a side to Edinburgh you *definitely* haven't seen before. If you're pregnant, have a weak heart or are of a nervous disposition, you might want to sit this one out. Otherwise, come with me ... *if you dare*.'

As I lead my group out into the night, I realise how grateful I am for the series of happy accidents that brought me here. This isn't the life I planned on twelve years ago, or eight years ago, or even five. But it's the life I've been given and it's filled with the most wonderful people imaginable. I look behind me and catch Hannah's eye. We share a secret smile. I didn't plan on falling for her, but I can't wait to see how things unfold between us. It won't always be easy, especially with Violet involved, but we'll get there one way or another. There is a new beginning unfolding in front of me and I've never been happier. Claire's letters, along with Hannah's unique magic, have brought me back to life and helped me see how beautiful life can be.

We'll take on the world together: Hannah, my wannabe astronaut and me.

Acknowledgments

It takes a lot of people to make a book happen and I was lucky enough to work with the brilliant One More Chapter team to bring *The Single Dad's Handbook* to life. Kimberley, Bethan, Claire, Melanie and Lucy – it has been a privilege to work with you all and thank you so much for giving my book such a lovely home.

Charlotte Ledger, you are extraordinary. Your passion for romantic fiction is unrivalled and you champion authors like nobody else. Thank you so much for being a brilliant editor. From that very first phone call when you said, "Evan and Hannah need to be together" to now, working with you has been a dream come true.

To my amazing agent, Sarah Hornsley, thank you for helping readers to find Evan, Violet and their friends. You're wise, thoughtful, kind and insightful. I couldn't be happier to be a part of #TeamHornsley. We're so lucky to have you.

Author friends are the best friends you'll ever have and I'm lucky enough to have some truly wonderful ones. Lia Louis, thank you for reading excerpts, obsessing over Ross Butler with me, and for all the encouraging voice notes. Andi Michael, the other half of Team Cheerleader, what would I do without you and your block capital messages?! Thank you for always being kind and supportive. Portia Macintosh, fellow *Pretty Little Liars* fan, thank you for everything, sistaaah. Holly McCulloch, Katy Colins, Polly Phillips, Jessica Ryn, Anstey Harris, Steph Chapman, plus so many more, THANK YOU for being my friends and welcoming me onto Book Twitter. You are truly marvellous.

Jodie, my best friend. You read so much of this book before anyone else and because of you, other people are now reading it too. Thank you.

To the best Booktuber and friend, Aoife Bennett, thank you for everything you do. The stories, the laughs, the pep talks. You're awesome. One day, you'll be writing a set of these, I just know it.

To all the lovely people who read *The Single Dad's Handbook* early and left fantastic reviews, you have no idea what that means to me. From the bottom of my heart, thank you.

The incomparable Maz aka Mum. Thank you for

reading my drafts, watching crime shows with me, and always insisting I write a book based on you (it'll happen one day!) Most of all, thank you for being my best friend. There's nobody like you. Kyle, the hospital scene wouldn't have happened without your amateur dramatics! Thanks for being the funniest brother anyone could ask for. Dad, for always telling me to keep going and asking if the movie rights have been sold. One day, hopefully, the answer will be yes!

Bonus Short Story

THE EASTER EGG HUNT

The human heart beats approximately thirty-five million times in a year.

I discover this fact on an early spring morning, as I watch the sun rise over my little corner of Edinburgh. Shards of light creep above the Salisbury Crags, bathing everything in a golden glow. Raising my eyebrows and taking another sip of coffee, I place my phone on my battered kitchen table, face down.

I'm not quite ready to face the world yet. Or perhaps it's the other way round: maybe it isn't ready for me.

A quick glance at the clock tells me I have precisely thirty minutes before the day has to start. I'm going to savour every last second. The house is quiet, Violet is still asleep, and I have a rare slice of time alone with my thoughts. This is as good as it gets nowadays.

My phone buzzes into life, some breaking news alert about house prices. Not something I need to bother myself with at seven o'clock in the morning. I look at the screen to dismiss the notification, but all of my thoughts scatter when I notice the date.

'Shit,' I mutter under my breath.

Sometime during the three hours since I came downstairs, I managed to convince myself that I could avoid what today means. If I didn't think about it, I could pretend it wasn't happening. Life, as usual, had other plans.

I heave a weary sigh and run my hands across my face, blinking back tears. Although I know I shouldn't, I look at my phone screen again. There she is, wearing those bright colours she loved so much. She's giving the camera her brightest smile, while I stand beside her, looking like the luckiest man alive.

I was, and I should've realised it at the time.

A year ago today, Claire died. My heart has apparently beat thirty-five million times since then, and I've no idea how.

Before I can think too deeply about this, Violet comes bursting into the kitchen. 'Good morning, Daddy! Can we go and find the eggs now? I think I know where the Easter Bunny hid them.'

My eyes widen with dread as my heart sinks. Is it *really* Easter today? I vaguely recall Violet mentioning it earlier this week, but I haven't slept well since Claire died and can't take things in like I used to. Now, I've got an excited four-year-old who'll be devastated that there aren't any chocolate eggs for breakfast. I lift her onto my lap, willing an answer to pop into my brain.

'Um…' *Quick, think!* 'I don't think he's been to our house yet, baby. We'll check later, OK? Go back to bed and I'll come and get you when he's visited.'

She doesn't answer right away, just looks at me as though she's searching my face for lies. I'm reminded with a jolt of pain just how quickly she's had to grow up since we lost her mum. Before she died, Violet was such a carefree, happy kid. Now she's withdrawn and serious.

'OK,' she says.

Her gaze falls to the floor; it's as though she knows I'm not telling her the truth. She climbs off my lap and I hear her footsteps retreat softly to her bedroom. I curse under my breath. How could I forget? Easter might be one of those mystical holidays that falls on a different date every year, but I should've known. I've been running around with my head up my arse for too long. Violet has lost enough this year; she doesn't deserve to have today spoiled by my terrible memory.

I need to fix this quickly.

Within an hour, reinforcements have gathered in my living room. My mum is perched on an armchair and my married friends, Dave and Lorna, are downing triple-shot espressos like their lives depend on it. The three of them look tired, dishevelled and low-key pissed off to have been dragged out of bed so early on a Sunday morning. I loiter next to the fireplace, trying to do a decent impression of someone who's had a good night's sleep in the last twelve months.

'So, are you going to tell us why we're here?' Lorna asks. 'Please tell me there will be bacon rolls soon, I'm starving.'

I decide not to tell her that I can't remember the last time I went shopping. 'Um … sure. Listen, I'm sorry to spoil your Sunday, but there's a problem and I need your help.'

Mum springs to her feet and places her hand on my arm. 'It's OK, darling, I know what you're going to say.'

I frown. 'You do?'

'It's a year today since Claire died,' she tells Dave and Lorna in what she thinks is a low whisper. When she turns back to me, I can't bear the sadness on her face. 'If you need some time to yourself today, we'll make it happen. I can take Violet for the day and—'

I hold up my hands, trying to ignore my heart splintering in my chest. 'No, Mum, it's nothing like that.

I'm fine, really, I feel much better than I thought I would. It's ... it's Violet.'

The panic level in the room rises several notches. Sharp intakes of breath, tensing of shoulders, furtive glances. I realise a couple of seconds too late that it's my fault.

'No, no, she's OK,' I assure everyone. 'Well, sort of. She's been pretty distant since… Well, since last year. Can't blame her, really, can you? Anyway, she's really looking forward to Easter today and ... well, I forgot about it. I didn't buy Easter eggs or organise anything fun for us to do. Nothing.'

Nobody says anything, but their expressions do the talking for them. *How could you forget something your kid was looking forward to? Just what kind of dad are you?* They'd never say it out loud, but I can tell they're thinking it. An imaginary knife twists in my gut. I should be doing better than this.

'So…' I clap my hands to break the awkward silence. '…I know it's a tall order, but I need your help. There are probably a million other things you'd rather be doing today, but anything you can do would be hugely appreciated.'

Dave, Lorna and Mum look at each other, weighing up what I've said. The fact they're here at all is nothing short of a miracle. I've lost count of the number of times

I've asked them for help since Claire died and every time, they show up. I don't deserve them.

'I suppose we could do an Easter egg hunt,' Dave suggests. 'Hide them around the house and garden. Violet would love trying to find them, wouldn't she?'

There are a couple of murmurs of agreement, but nobody looks convinced. Panic begins to rise in my chest. Maybe this is one ask too many. Maybe they expected me to have my act together by now.

'Where would we get them, though?' Lorna asks. 'I know we bought a couple for her, but the shops will be sold out, won't they?'

'Not necessarily,' Mum chimes in. 'The shops always have some on offer if they've got excess stock. They keep them right next to the tills.'

She claps her hands in delight and flashes me a supportive smile. I just about manage one in return, but I know it won't reach my eyes.

Dave walks over to me and claps me on the back. 'Just tell us what you need, mate. We'll sort it out, won't we?' He looks at Lorna and Mum, who both nod in agreement. 'And listen, if you need to talk about anything, just let us know.'

I meet his stare and a moment of understanding passes between us. We don't have to say anything to know we're on the same page. I paste a smile to my face and make a thumbs-up gesture.

'Really, mate, I'm doing OK.' *Liar.* 'I didn't think I'd be able to get out of bed this morning but look at me!'

He raises an eyebrow. 'Yeah, standing in your dressing gown trying to organise an Easter egg hunt for your kid because you forgot. Living the dream, aren't you?'

Someone else might have taken offence to that. In fact, under different circumstances, I might have as well. But Dave and I have known each other for years and there isn't the slightest trace of unkindness in his tone or expression. So, instead of getting angry, I laugh. Proper, doubled-over belly laughter. I'm not sure what I find so funny, but this makes a nice change from crying and random bursts of fury.

'OK,' Dave says, chuckling uncomfortably. 'It wasn't that funny.'

'No, it was,' I wheeze, trying to catch my breath, 'because I just realised it's impossible for things to get any worse! I mean, *I forgot Easter*. Violet told me over and over again how much she was looking forward to it and I just … didn't take it in. It completely slipped my mind!'

The laughter nudges into maniacal and I soon attract confused stares from Mum and Lorna.

'All right, man, give yourself a break.' Dave slaps me on the back again. 'It's not like you forgot Christmas! Violet had a lovely day then, didn't she? Why don't you go and get dressed, then we can sort out this Easter egg hunt?'

His smile is strained at the edges and there is fear in his eyes. That startles me and brings the laughter to a sudden halt. Dave arrests people for a living; as far as I know, he's never been scared in his life. Until now.

'Yeah.' I straighten myself up and pull my dressing gown tight across my chest. 'That's a good idea.'

I walk over to the door and turn to face them one last time. 'Oh, and Mum bought most of Violet's presents last year because I could hardly get out of bed. That's why Christmas was nice.'

I leave the kitchen and head for the stairs. The murmurs start when I'm about halfway up. Hushed words from three voices, clashing in the air, laced with concern.

What are we going to do about him? He needs help.

While Mum stays behind to look after Violet, Dave, Lorna and I hit the big Tesco near my house. I'm still in a zombie-like state, but manage to navigate the aisles with relative ease. I only bump into the racking a handful of times, so I'm calling that a success. As I'm browsing the limited selection of Easter eggs and trying to determine whether Violet would prefer a Bounty or Snickers one, Lorna joins me.

'We need to talk.'

'In a minute,' I reply. 'I'm trying to choose some Easter eggs.'

She holds up her basket. 'Already covered. I picked up a Trolls one near the front of the shop and they had some Cadbury's Buttons ones near the tills. Evan, this is serious. We're all worried about you.'

My gaze snaps to hers and I take a deep breath, bracing myself for impact.

Lorna continues. 'Claire's death hit you really hard; we get it, honestly. But you can't keep going on like this. It's not good for you or Violet. Let us in a bit more; it's OK to ask for help, you know.'

I raise my chin and stand up straight. 'I *have* asked for help, and I'm doing fine with Violet. She has everything she needs.'

Her head tilts to one side and she flashes me a "who are you kidding" smile. My insides writhe with pain. It's one thing for my friends to think I'm falling apart – I am – but I hate the idea of them worrying that I can't cope with Violet.

'I know she does.' Lorna puts her hand on my arm. 'And I know you'd do anything to make sure she's OK. You've called us a few times for a chat and that's great, but we can do more if you need us to. Like today! You don't have to do everything on your own and you definitely don't have to pretend you're not struggling today if you are. The first anniversary is always tough. I was the same when I lost my mum.'

It takes everything I have not to break down and admit how I really feel. Instead, I gently remove my arm from her grip and use every ounce of strength to smile.

'I'm not struggling. Honestly, I feel absolutely fine. In fact, I'm *better* than fine. I feel great! So, you, Dave and Mum can stop worrying about me, OK? There's nothing to worry about.'

I grab a Bounty Easter egg and stalk off towards the checkout. My eyes are burning with tears and exhaustion, but I'd rather run through the store naked than cry in front of Lorna. If I just keep telling myself I'm OK and don't let myself feel the grief currently threatening to overwhelm me, everything will be fine.

The second I walk through the front door, I swing into action, picking up Violet's stray socks from the stairs and moving coats from the bannister to the hall cupboard. I have to show Lorna – show *everyone* – that I'm a capable dad. She and Dave have gone home to pick up their Easter eggs for Violet, so I've got roughly ten minutes to make some sort of change. I head straight to the kitchen, scoop Violet into my arms and pepper her face with kisses. She giggles with surprise; it's a beautiful sound.

'What's got into you?' Mum chuckles. 'You're very … alert!'

I shrug and put Violet down on the floor. 'Nothing, I'm just happy it's Easter that's all. Best day of the year, right?' I look at Violet. 'But first, we need to find some eggs, don't we? Gran will help you get ready while I check to see if the Easter Bunny's been to our garden. Go on, hurry!'

A bright, beaming smile spreads across Violet's face and for a brief second, I see the kid she used to be. My already-broken heart cracks a little more as I think about what the last year has done to her. She scampers off towards the stairs, while Mum pauses in the kitchen doorway.

'You are … you know, all right, aren't you? Because if you want to sit down and talk—'

'You'd better go; Violet will be waiting for you.' I shoot her the cheesiest grin I can muster on three hours' sleep. 'Move on, show's over, nothing to see here!'

Mum's eyes narrow. 'You can't ignore today, you know, no matter how hard you try.'

When I don't reply, she turns and leaves the room. I take a deep breath, rub my eyes to get rid of the crusts of sleep, and survey the kitchen. It'll have to be tidied before we go outside to hide the Easter eggs. Usually, I leave it in a vague state of disarray, but today has to be different. *I* have to be different. I gather up Violet's cereal bowl, Mum's coffee cup and the butter-smeared plate she must've used for toast. I clean and tidy at a frantic pace, sweeping up crumbs, washing and drying dishes. Maybe this will show everyone once and for all that there's nothing to worry about.

Dave and Lorna walk in just as I'm attempting to switch on the washing machine. They take in the newly tidied surroundings with a mixture of shock and amazement.

'Wow, you've been … busy,' Dave says, attempting a smile that dies on his lips.

'Yeah, I thought the place needed a bit of a tidy. Looks better, doesn't it?'

He gives a slow, uncertain nod then places two carrier bags on the table. 'Definitely, yeah. We, erm, brought the Easter eggs.'

I clap my hands. 'Awesome! Now we can get on with hiding them, can't we? Violet's going to love this. Hey, do you think there are any costume hire places open today? I want to see if I can rent an Easter Bunny costume!'

Lorna frowns. 'You'll be lucky; it's a Sunday and most places are probably closed for the Bank Holiday weekend. Anyway, the Easter bunny costumes will have been hired out weeks ago. Why don't you sit down for a bit? We can go and hide the eggs in a minute.'

I shake my head. 'No can do, Violet's off getting ready and she'll be down any minute. Let's go!'

'Then why are you going on about hiring a costume?' Dave asks, the furrow in his brow deepening. 'You're not making any sense, mate.'

I grab the carrier bags from the table and gesture towards the door leading to the back garden. It's taking everything I have to keep up this happy façade, but I have to show them that, at least where Violet is concerned, I have my shit together. If organising an Easter egg hunt will restore people's faith in me, I'll do it.

The hunt is on.

Six chocolate eggs have been secreted around the back garden for Violet to find. One is in the shed, a couple are in the large, unkempt bushes that line the perimeter, and there's even one in an upturned wheelbarrow. She's currently running around the garden in a state of pure delight, looking in every nook and cranny for the chocolate she wants so badly. It's a joy to watch. I'm standing by the back door, watching her, while Dave and Lorna are in the kitchen making cups of coffee. Mum is standing next to me, flinching every so often when Violet disappears out of sight.

'How long do you think she'll take to find them?' I ask. 'My bet is another fifteen minutes.'

'Maybe we should help her,' Mum suggests. 'She doesn't seem to be getting very far. Has she, um, said anything about her mum? You know, since it's the first anniversary.'

She says that last sentence as if the words are incredibly rude and she doesn't want to offend me. I look at Violet, who's pinwheeling around the garden in search of Easter eggs, looking like any other excited four-year-old. Except she isn't. Not all kids her age have had their world ripped in half. She wanders over to the upturned wheelbarrow and, when she thinks no one is looking, her bright smile disappears. My heart breaks a little more.

'Not yet. But she'll be fine, I know she will.'

I'm saying that to convince myself as much as my mum. It hasn't worked on her, judging by the look on her face.

'Come on,' she says softly, edging closer to me. 'It's just the two of us now, so you can be honest. How are you feeling? You must have thought about Claire today.'

Hearing her name brings a lump to my throat but, before I can reply, my phone rings. It's a FaceTime call from the last person I expected to call me today.

'Hannah.'

She waves at me, smiling brightly. 'Hey, you! I just

thought I'd give you a quick call so I can make you insanely jealous. Look at this view!'

She quickly spins her phone around to show me a shimmering sea, where people are surfing, sailing or on jet-skis.

'Isn't it brilliant? God, I love it here.' Hannah sighs blissfully and winks to show she's joking. 'Anyway, how's Edinburgh? Is my favourite four-year-old around? I want to say hi.'

I look at her for a moment. Freckles dance across her sun-kissed skin and her eyes are bright with joy. Envy slinks through my veins, followed swiftly by anger.

'She's busy right now.' My voice is strained at the edges as I try not to show how utterly furious I am with her. 'You know, since it's the first anniversary of Claire's death. We're trying to do something fun for her, so she's looking for Easter eggs in the garden.'

Hannah's smile instantly vanishes and her hand flies to her mouth. 'Oh God … oh shit, I … I messed up the time difference. I'm so sorry, Evan. How are you doing?'

I shake my head. 'Don't worry about it. I'm doing OK, just getting on with things. You look like you're having a whale of a time though. Must be lovely to go off globe-trotting.'

She shifts uncomfortably and looks away from me. 'You know why I had to leave. I'm sorry, I wanted to stick around, I just—'

'I said don't worry about it. We're all fine here, so you just keep doing what you're doing. You don't even need to think about us.'

Bitterness is creeping into my tone now. Part of me wants to pull it back, so we can have a civil conversation, but then I remember the way she left. The promises she made and broke.

'That's not fair. I think about you and Violet all the time. I just couldn't stay like I wanted to.' She swallows hard and chews the edge of her thumbnail. 'Oh, and you're not OK. Whatever bullshit you're trying to pull, it doesn't work on me. I know you; when you're sad, you shut people out. That might be OK for a regular bad day, but this is different. You lost your bloody wife, Evan. You can't run away from it or pretend it doesn't hurt.'

Tears sting the back of my eyes and a lump rises in my throat. 'Sorry, but you can't tell me how to grieve. I don't want Violet to see me upset, so just let me deal with this in my own way.'

Before Hannah can reply, Violet comes barrelling over, carrying a Cadbury's Buttons Easter egg.

'Auntie Hannah!' She squeals with excitement. 'Look what I found! The Easter Bunny left it for me.'

'Wow, look at that! Easter eggs for tea tonight, I think.' She winks and Violet's grin widens. 'If it's OK with your dad, that is.'

They both look at me. 'Well, I can hardly say no to that, can I?'

Hannah holds my gaze for a second before turning to her favourite four-year-old. 'Listen, kid, I hope you're causing as much trouble as possible and keeping that dad of yours on his toes. He needs it. I'll see you really soon, OK? Save a bit of that chocolate for me.'

Violet nods, blows a kiss, then shoots off in search of more eggs.

'Did you mean what you said about coming to see her soon?' When Hannah doesn't reply immediately, I continue. 'Please don't make promises you can't keep; she really misses you and—'

She holds her hands up. 'Before you go down the protective dad route, I'm actually thinking of coming back for a visit. I wouldn't have said that to Violet unless I was serious. How about we make a deal? I'll look into flights home, if you admit you need help and let yourself grieve for Claire. I've still got another few months left at my job here, so I can't come back right away, but I'll start looking soon. Plenty of time for you to keep up your end of the bargain. What do you say?'

She holds out her hand for me to shake, even though she's on the other side of the world. I run a hand over my face. Hannah is the one person I can't hide from.

'Fine. Deal. But you'd better book that flight; I'll never hear the end of it from Violet if you don't.'

We exchange a smile, our first since she upped and left last year.

'Take care of yourself, OK?'

'You too.'

We say goodbye and I stuff my phone back into my pocket. Mum looks at me, her arms folded over her chest.

'Anything you want to tell me?'

She smiles and waits for me to reply. My attention is fully focused on Violet, who's rooting around in some bushes at the bottom of the garden.

'Daddy, look what I found!' She yanks a colourful box from the foliage and waves it triumphantly above her head. 'Come and help me find the rest.'

I smile at Mum. 'It can wait until later. I've got to see a four-year-old about some chocolate.'

I stride across the garden to where Violet is waiting for me. Together, we run into the shed and begin looking around for the Trolls Easter egg I hid in here a little while ago. I know it's in the toolbox; she doesn't. I'll grieve for Claire later, probably when Violet's in bed. I'll watch our wedding video, listen to our favourite songs and think about the memories we made together. Violet will probably mention her later; I'll cross that bridge when I come to it. Right now, it's all about making things fun for her, giving her some time off from missing her mum. I'll laugh and play and join in with her games as best I can, even though I'm crumbling inside. I only have to hold it together for a few more hours, then I can fall apart.

I look at Violet, frantically combing through a corner of the shed. Easter eggs aren't the only thing we're searching for, I realise, we're also searching for a new life. The one without Claire that we never planned to live. I think about the article I read about heartbeats earlier this morning. Where will Violet and I be, thirty-five million heartbeats from now? Will we find a way to move on, that new beginning that seems so out of reach right now?

'Found it!' She grabs the Easter egg from the toolbox and hands it to me with a triumphant grin.

I smile. Maybe there's hope for our new start after all.

Bonus Recipes

Evan and Violet really bond when they bake together, even if there are some mishaps along the way! I love to bake myself, so I thought it would be fun to include a few of the recipes from the book. If you try these at home, post the results on social media and tag me and my lovely publisher using the following handles.

- **Twitter:** @Lynsey1991 and @0neMoreChapter_
- **Instagram:** @lynseygram and @onemorechapterhc

And don't forget to use #**TheSingleDadsHandbook**.

Happy baking!

Chocolate Brownies

170g melted unsalted butter
100g light brown sugar
150g caster sugar
2 large eggs
125g melted dark chocolate
100g plain flour
30g cocoa powder
1tsp salt
300g chocolate chips (milk, white, dark or a mix!)

1. Preheat the oven to 180 degrees and line an 8x8 baking tin with parchment.
2. Add the melted butter to a bowl with the brown sugar and caster sugar. Mix until it's smooth.
3. Add two eggs and mix until fully combined. Then stir in the melted dark chocolate.
4. Sieve in the flour, cocoa powder and salt then fold into the mixture.
5. Fold in the chocolate chips then put your mix into the baking tray and put into the oven. Bake for 25-30 minutes.

Note: Baking times may vary depending on your oven. Start checking them with a skewer at 25 minutes. If the mixture is still really wet, leave them for around five minutes and check again. Keep doing this until only a tiny bit of mixture comes out on the skewer. Then leave to cool and enjoy later!

Fairy Cakes

4oz / 113g margarine
4oz / 113g self-raising flour
4oz / 113g caster sugar
2 medium eggs
½ tsp baking powder
1 tbsp milk

Decoration
Icing sugar
Water
Sprinkles

1. Preheat the oven to 180 degrees and line a cupcake tin with paper cases.
2. Add the butter and caster sugar to a bowl and whisk until the mixture is pale and fluffy.
3. Beat the eggs in a cup and fold them in, one at a time.
4. Sieve in the flour and baking powder and mix until you have a smooth, glossy batter.

5. Add a tablespoon of milk. Trust me! This loosens the batter and makes the cakes even lighter and fluffier.
6. Spoon the mixture into cases and bake for about twenty minutes. Leave to cool fully.
7. For the icing, pour several spoonfuls of icing sugar into a bowl, add a splash of water and mix to form a spreadable paste. Using a teaspoon, apply some to each cake and add your favourite decorations – sprinkles, sweets, whatever!

Note: This mixture makes a tray of about ten cakes, but the recipe is easily scaled up if you want to make more. An eight-ounce mix will give you almost twenty – loads to share!

Blondies

170g/6oz melted unsalted butter
200g/7oz light brown sugar
150g/5oz granulated sugar
2 large eggs
250g/9oz plain flour
1 tsp baking powder
½ tsp salt

1. Preheat the oven to 180 degrees and line 23cm x 33cm baking tray with parchment.
2. Whisk the melted butter, brown sugar and granulated together, then add both of the eggs. Mix until fully combined.
3. Add the flour, salt and baking powder and whisk to form a batter.
4. Spread the mix evenly onto the baking tray and bake for around thirty minutes. The top should be set and light brown. Leave to cool completely in the tin.

Note: This recipe is for plain blondies, but you can add chocolate chips for some added texture!

One More Chapter is an award-winning global division of HarperCollins.

Sign up to our newsletter to get our latest eBook deals and stay up to date with our weekly Book Club!
Subscribe here.

Meet the team at
www.onemorechapter.com

Follow us!

 @OneMoreChapter_

 @OneMoreChapter

 @onemorechapterhc

Do you write unputdownable fiction?
We love to hear from new voices.
Find out how to submit your novel at
www.onemorechapter.com/submissions